WRITER'S DEATH

WRITER'S DEATH

Agnes Taylor Mystery
Book 2

EVA BERNHARD

EB Press

Books by Eva Bernhard

Agnes Taylor Mystery Series

Absent Beauty - Short Read Prequel

Silent Sands − Book 1

Writer's Death − Book 2

Snowbound − A Holiday Mystery − Book 3

Stormy Night − Book 4

Louise Penfold Mystery Series

Death at Rosewood Manor − Book 1

Death at Eagle Roost − Book 2

ISBN 978-1-997787-11-2 (Standard Font Hardcover)
ISBN 978-1-7777877-4-5 (Standard Font Paperback)
ISBN 978-1-7777877-5-2 (EBook)
ISBN 978-1-0690966-2-3 (Large Print Hardcover)
ISBN 978-1-0688740-2-4 (Large Print Paperback)

Editorial Services by Pam Clinton (pam@pccProofreading.com)

Cover Design by EB Press with images from Stock.adobe.com.

This novel is a work of fiction. Bowman College, its environs, and all those associated with it only exist in the author's and readers' imagination. Characters in this novel are entirely fictitious. Any resemblance to actual persons, living or dead, would be purely coincidental. Historical or real persons mentioned in passing are used fictitiously. Opinions expressed by characters are not intended to represent any real person's views but solely serve the purpose of fiction. Locals, events, companies, businesses, institutions, organizations, and similar entities are either fictitious or used fictitiously.

Chapter 1

"Got you!" The laptop screen in front of Agnes illuminated the satisfied glow on her face as she pumped a fist in the air.

It had taken her twenty minutes to catch the cheater. With a groan, she stretched to unkink her sore neck and flip back her dark hair. Her yawn echoed hollow in the barren underground office, dimly lit by a green-shaded banker's lamp.

The screen's taskbar read 10:14 PM. Almost 45 minutes to go until Jac would show up so they could walk home together, she thought, glad at the prospect of calling it a night. The self-imposed, lonesome late shift at the college campus allowed Agnes to get on top of the virtual grading pile. Or so she'd hoped until an eerie sense of déjà vu ground progress to a halt.

Past her mid-thirties, philosophy professor Dr. Agnes Taylor never considered herself gifted with an unusual memory capacity. But even when grading digital mountains of student essays in the online dropbox, an occasional feeling of 'I've read this before' made her sleuthing nose quiver.

This time, the report generated by Turnitin, the plagiarism detection tool Bowman College, like so many other Canadian educational institutions subscribed to, highlighted no copied paragraphs or phrases in the submission. Her gut begged to differ.

On a hunch, she'd downloaded and scrolled through the student's doc in MS Word. Nothing suspicious in an obvious way.

Ready to give up, her cursor had idled over 'Review' on the menu ribbon. The mouse clicked. Up popped the review panel. Prompted by intuition, she'd clicked 'Tracking.'

Amazed, Agnes stared at the text. Countless phrases were underscored in red.

The doc's revision history showed two names. One was the student who submitted the essay. The other was the originator of the doc, a student from another section of this course. She'd skim-read those submissions as they trickled in but hadn't yet checked Turnitin results. Her subconscious must act like a sponge, she realized. Her hunt in MS Word yielded clear evidence of randomly rephrased bits and pieces to fake an authentic submission.

"If you insist on cheating," she said into the silence of the room, "at least use your brain and turn off tracking."

"Darn it," she said under her breath. The screen flickered back at her.

The excitement of the chase was one thing. The paperwork involved quite another. An officially recorded academic integrity breach case required investigating further, filling out endless forms, sending emails, meeting the students, and listening to all kinds of excuses. The cheaters would receive a zero grade on the assignment or more serious sanctions if it wasn't their first breach on record. A waste of everyone's time.

"Do us a favor and put in an honest day's work," she muttered.

Academic dishonesty, she felt, was so unfair to other students who worked hard for their grades, and it jeopardized the value of higher education.

Footsteps echoing in the deserted hallway startled her out of her musings.

The sound brought back an acute awareness of the musty air in the grotty, windowless basement office. Most of the instructors sharing the workspace in the muddy-gray concrete heap housing the Humanities department left the door wide open to make the space less claustrophobic.

When alone at night, door open or closed, it felt kind of creepy.

Agnes shivered and pulled the lapels of the cardigan over each other to feel the warmth of a woolly hug. An indifferent dresser, she chose clothes haphazardly to tone down her curves but never sacrificed comfort.

Too early for Jac.

Eyes trained on the gaping doorframe, illuminated by the dim nightlight in the corridor, Agnes waited, a vague sense of unease mounting.

"Silly, don't get fanciful," she scolded herself. This wasn't the first time working late on campus since she got the one-year contract teaching job a few months ago. Nothing distracted from concentrated labor here, unlike at her transient home shared with Jac and two male graduate students who enjoyed philosophizing over beer and pizza.

Night-times, the cavernous office was quiet. Silent like a tomb...

Except for the footsteps, gaining in speed.

Security on yet another duty round, she told herself.

A burly officer had come by twice, reassuring yet disruptive. Each time, he'd startled her by flicking on the overhead fluorescent strip. She hated its glaring brightness. The man's bulky presence, clad in a midnight blue uniform illuminated by the merciless blueish-white light, made the room shrink and the decrepit furniture appear even shabbier.

The clacking steps sounded different. Less clunky. Not bulky safety boots.

They grew loud and stopped.

For a moment, Agnes frowned at the elongated, dark figure standing motionless in the opening, backlit by the weak hall light. Only when it moved toward her did she exhale in noisy irritation.

"Jeez, Jac. Do you have to scare me like this?" With irrelevant attention to detail, she added. "Are those new boots?" Sleek, high-heeled lace-up ankle boots explained the clack-clacking.

When Jac stood silent, Agnes's frown returned. "What's wrong?"

Her friend swayed as if dizzy. Agnes jumped up and rushed forward.

"Here. Come sit down. I'll get you some water."

Arm slung around Jac's quivering back, she led her to the nearest swivel chair. In the desk lamp's yellowish beam, Jac's face looked ghastly. The edgy features and pointed chin, framed by a sleek bob of ice-blond hair, appeared bloodless, tinged greenish in contrast with the black of Jac's tailored wool coat. Sophistication incarnate, Jacqueline Xavier appeared disturbingly rattled.

Agnes leaned over and grabbed a water bottle from the metal shelf cluttered with discarded ancient monitors, file folders, and other abandoned paraphernalia. She unscrewed the top and eased the bottle against Jac's lips. Like a child, her friend swallowed tiny sips.

"Are you ill?"

Images of Jacqueline, a lightweight petite, being attacked in the desolate building while working alone in her office upstairs flitted through Agnes's mind.

"Did anything happen to you?" she asked, trying to hide her growing alarm.

Her friend's hand reached up to grasp hers in a gentle clasp. Pale and drawn, Jac whispered, "Not to me. It's Dorian."

"What? What about Dorian?" They both taught Dorian

Gable. Professors in the department recognized him as the most promising, yet exasperating, student in the creative writing program. A brilliant third-year student with an entire slate of personal issues.

"What did he do now?" asked Agnes.

"He's dead."

Chapter 2

Jacqueline Xavier felt her face crumble. When she'd received the brief message minutes ago, alone in the comfort of her cozy faculty office, it had shaken her to the core. Any young person's passing was tragic. Dorian Gable, however, was a star student of her beloved Creative Writing program.

Into Agnes' stunned silence, she said, "They found him on his bed." Tears welled up as she spoke. When her friend Agnes pulled her close, Jac dissolved in a flood of emotions.

"How? A young kid like that doesn't just die," said Agnes. "Was it... He wouldn't..."

"I don't know. Cassandra didn't say."

"Did she call you?"

"No, she emailed. Only a few words. I had contacted her earlier today to schedule an advising appointment for her. To get this in response... I still can't take it in." Jac twisted her head to face Agnes, who still held her close. "Of course, I tried to reach her and left a message. No response. Then, I rang Martha Muller, but her phone was turned off. As our Associate Dean, she needs to be told."

"Does Dorian live in residence on campus? Do you know? Security could—"

"No, he lives in town like most of them do. I looked up his address on file. I don't have access to other private data. My God, if only AD Muller could be reached. Though with the privacy policy…"

"I know, requires consent. It's terrible, but we can't do anything tonight. Let's get you home." Withdrawing her arm, Agnes rose.

It left Jac bereft of comfort. Benumbed, she watched Agnes shut down the laptop and stuff various belongings into a back-pack. A wave of affection for this loyal friend from their under-grad days suffused her.

As so often, when the present raised her anxiety levels, Jac allowed her mind to withdraw into soothing, often random thoughts.

Fragmented images arose of their younger selves a dozen years ago. They'd connected during a group project as sopho-mores at York University on the outskirts of Toronto. Both were taking a course in Canadian literature. For Agnes, as a philos-ophy major, it was an elective. A Lit major from the get-go, Jac chose it as her core subject area.

The group, as so many mandatorily assigned student groups, was dismally dysfunctional. Only Agnes and she pulled their weight and brought in an A+ grade for the presentation on Timothy Findley's *Wars*. Their mutual outrage at the freeloaders in their group bonded them despite their marked differences in character and temperament. Their deep friendship helped them survive years of struggles in academia at different ends of the country.

As they now walked side by side through deserted corridors to the stairs leading to the front of the building, Jac's mind continued to freewheel, keeping the present at bay.

Back in August, after Agnes's return from Germany, Jac persuaded her to apply for contract teaching at Bowman College, a few hours' drive from Toronto.

When the Humanities department offered a one-year

contract, Agnes, the urbanite, signed up to teach "in the boonies" and jumped at the suggestion to share living quarters. Rents in the province of Ontario were at a premium, even in small towns. To economize, Jac sublet three bedrooms of the dilapidated two-story she'd moved into over two years ago.

The summer holiday in Germany with Sera, the mother Agnes had been estranged from for two decades, must have worked wonders. Despite the dead body they'd found on a beach...

The mental image of death yanked Jacqueline right back into the glaring present.

They'd reached the central part of the main floor that connected the office and the classroom wings. Despite the late hour, over a dozen students huddled around the Pit, an atrium with bleacher-like steps to a sunken squad. Excited buzz met them as they passed along the top.

Upon seeing them, two girls rushed up the steps. A pair of males tagged along.

News traveled fast on the campus grapevine. As a faculty member and program coordinator, Jacqueline felt duty-bound to provide support, no matter how much she stood in need of it herself. She disengaged her arm from Agnes's and straightened her spine.

"Professor," one girl, a tall, short-haired brunette, called. "Isn't it horrible? Did you hear?"

Jacqueline waited until the two came abreast with them. "Yes, Renata. It's a terrible shock for all of us." Sadness colored Jac's voice while she fought growing emotional. The girl's sensation-hungry demeanor offended her.

The other girl, Cleo, said in hushed tones, "We'd never thought he'd kill himself over it."

Mon Dieu, please don't let it be suicide, Jac prayed silently.

"Over what?" asked Agnes.

Renata said, "The thing with Prof. Nessbit."

Jacqueline saw Agnes's brows shoot up.

The young fellow who'd sidled up to Cleo's right chimed in, his guttural voice booming in the sparsely populated foyer, "They hushed it up, of course."

"Kalen, I don't think you want to perpetuate such groundless claims," said Jacqueline. She wouldn't stand for slander, even if it targeted an odious colleague like Herbert Nessbit.

Kalen, dark hair curling out from under a baseball cap and a muscular six-foot frame clad in sweats, snickered. "Sure. Sure. You've gotta stand by the man, Jac. Us students know better."

On the other side, next to Renata, skinny little Joel's eyes sparkled behind his granny glasses. His hands twisted the hem of the bulky pale-blue sweatshirt, shapelessly drooping over his grubby jeans. To make himself taller, or merely a nervous habit, his feet—stuck in untied scuffed trainers—rocked to their toes and back down incessantly.

"Dorian himself told us Prof. Nessbit denies ever having seen Dorian's manuscript," Joel said. The squeaky voice always reminded Jac of the mice who wintered in the basement of her shabby-chic brick pile of a home. Such uncharitable stray thoughts she suppressed as quickly as they arose.

"If Dorian believed to have a grievance, I'm sure he would have taken appropriate steps," she hastened to squelch further speculation. Her firm tone resulted from much practice rather than conviction. Except for Nessbit, everyone agreed Dorian to be a gifted writer. Brilliant, but hopelessly muddled in practical affairs.

The rumor was common knowledge. Since Dorian lodged no official complaint, neither she, as coordinator of the Creative Writing program, nor Martha, the Associate Dean of Humanities, could take any action. After all, educational institutions were rife with gossip about professors. In the age of social media, rumors spread like viruses, forever mutating into more contagious strains. Until the next one succeeded them—or they turned actionable.

On the surface, this one was innocuous enough. It dated

back a month or two. A habitual procrastinator, Dorian delayed submitting a creative writing assignment for Herbert Nessbit's class. In his idiosyncratic style, he'd hand-written his piece. Long after the due date, he'd dropped it off after office hours on the department secretary's desk with a note to Nessbit. Or so the story went. Denying receipt, rumors claimed, Herbert assigned a zero grade for non-submission. Hardly grounds to take one's life, Jac reassured herself.

The chatter in the Pit increased in volume and shook Jac out of her reverie. More students had joined their group and barraged Agnes with questions about how Dorian died. Neither Agnes nor she had the answer.

Time to take charge, Jacqueline exhorted herself and straightened her posture. Her much-practiced lecture-voice sufficed to catch everyone's attention.

"Tomorrow, we will receive the college's obituary email." This was standard practice in cases of a community member's passing. "Let me urge you to take advantage of our Student Services' resources. The counselors are there to help us come to terms with the grief that all of us experience. Losing a friend is a terrible thing—and one so young—"

"Well, well. The ghouls have gathered." The forceful male voice echoed across the foyer, cutting off Jacqueline's advice to the students at large.

Every head swung around to face the newcomer, who stood raised above them on the curving staircase leading to the upper floor.

Exasperated, Jac strode across to him. Up close, she fixed him with a deep frown and said, "For once, try to curb your sarcasm, Timothy. This is hardly the time—"

"Sorry, Jac. You should see them all from above. Like vultures at a roadkill. Turned my stomach." In a gesture that struck Jacqueline as theatrical, the back of his hand—long, tapered fingers loosely extended—stroked over his brow, lifting the chestnut strands of his artfully messy hair.

Timothy Charles Elliot—Chuck to his buddies and favorites among students—preferred to be called TC by everyone else. Employed by the college on a term-by-term basis long before Jac arrived, he'd competed for the position she snapped up as an outside hire. Whether he'd ever forgiven her, she couldn't tell.

"When you call me Timothy, I know I'm in the doghouse." His rueful smile sought to appease Jac. "If only you'd call me Chuck."

That she was not prepared to do. But she relented somewhat. "This is far too serious, TC, for us to quibble over extraneous points. The students need our sincere support."

"Agreed, agreed. I'll do my best. No matter how Dorian's passing has shaken me," he added softly. "After all, I thought of him as a young friend."

With Timothy in tow, Jac retraced her steps to join Agnes. Most of the dispersed groups now gathered in the vicinity. A sense of being watched made Jac glance sideways.

In a flash, she caught the brooding eyes of a hunched figure on the corner parapet of the Pit. The head slowly bent low as though engrossed in a vision of his bony knees. Stringy dark hair fell forward to hide the translucent, rodent-like features. Lester, unmistakably, Jac thought. Always watching, rarely speaking, at least in her class. And if, in a low muttering tone.

It reminded her of an upcoming advisory meeting scheduled for him. Tomorrow? Or the day after? She'd have to check. The thought of meeting him in her office, one-to-one, simultaneously filled her with dismay and guilt at her reaction. Lester's demeanor matched the creepy, noir prose he produced in abundance.

Now, he pretended not to notice anything around him. The vantage point he'd chosen to huddle, she estimated, gave him a perfect view of anything going on in the Pit.

Resolutely, she turned away, momentarily catching Timothy's sardonic smile, a telling comment on her discomfort. She scowled at him and focused on her waiting friend instead.

From several yards away, Jacqueline could see the concern in Agnes's face as she spoke to the students near her. In the merciless, artificial light, Agnes's features—framed by dark brown, almost black hair curling onto her shoulders—appeared pallid with exhaustion. If only Agnes would exert her undoubted aesthetic sensibility to improve her wardrobe, Jac mused, visualizing how she herself might accentuate such an attractive hourglass figure.

Irritated with the frivolous, escapist thoughts, Jacqueline addressed the group around her friend, "We all need to get home. Campus will close shortly."

"Dr. Xavier," said a timid girl who remained at the fringe, "Can you tell me? He didn't...suffer?" The boldness of posing a question, Jac suspected, made the sensitive lip quiver in her dark face.

"I'm sure he passed away peacefully, Nicole." A merciful fiction. No details had emerged yet.

How to end these fruitless speculations and prompt the students to disband was now the question.

Timothy wasn't helping.

Rather than stifle the scuttlebutt, he added his five-cents-worth to the rumor mill.

"Of course, there can be no question of Nessbit suppressing a student's submission," Jac heard him say. "Yes, Kalen, we both know Dorian insisted he handed in his manuscript. He told me so himself. But things can get lost."

"Don't you find it suspicious Herb's got a book coming out? Someone says so on Snapchat. Man, the guy published f-all in eons," Kalen boomed.

"We'll know for sure when his mystery opus is on the market," said Joel, rubbing his nose and dislodging his glasses. He caught one arm just in time to prevent their fall. An optician should adjust them, Jac thought.

"How do you make that out?" Cleo sneered at Joel. "There's no copy of what Dorian wrote. The as—I mean, Dorian didn't type it and, I bet, didn't xerox the stuff before dropping it off. Never did, did he?"

"Wouldn't he have drafts and notes, though?" asked Agnes.

Jacqueline nudged her friend unobtrusively to prevent further speculation. It did nothing to stop Timothy Elliot.

"Dorian was unique in that," he said with authority. "Wrote straight from the heart. Stream of consciousness. Wildly authentic. Any writer would give his—or her," he added with a bow to Agnes and Jac, "soul for that gift. A veritable genius." His tone grew reverential as he spoke.

"Genius? Yeah, right." Cleo snorted. "Why is everybody raving about his stuff? His plots are so pedestrian."

Kalen cuffed her. "Jealous cat."

"I think we really ought to—"

Two security guards, a brawny male and an unsmiling female, both in the college's dark blue uniforms, entered Jacqueline's line of vision, causing her to break off.

The perfect reinforcement for her desire to shoo everyone off the premises. Let them take over.

Chapter 3

Before rushing to campus on Tuesday morning, Agnes checked her college emails and found a listserv message informing the campus community of Dorian's death. No details as to the cause of his 'passing,' as they referred to it.

Nothing unusual in the omission. In her experience of educational institutions, such emails rarely revealed anything. At the most, they might say, 'after a long illness' or 'unexpectedly.' Suicide would not be advertised.

But it was on everyone's mind. Students suffering from mental health issues were not uncommon. Mandatory training for faculty included units on spotting severe distress symptoms and 'risk of self-harm' in students.

This is different, Agnes thought, while she grabbed her stuff and hastened to leave for her eight AM class. There's something else going on.

The students last night had bombarded her with questions about how Dorian died. Yet, she'd sensed they knew something she didn't.

Then she heard one of them say, "Duh? He offed himself. Toxy says so on Snapchat."

As she'd turned to discover who'd spoken, Jac diverted their attention and told them to expect the obituary via college email. Well, they'd got it in their inbox now.

An hour later, the crowded corridors on campus were abuzz. Students milled in groups and pairs or stayed at the fringes on their lonesome. With a reusable coffee mug in one hand, her other hand clutching the strap of her backpack, Agnes barely avoided being jostled by oncoming foot traffic.

Preoccupied with what lay ahead today, Agnes's mind fretted. Three hours of existentialist philosophy in fiction. Death and suicide among the topics. And with Dorian's seat empty in the back. No one will sit there. Got to say something about his death. Word it carefully…

Her stomach fluttered at the thought of students' questions about what happened to their peer.

Someone's "Good morning, Dr. Taylor," cut into her rumination. Still distracted, she raised her coffee mug in greeting but only caught sight of the student's back as he rushed by her.

Just as she passed the connecting entrance to the office wing, she spotted a familiar tan fedora hat rounding the corner. Below it, she glimpsed puce, somewhat pudgy cheeks mottled with three-day bristles.

When their glances connected, she received a haughty, sneering nod, and Herb Nessbit brushed past her. For a moment, her gaze followed the retreating stocky figure dressed in dark brown corduroys, topped by a vintage tweed blazer, the obligatory cashmere scarf flung casually over one shoulder. Today, it was the dove-gray one.

A wry smile pulled up the corners of Agnes's lips at the thought of Herb's author branding efforts.

Then she recollected the nasty allegations students made against him last night. Tough time for the poor guy, she thought.

Minutes later, when she entered her classroom, the buzz

she'd heard from several yards away hit her full force—only to die in ripples as students perceived her. Some nudged or shushed their neighbors.

One voice still boomed on. None other than Kalen—presumably airing more conspiracy theories.

Agnes's "Hello, everyone," fell into a brief lull and made Kalen's face swivel toward the podium.

Unabashed, he inquired, "Hey, Agnes. What's new?"

"Give me a moment to set up, Kalen," she said, in no rush to admit her ignorance in case he meant info about Dorian's untimely death. "I'll say a few words to the class once everyone's settled."

Her hands busy with the routine tasks of checking the electronic equipment, Agnes marveled at how quickly she'd adapted to the oddities of college culture.

Back when she first started teaching, fresh from a postdoc year at a major university, the casual way college students treated faculty had made her gasp.

Sure, Canadian colleges were job-oriented and offered brief diploma and certificate programs, plus some bachelor's degrees. At least, many of the BA students abided by university-style conventions of politeness and addressed profs by title. Not Kalen, though, who applied levelling equality, treating everyone as a buddy.

Unless students were downright rude or offensive, Agnes didn't care about niceties.

While she connected her laptop to the data projector and checked the podium controls, a few latecomers strolled or rushed in, according to personality.

A hush caught her attention. The atmosphere grew numb. Wary faces turned towards the door. Other eyes veered to close neighbors or sought the comfort of cell phones.

The cause of the freeze now paused in the doorway.

Goose bumps rose on Agnes's arms. Enter Kafka, her mind commented. She suppressed a sigh.

The nickname, coined by Kalen, stuck to Lester since he'd given a truly Kafkaesque presentation on Franz Kafka's *Metamorphosis*. 'Gregor' would have been more appropriate, Agnes figured. There was something creepy, bug-like, about Lester, she mused as he crept in to sit at his accustomed place right in front of the podium. The rounded back and bent shoulders of the habitually hunched gait, emphasized by black-bluish garb, reminded her of the story's main character, who woke up morphed into a beetle.

Annoyed at her invariable reaction to this student, Agnes shook off the imagery and forced a welcoming smile. The responding twisted, mocking snigger—as though he'd penetrated deep into her consciousness—made her shudder. To mask it, she rubbed her arms to mime a chill and bent low over her laptop.

"Eh, Kafka. What's up? Done some sinister plotting again?" Kalen's bantering bellow broke the spell and drew a laugh or two.

An insider joke? she wondered.

Lester didn't bother to turn around, but Agnes was close enough to see his sneer.

Conversations picked up again in a low hum. Under the guise of connecting her device to the podium console, Agnes observed the class to gauge their state of mind. Some appeared very subdued. Others fidgeted with suppressed excitement. A few of the latter darted quick glances toward the back corner. Not only Dorian's accustomed seat by the window wall was unoccupied, but also a cluster of seats surrounding it.

Something tugged at Agnes's memory, prompting her gaze to wander over the window wall on one side of the room. The wet and gray weather fit the day. No point turning on the overhead lights; it made any projection onto the screen illegible. On sunny days, they closed the blinds to shut out the glare. A pang of regret always accompanied turning her back on such glorious mornings. Not today. Closed shades seemed appropriate despite the overcast sky.

As she moved to draw the first blind, a couple of students got up to follow suit with the ones further back. She smiled her thanks. In doing so, her glance met a tentative smile from a girl in the first row, right by the window. Melanie, a conscientious, quiet student who rarely participated in discussions but performed consistently at A+ level.

What had eluded her recall moments ago resurfaced. Her subconscious must have alerted her to Cassandra's absence.

That's a first, thought Agnes. Cass never misses class or arrives late.

For the last few weeks, Cassandra had sat in the first row with Melanie. Early on this term, Cass and Dorian appeared inseparable, always sitting in "their" corner way in the back. Half-conscious of the switch to the front, Agnes had assumed Cass found it difficult to make out the PowerPoint slides on the screen from way back.

"Time to start." Agnes raised her voice to cut over the renewed chatter while her finger touched 'unmute' on the multimedia console to reveal today's agenda on PowerPoint. Conversation ceased.

"Good morning, everyone." She took a belly breath to steel her nerves for the next bit.

"Before we get into today's material, let me say a few words. It is with the greatest regret we heard about the sudden passing of one of our class members. Dorian Gable was not only a gifted student but a dear friend to many. We will sadly miss him."

An ominous murmur arose from several directions.

In front of her, she heard Lester mutter, "Rip the genius."

Or did he mean R.I.P.?

Worried about open dissent, Agnes hurried on, "You've all received the college's email this morning. Please get in touch with our counselors as needed. They are best able to support us in our grief. Remember to talk to me or any faculty member if you need help."

Anxious now to get on with the today's agenda, Agnes scanned the sign-up list for student presentations.

Oh no, not good at all, her mind groaned as she saw Cassandra's name and topic at the top of the list. A presentation on Herman Hesse's *Steppenwolf* was bound to stir up emotions. After all, the protagonist Harry Haller planned to commit suicide at fifty…

Maybe all for the best if Cass skips class today, Agnes figured.

"Has anyone seen Cassandra this morning?" she asked the class. "No? Okay, let's rearrange things and determine who presents first after my lecture."

"Not me," said one presenter. Two others echoed him.

"I'll go first if she doesn't show up," called out a tall guy, ruffling his black curls. "Get it over with fast." From his place by the door, he faced the others in mock despair.

"Thanks, Yash." Agnes smiled in his direction. Though the first one out once class ended, Yash never missed a day. One of her keenest and most reliable participants in any learning activity, a fact she much appreciated.

A soft voice to her left diverted her attention.

"Can I speak to you outside for a second? About…Cass?"

The anxious look on Melanie's face prompted Agnes to nod in agreement, no matter how reluctant to delay the start of her lecture.

"Okay, guys—and gals," she added. "Time to refresh your memory of the assigned short story by Simone de Beauvoir. Skim read it while Melanie and I have a quick chat. We'll be right back."

Curious glances followed them as she steered Melanie out into the hallway, empty now at a quarter past eight. A bench in beech-colored bentwood a few yards across from the door, overlooking the landscaped campus grounds outside, suited for a private conversation.

It took a moment before Melanie spoke, her voice barely loud enough for Agnes to hear.

"I'm so worried about Cass. She's going to pieces over Dorian killing himself…"

"Does she know he wanted to die? I mean, is she sure it wasn't a terrible accident?"

Chapter 4

Jacqueline put down the receiver of her clunky black office phone and checked the time on the display. 10:18 AM. Elbows on the desk, her fingers reached up to her temples, massaging them in tiny circles. The throbbing persisted.

The call from the associate dean, Martha Muller, did nothing to relieve the uncertainty about what had happened to Dorian Gable. Jac was to drop by for a quick word about administrative directives determined earlier this morning by the dean in consultation with AD Muller. The death of a student involved all levels of the admin hierarchy, Jac realized. Especially if indeed self-inflicted.

Harrowing most of all for the parents.

Her own sadness at the loss of a young person she'd known for two years paled by comparison. Yet, a deep-seated worry overshadowed grief and sent burning spears of apprehension and shame through her torso.

If a professor's actions drove the student to take his own life, the consequences would be horrendous.

It was she who had convinced the committee two years ago to hire Herbert Nessbit, a rising star in literary circles. She had wanted him as the flagship of her pet project, the Creative

Writing program. From the moment she'd joined the college, most of her time and efforts went into its development, inauguration, and day-to-day implementation.

Colleagues already looked askance at her when Nessbit's stardom waned after his initial publishing success. No one openly questioned her judgment, but still.

A scandal before the Ministry of Education's review of the program in a few months' time might result in severe funding cuts. The college executive would look for someone to blame. The thought caused Jac to groan out loud. She'd lose all she'd worked for. Her dream of rising to the higher ranks of the college's executive would come to naught.

Stop this futile fretting, she ordered herself and rose, straightening her indigo pencil skirt. Her hands stroked down the silky sleeves of the taupe blouse. The cool fabric against her skin soothed. Power-dressing, adopted during her sojourn in Paris, helped restore her sense of purpose.

The aura of competence it suggested to her mind and others was addictive, she admitted as she slipped her mobile into the pocket of a collarless jacket.

Just time enough for a refill at the water cooler on the way to Martha's office. She grabbed the tempered glass reusable bottle from her desk and headed out.

The empty hallway magnified the clacking sound of her heeled lace-up booties on the hard, vinyl-tiled floor. It evoked a vague memory of Agnes's comment last night about new boots.

As she walked by Herbert Nessbit's office, his door stood ajar, granting a glimpse of the man within. Head thrown far back, his face was in shade against the backdrop of the uncurtained window behind him. If it were not for the closed eyes, he'd appear to be contemplating the ceiling. The desk was empty except for a camel fedora facing its owner.

On an impulse, Jacqueline stretched out her hand to push open the door. Someone needed to set the rumor straight before it killed her brainchild.

Wincing at the unfortunate metaphor, Jac called out softly, "Herbert? A word?"

The eyelids opened a slit. She waited in vain for an invitation to enter. Not letting that deter her, Jacqueline stepped closer. His head swiveled around; bloodshot, bleary eyes turned toward the intruder.

Jac's lips tightened. Everyone knew Herbert liked to imbibe. But this early?

"What do you want?" The gravelly voice was so at odds with the high-brow image he loved to nourish, Jac thought. Perhaps he veered towards a Hemingway vibe these days?

Put on the spot, Jacqueline realized how unprepared she was to tackle a sensitive subject as a rumor which boiled down to gossip. One couldn't very well ask him pointblank to tell the truth about—What? Stealing students' work? Misappropriating it? Lying about not receiving it? Up to now, she'd dismissed all the rumors as mere spite.

Careful to sound non-confrontational, she said, "Just wanted to see how you are. A student's passing is such a shock to all of us."

"Oh, *please.*" He drew out the word and rolled up his eyes to show more red. "Spare me."

When Jac hesitated to respond, he scoffed, "A student's *passing.* 'Death,' the word is. Ridiculous euphemisms. Our genius offed himself. *Exitus. Finito.* End of story."

Jacqueline swallowed. It didn't rid her of the distaste. The man evidently was in shock. Horrified at the gossip about himself, no doubt. To realize what students thought him capable of must deeply hurt.

Compassion softened her tone as she said, "Herbert, no one among the faculty believes these ghastly rumors. We need to put an end to them before they harm you and the program."

"Your pathetic program. Think you'll churn out pocket geniuses here? At a piddling college?" His laugh echoed incongruously in the narrow confines of the cubby-sized office.

In an effort not to lash out, Jac gazed at the sparsely filled metal shelves that took up two sides. Next to the door to her left stood a well-worn, gunmetal filing cabinet, the top drawer ajar. She suppressed an urge to push it shut and focused on the institutional green, low-pile carpeting, threadbare in the high-traffic path to the desk.

The narrow window faced the staff parking lot. Two stories below, she knew, were the dumpsters and loading dock.

Not an inspiring environment for a writer. Unless he produced stark prose in the noir thriller genre.

As Herbert's sputtering subsided into huffs, Jacqueline reluctantly let her gaze return to the ungainly sight. She wished herself a foot taller to look down her nose sternly when she addressed him.

"May I remind you, Herbert, the Humanities department entrusted you with a much-coveted position. For your sake as well as ours, you must have a vested interest in the Creative Writing program's prospering and in stopping damaging rumors."

Like a parrot, he screeched, "Stopping them? How? It's a conspiracy. Against me. I'm being victimized!"

Wild-eyed he stared at her and spluttered, "Don't you see?"

His hands waved as if fending off attacking birds.

"Just leave me alone!"

Concerned someone might overhear his outburst, Jac judged a retreat to be the best policy. Her mouth forming shh–shhs, she drew out her phone to lend credence to her words, "Goodness, I forgot the time. My meeting with Martha…"

Her hasty, "Catch you later," she realized to be ill chosen as she drew the door shut upon her exit.

Chapter 5

Impatiently, Agnes checked the time yet again on her mobile. Not a single student came to her office hour after the morning class. Instead, she'd filled out the paperwork for the cheating case and emailed the students to set up separate meetings. Now, she couldn't wait to get out of the dismal office to meet Jac for a quick bite before her next class.

It'll be tight to make it back on time, she thought as she grabbed her wallet and locked her other belongings in the filing drawer of the metal desk. In the SMS, Jac said to meet at their favorite coffee shop.

A few minutes later, Agnes was rushing along the main path of the park bordering the campus grounds. The fine gravel, soggy from a bout of rain the other day, squished under her boots. They'd need cleaning before going to class, she figured, glad the half-inch heels didn't dig deep into the grayish mud. Her work-a-day pants' mottled pewter color hid spatters well.

Twice a year during mud season, everything turned tawny and lifeless in southern Ontario. Add a gloomy sky and November's downright depressing, Agnes grumbled to herself and shivered.

When she opened the door to Perfect Grounds, housed in a

black and white clapboard one-story with gingerbread trim lining the gable, she spotted Jac on a window bench. Her friend catered to her preference, always reserving the seat facing the view outside for Agnes.

Jam-packed at a quarter to twelve, not only with college patrons but businesspeople and office clerks from along this most popular street in town, the place buzzed. Its homemade soups, sandwiches, oven-warm baked goods, and gourmet fair-trade coffees ensured its claim to local fame.

Agnes's stomach growled as the scents of fresh-baked bread and potent dark roast brews hit her. As she weaved past the bistro tables, a server in black jeans and matching T-shirt, a raised cup logo emblazoned in royal blue across the chest, hailed a welcome. Steam rose from the tray he carried aloft. The aroma of curried cauliflower soup tantalized her tastebuds.

"Hey, Kristian, I'd love a bowl of that, too," Agnes told him.

"Be over in a bit with your order. Kitchen's short-staffed today. Latte with it, as usual?" A sideway jutting of the chin, and he added, "Jac told me to hold hers back until you got here."

A wane smile greeted her when she pulled out a chair across from Jacqueline.

"Dawn departure catching up with you?" Agnes kept the tone light but, up close, noticed her friend's delicate skin showed worry lines. Dark under-eye circles spoke of exhaustion.

"Sorry, Jac, I'll stop my flippancy. Did you hear further details about Dorian? The underground gossip sizzled this morning."

"Agnes, this is too serious—" Jac's features contracted in evident dismay.

"Hey, no worries. Just the usual empty talk below stairs." Irritated with herself, Agnes's fingers toyed with the laminated menu card while she cursed her habit of voicing ill-timed thoughts.

Jac reached across the narrow table to still Agnes's hand.

"I'm so anxious. This could kill—I mean, seriously harm the program."

The raw emotion on the other's face took Agnes by surprise.

"I understand, Jac. Let's not forget the real tragedy is the kid's life. Accident or suicide," Agnes added quietly, "it's devastating for his loved ones."

When Jac murmured contrite agreement, the magnitude of their loss hit Agnes with full force. Week after week, she'd seen Dorian in class. Several times, he'd sought her out to talk philosophy.

"Camus was his favorite."

Only Jac's puzzled "What?" told her she'd spoken out loud.

"*The Stranger* by Camus fascinated Dorian. Grabbed his creative imagination. Someone killing for no apparent reason—"

"My God. Are you saying he obsessed about death?"

"Not really… Mightn't have been death *per se*," said Agnes. Her mind grappled with the picture of Dorian during their after-class chat. They'd sat on the bench outside the classroom. Both had contemplated the bare trees swaying in the wind, rain beating against the glass. When engaged in philosophical discourse, Agnes habitually stared unseeingly at anything but her conversation partner. The mind turned inward to focus on the subject matter rather than the speaker.

The sound of Jacqueline shifting restlessly on the bench seat brought Agnes back to the present.

"We did, of course, also read excerpts from Camus's *Myth of Sisyphus*," the thought of Dorian prompted her to add. "Remember, the one starting with the famous line, 'There is but one serious philosophical problem and that is suicide.'"

"Oh no! You think—"

"No, Jac. Come on, we both know Albert Camus does not advocate taking one's own life. What fascinates him—and, as I understood, also Dorian—is the existential dilemma to judge whether life is worth living. My sense is Dorian responded with a resounding 'ye.'"

"But Agnes… Do you believe he didn't kill himself?" Jac's hands plucked at each other on the tabletop. "It is so frustrating. Even Martha heard no details and our privacy policy, of course, prohibits requesting such information from next of kin."

"Right now, it's all wild scuttlebutt speculation. No grounds for belief one way or another. A dreadful accident seems far more likely to me than suicide." On second thought, Agnes admitted, "Mind you, Cass might disagree."

"Did you talk to her? I couldn't reach her all morning. Just left messages—"

The arrival of their order interrupted. Against her usual manners, Jac grabbed her phone and ignored Kristian, who unloaded steaming bowls. Their wafting fragrance made Agnes's mouth water. Butter curls in a white porcelain dish, placed in the middle of the table within easy reach for both, just waited to melt on the still-warm Calabrese bread.

When he put her latte in front of her, Agnes complimented the barista's creativity. "I love it. A perfect swan."

"Enjoy," Kristian said. "The coconut curry might put a smile on Jac's face. She's not her usual self today, is she?" A commiserating glance at Jacqueline made up for talking about her as if not present.

"Oh, she'll perk up after a few spoonfuls of it," Agnes said lightly. "One of those days, you know."

After Kristian left them, she coaxed Jac to dig in. "Smell this? You'll love it."

"Never mind that now," Jacqueline waved off the small talk. "What were you saying about Cass?"

"Oh that," muttered Agnes through a mouthful of delicious, buttered bread. A sip of coffee made her sigh contentedly. Into Jac's expectant silence, she explained, "This morning, Cassandra didn't show up for her presentation. The death must've hit her hard."

"Not surprising as a close friend of Dorian's. If you didn't see her, what makes you say she believes it's suicide?"

"Let me finish." Belatedly, Agnes glanced around to see if people at other tables could listen in. Conversations around them, plus the ambient noise, however, discouraged eavesdropping. So, she continued, "Mel asked me for a quick word outside during class and told me about Cass. According to Melanie, Cass is devastated because she broke up with Dorian a few weeks ago and now fears it drove him to take his own life."

"Then it has nothing to do with Herb. The rumors are unfounded." Relief colored Jac's voice for the first time since Agnes arrived.

"Hate to disillusion you, but it does not follow."

"Why? If disappointed love is the cause, then all the talk is just malicious spite."

"We don't even know yet it's self-inflicted, let alone causation."

"But Cass says—"

"First off, I've no clue what Cass might say or not. All I passed on just now is what Melanie surmised and shared with me this morning." Agnes swigged some water to clear her palate and mind.

"From what I understand," she said, "the only two facts are: One, Cassandra and Dorian broke up. Two, Cass is in emotional turmoil or 'going to pieces,' as Mel puts it. A third claim is again a mere inference Mel shared with me when we spoke. Namely, Cass has a new boyfriend she's cagey about. Might not even be true. Without ever having seen the guy, Melanie infers he must be older, and Cass feels guilt and remorse."

"A reasonable inference—"

The bus person who set a fresh jug of water on their table stopped Jac.

Thirsty after the well-salted soup and so much talking, Agnes refilled their glasses and emptied hers in a few gulps.

"Isn't it?" asked Jacqueline.

"What?"

"Reasonable. What Melanie assumes."

"Use your good brain, Jac. Unless Cassandra tells us herself, which she's unlikely to do, it's guesswork." To ward off an objection, Agnes went on, "Even if Mel were correct, it doesn't impact either Dorian's death or the rumors flying about."

"I'm sorry. This makes no sense to me."

"Think it through. If suicide, it could be for multiple reasons. On the flip side, if accidental—which I believe more likely—the gossip about the issue with Herb might still rest on actual events."

Across from her, Jacqueline slumped back against the window. Very uncharacteristic for someone so elegant, Agnes's mind acknowledged.

The defeated tone matched the loss of posture when Jac concluded, "In short, my worry about the program is justified either way."

"Well… Ask Herb what happened. No one else can tell you."

"I tried." Jac's voice pitched higher, and she pushed the half-eaten soup away.

Concerned they might draw the attention of other patrons after all, Agnes glanced at the neighboring tables on either side. No one appeared interested.

To change topics, she said, "Hey, don't waste that delicious coconut curry. No point in letting things spoil your appetite. You already look peaky today." Determined to set a good example, she finished her own soup.

When her friend merely massacred the Calabrese instead, she urged her, "At least dunk it first."

Absentmindedly, Jacqueline dipped a piece of bread and bit off the curried end before it could drip onto the table. For a moment, Jac regarded her speculatively, bread held aloft.

Agnes's mind veered toward the question of dessert. Maybe

better not. Too much food would make her sleepy. Not good when the afternoon class had a test. Vigilance paid.

Into her musings, Jac said, "The only way out is for you to investigate. Disprove this mean gossip."

"Come again?"

"You heard me. Prove Herb innocent of whatever urban legend holds him guilty of."

"Me? I've got no clue about any of this. Hardly know the man. What do you take me for? Some private eye?"

"You've done it before. If you can investigate a murder, tracking down a rumor is child's play for you."

"I did no such thing!" Nor do I want to remember any murder, Agnes added silently.

"Your mom said last summer was already the second murderer you helped unmask. To have her tell me about it, rather than you sharing, really hurt. But I respect your sensitivity on the subject. So, I never alluded to it before."

"When did Sera say this?" asked Agnes, curious now despite wishing to bury the memory.

"Remember the night we went for dinner during her stopover in Toronto on the return flight from BC? We chatted about the summer holidays while waiting for you."

Dimly, Agnes recollected being stuck in inbound traffic to the mega-city—mega by Canadian standards. Sera's cross-country flight from Vancouver on the Pacific Coast of British Columbia to Halifax in Atlantic Canada allowed for a one-day stop in Toronto to visit old friends—and do dinner with her daughter. For decades, Agnes had dreaded her mom's flying visits. Not so since their vacation in Germany.

"Anyway," Agnes now said, "I didn't investigate. If anything, I played Watson to someone else's Holmes. Forget it." No wish to expand on the topic, she decided.

Though, the summer experience had reawakened her taste for mysteries. Ever since she's reread all of Conan Doyle and deep-dived into Christie's mega output. The genre enamored her as a teenager. By the time she studied at Uni, she'd shed the habit as shamefully frivolous. Nowadays, she reassured herself, the interest in it was purely philosophical. Human nature, reasoning, and ethics, after all, were the province of philosophers.

"Watson or Holmes, I don't care," Jac echoed her silent musings. "Philosophers are experts in logic and deductive reasoning. An ideal prep for ferreting out things."

"Holmes relies a lot on induction based on empirical evidence, rather than deductive logic."

"Don't split words. For once, put your training to good use and disprove these rumors."

"Oh? Thanks a bunch. Here, I thought my PhD was useful in teaching philosophy. Besides, the difference between induction and deduction matters a—"

"Agnes, cut it out. What matters, this mushrooming rumor harms all of us. Apart from jeopardizing all I've worked for, it'll ruin Herb's career."

"Ah, talking about dear Herb?" A resonant voice cut in.

Like a gossip caught red-mouthed slaughtering someone's repute, Agnes felt her cheeks burn. Without turning to look, she'd already recognized the newcomer. The heady mix of amusement and self-confidence was all too familiar to her.

They weren't exactly friends. TC lingered for a chat when he dropped by the basement office where the part-timers congregated. Though he himself didn't use the 'underground' as Agnes dubbed the dingy office. The guy must have a desk somewhere upstairs, she figured. One ran into him at reception or in the hallway up there. She never asked.

His witty conversation and handsome features made him intriguing company.

After finishing his master's degree, TC unfortunately enrolled in an online university's PhD program where faculty proved anything but supportive, as he'd mentioned at one point.

With a heavy teaching load at Bowman College, no wonder his dissertation progress stalled.

Early on this term, she jokingly told him she'd soon be writing her own 'notes from underground.' He got the reference right away, countering he hoped she wouldn't turn out quite as spiteful as the underground man. One would expect nothing else from a guy with a double major BA in literature and philosophy.

Her class had been reading Dostoevsky's *Notes from Underground*. Come to think of it, Dorian had pointed out how amazingly skilled the Russian author was at drawing fascinatingly unlikeable characters as the unnamed protagonist. Following the current predilection for likable characters, most of his classmates had demurred. Only Lester vehemently agreed. But then, peers found Lester the most unlikeable of all.

The memory made her look up at TC now with a wry smile.

His eyes held hers as he asked, "Mind if I join the colloquium?"

Chapter 6

What could they do but accede to the request? Teeth set on edge, Jacqueline fumed. No need for Agnes to smile quite so radiantly in pointing to the vacant chair, thought Jac. Her own scowl did nothing to discourage him. Try as she might, her facial features didn't lend themselves to intimidating expressions, as her friends and loved ones often told her.

So unfortunate Timothy's catching the last remarks about Herbert. She deplored her failure to spot him in time. Too many people blocked her view when the neighboring table changed shift, so to speak. How much else, Jac wondered now, had Timothy overheard before he made his move? The Perfect Grounds takeout cup in his hand showed he didn't enter merely a moment ago.

The way he crossed his legs and sat back left no doubt he meant to stay. It irked Jac into pointing out, "Why the paper cup if you intend to linger?"

"Are you appealing to my green conscience? Scout's honor: I recycle. Habitually." TC flashed her a smug glance before turning his chair slightly toward Agnes to ask, "So, what's all this fuss about our friend Herb?"

The practiced boyish smile might well mislead Agnes, who

was easily charmed by attractive males. To forestall Agnes's response to the charmer and his question, Jacqueline leaned in to say, "Surely you are aware of the latest student gossip, Timothy? As a long-standing employee of our department, you must realize the negative impact of such malicious chatter."

The puzzled glance she received from Agnes brought home how pompous she must sound. No matter. Time to take a firm line with Mr. Timothy Charles Elliot, MA.

"Oh, it's Timothy today, is it? I'm in Dr. Xavier's bad books again." The mockingly raised eyebrow was solely for Agnes's amusement.

Attuned to Jaqueline's wintry mood, Agnes said gently, "Nothing personal, TC. We're all on edge because of Dorian. People in admin, like Jac, bear the brunt of it."

Immediately, Timothy grew solemn. A face for every occasion, Jac thought wryly. As she would have predicted, the words and tone followed suit. In a pinch, he was her match for academic pomposity.

"Forgive me. Flippancy was uncalled for." A deep sigh. "Put it down to my way of coping with grief. I truly admired Dorian as a gifted friend—or may I say 'protégé'?"

With pensive care, he placed the paper cup on the table and lowered his eyes as if in respectful mourning, it seemed to Jac. Her conscience chided her not to be uncharitable.

Agnes reached out but then dropped her hand before it touched Timothy's arm. Instead, she said, almost too softly for Jac to catch, "We understand how deeply it affects his close friends. Like you, TC. And Cass. She's—"

About to give a nudge with the toe of her boot, Jac caught her breath in relief that Agnes broke off before committing an indiscretion. The way the man's head came up to glance shrewdly at Agnes evinced curiosity.

Yet, when he said, "One feels so utterly helpless," Jacqueline admitted to herself that the sadness must be genuine. She mustn't let her own dislike of the eternal ABD cloud her judgment. Did Elliot know his never-ending 'All But Dissertation' status in an obscure online PhD program he'd chosen earned him that nickname among full-time faculty?

Jac covertly glanced at Timothy still bent over his paper cup in devout silence. Though he tried to sabotage her chances during the hiring process they'd both competed in, she should rise above bearing grudges years later. After all, Timothy lost out in the end. Contrite, Jac vowed to live up to her own sense of professionalism.

To make amends for her earlier curtness, she murmured, "We all appreciate how much you care about our students." Such supportiveness, however, should not reflect in top grades for his favorites, she felt. Sorry about the mental relapse into caviling, she hastened on, "You're not alone. It's devastating we can't do anything about—"

"But Jac," Agnes cut in, "didn't you just ask me to disprove—"

"I'm sure TC wouldn't—"

"What wouldn't TC?" the man cut in. "You were going to say, Agnes?" With another of his irksome smiles at Jac, he inquired, "Shouldn't I at least be aware of what I wouldn't?"

The gambit appealed to Agnes, who remarked with a grin, "Got you, Jac." She leaned forward, the heavy dark hair curtaining her face from the man beside her as she whispered, "He's better suited than me to delve into things. You need someone close to Dorian and everyone involved."

Of course, Elliot heard every word, though he leaned back and studied his nails. Left with no choice but to do the polite thing, Jacqueline opted to explain, albeit dismissively. She straightened her back and addressed Timothy in measured words.

"I rashly asked Agnes's help in pinpointing the source of this spiteful gossip about Herbert and Dorian. Since then, I've realized there is no way of tracing it." After a quick pleading glance at Agnes not to argue, Jac continued, "Forget what I said. Nothing can be done about it."

As though she hadn't spoken, the insufferable man turned to Agnes. "You were saying 'disprove.' Was the idea to show Herb had nothing to do with Dorian's death?"

When Jacqueline commenced to answer, his palm went up. "Let Agnes speak for herself. She has a stake in the department now, too."

"Kind of," said Agnes, looking her apology at Jac. "I believe accidental death to be far more likely. Jac's major worry is the potential harm to the Creative Writing program. Plus, to Herb. Hence, the idea to prove Herb never received Dorian's story submission, thus saving everyone's reputation. Errors happen." Again, she glanced at Jacqueline before she added, "Some believe Dorian's death harks back to a breakup."

Jac closed her eyes to prevent groaning out loud. While she's sought to stifle Timothy's curiosity, Agnes was fueling it. His features betrayed rapt attention despite the laid-back posture he assumed.

"You think a lover's quarrel made him take his own life? A romantic end, far more apt for a creative genius." In complete disregard of Jacqueline's presence, his gaze courted Agnes.

This was getting worse. Jac's irritation mounted. She no longer cared if she sounded waspish. "As a close friend of Dorian, you, of all people, should know the truth behind all this."

The glance her remark earned her was far from friendly. He obviously resented interference in his growing rapport with Agnes, who annoyed Jac further by suggesting brightly, "All the more reason to let TC find out what's going on. If a degree in philosophy qualifies for a truth-finding mission—as you claimed earlier, Jac—then he's quite as well-suited. Add to that his familiarity with students and faculty, etc., he clearly is your man for the job."

Shot yourself in the foot, Jac wanted to shout at her friend.

If you argue along those lines, he's also better suited for the permanent position the department will post soon. Academia was tough enough. You didn't need to undermine your chances.

To his credit, Timothy humbled himself for once. Or is he trying to please Agnes? Jac wondered. For he responded, "No way a double major and MA are on par with a full-blooded philosopher's credentials. You've got the advantage there, Dr. Taylor."

The effect of Timothy's words and deep blue eyes on her friend showed in the rosy color suffusing Agnes's creamy complexion, a glow to enhance her attractiveness. Those two are falling for each other, she realized with sudden certainty. In a flash, she foresaw endless complications to her own friendship with Agnes.

Timothy's voice, however, was merely playful when he said, "Tell you what—why don't I assist you in this mission? Two heads are better and all that."

Agnes sparkled with enthusiasm. "Hey, let's create a team instead." She turned a delighted face to Jac. "Don't you agree TC and I can take turns playing Holmes and Watson on the Philosopher Team?"

Jacqueline ground her teeth, thinking there's only one team he plays on, and that's Team Timothy.

Chapter 7

Another fifteen minutes to go until the end of test time. Agnes felt bored out of her mind watching the last stragglers struggling to find answers. Most of their peers finished in half the allotted span.

While she monitored the classroom from sheer habit, her mind drifted off again.

The first hour of class had been a blast. Keyed up from an exciting chat with TC about their mission, she'd dazzled the class with a spirited lecture. Written over two thousand years ago, Seneca's letter 'On Friendship' still resonated. The Roman philosopher's point that a friend is someone we trust, which presupposes we thoroughly know their character, caught the students' interest. Never mind Gen Zs alleged indiscriminate craving for social media 'friends.'

A warm glow spread to Agnes's face, recalling TC's eagerness to assist her. Maybe they could become friends. Why Jac changed her mind beat her. After being so keen for Agnes to disprove the rumors. Odd. On the way back, while Team Philosopher tossed ideas, Jac didn't say a word. Okay, some were rather wild, like infiltrating the rumormongers.

A throat-clearing brought her back to the present. She

scanned the room. Its setup, twelve so-called puddle tables intended for four occupants each, was not conducive to administering exams. Students faced each other rather than the media console podium at the front. Great for group discussions and collaborative work, but a nightmare for proctoring a full class. A row of windows toward the busy hallway aggravated the distraction. Well, better than a completely windowless room, she admitted. Those were claustrophobic. The motorized blinds, forever stuck in their casing under the ceiling, no longer worked in this room to shut out the chance of peers outside catching the attention of their buddies inside the classroom. Or anything else going on out there...

Just like now when her idle glance caught sight of someone going by—or more accurately, she decided, stealing by. Because whoever it was seemed to walk on tiptoes, rounded back hunched forward. A baseball cap pulled down, its bill covering the nose, increased the incongruous appearance. When the head swiveled toward the window where two girls sat across from each other, bowed over their test sheets, reflected light flashed for a second. Must be wearing glasses, Agnes deduced.

Still amused, her finger reached for the touchpad to wake up her laptop. Eyes on its screen's clock display, she announced, "Another five minutes. Please finish up."

Enough time to check college emails. Ah, one from Cassandra. Glad she's getting in touch about the missed presentation, Agnes thought. When she clicked to read and respond, she found a frantic plea to meet 'ASAP.' Sent an hour ago.

Cautious about students' anxieties, Agnes suggested coming to her office in half an hour and promptly received a request to meet off campus instead. Not standard procedure for student consultations, but what the heck, the bereavement warranted exceptions. Busy fingers already responded to suggest a bagel caff *en route* to Jac's house. Students liked the place. Would get her home not much later than planned, and she could grab a smoked salmon cream cheese bagel as a pseudo dinner.

Cass's answer flashed up in seconds: 'I wait out front.'

The three students near the podium got up to hand in their test sheets and scantron cards.

"Thanks. How did it go?" she asked.

One of them, who never uttered a word in class, shook his head and smiled shyly. The other wriggled her hand, saying, "So-so." The third couldn't wait to get out.

Bodes ill for results, Agnes sighed as she contemplated their departing backs. Two more filed out after dropping off their tests unceremoniously. The girls at the window seats took the longest to gather their scattered belongings from the floor.

Better get out of here fast, Agnes said to herself once alone. While she packed up, she scanned the space for stuff left behind, as often happened in the rush to leave after a test. Not today. A glance at her mobile told her there'd be barely time to feed the scantron machine at the office before seeing what was up with Cass.

The moment she reached the door, it slowly opened as of its own accord. In reflex, she took a step back. The person who slouched in the doorway startled her even more. The bill of a now familiar blue cap confronted her in lieu of a face.

"What are you—" She stopped as the chin went up to reveal granny glasses.

"Joel! You shouldn't—" The rest remained unsaid. For she realized slinking about might be the kid's normal mode of loco-motion. Though she'd never consciously noticed. An inconspic-uous student in every way.

Instead of his usual diffidence, he conveyed a sense of eminent self-importance as he straightened up. A furtive glance in both directions of the hallway and he eased the door shut.

"Can we speak, Dr. Taylor? I have a report to make."

The tone caused Agnes to suppress a grin. Cloak and dagger stuff in the offing. Her mind brought back the image of the scene in the Pit the night before and wiped the growing smile from her lips. Perhaps Joel knew something.

Torn between curiosity and concern about being late for Cass, she turned to rest the heavy backpack on the podium.

"What's up?" she prompted.

"I must bring an incident to your attention that occurred in this room…" He consulted the mobile clutched in his right hand, "Seventeen minutes ago."

"In this class? You weren't in—" Oh no, she thought, but outside the hallway window.

"I observed an obvious breach of academic integrity." Said with marked disapproval. "Two females exchanged their grading cards and—"

"Stop, Joel. We don't go by hearsay." Or ratting on peers, her mind supplied.

"The evidence is irrefutable," Joel piped up in his treble voice, thumbs fumbling the mobile close to the thick lenses of his glasses. "I videoed it."

"Don't! Sorry, Joel. Don't show me. The college community would be rightfully upset if people felt someone might secretly record them while on campus. Our AD wouldn't accept this kind—" Better not call it 'denunciation,' she figured. Already, Joel's face crumbled in dejection and hurt.

She hastened to reassure him, "You meant well. Thanks. I'm so glad you came to me," thinking, instead of plastering it all over social media channels.

"My program teaches surveillance techniques," Joel informed her, standing very straight now, chin up, two fingers of his left hand pushing the slippery glasses back in place. "The profs expect us to gain practice." Then his shoulders slumped forward, and his voice quivered. "How else can I prepare for my career as Private Eye?"

"Oh, are you in the private investigation and security program? I didn't realize." Her general education classes drew on cohorts from lots of programs. "Um, so interesting," she added to his vigorous nodding.

The little guy's feet moved incessantly to an inner beat, up and down. It made one's head want to follow suit, she found.

"You've got to tell me more about it sometime," she said soothingly. "I'm sure they wouldn't want you to practice on unsuspecting peers, though."

"If your target suspects it, surveillance doesn't work," Joel pointed out—reasonably, she admitted to herself.

"Well, keep it under your hat...*er*. I mean, don't spread your observations for now, please. Confidentiality is part of your job, isn't it?" A slow answering nod from him, reinforced by her smile. "We'll talk again soon. Got to run to a meeting." Mental note: check with Jac or Martha about how they handle this around here. Argh, cheaters eat up far too much of everyone's time.

She slung her backpack onto one shoulder and invitingly opened the door.

Still, Joel did not look mollified. Hunched forward, though not walking on tippy toes, his disappointment was palpable.

The slight figure slunk out into the hallway. From under the cap, she heard a murmur, "What's the use?"

Chapter 8

Jacqueline stared unseeingly out into the gray drizzle. Arms tightly wrapped around her torso, she hugged herself, fingers plucking at the soft merino wool of the black cardigan, a long-time favorite she kept at the office both for warmth and comfort.

Usually so calming, the view onto the park-like campus grounds did nothing to soothe her mind this afternoon. Nor did the serene ambience she'd created in her workspace.

The austere standard office outfitting was softened by wooden bookshelves and cushions in pastel light greens, sunny yellows, accentuated by shades of white that she'd introduced. Renoir prints in minimalist frames surrounded her with peaceful scenes. The much-loved *Road in Louveciennes* invited viewers to join a family on their country walk among luscious trees. His *By the Seashore* vied for her attention across her desk. Today, the quizzing glance of Renoir's girlfriend seemed to mock her until she'd jumped up to pace, ending up by the window.

Was knowing better than ignorance? Why had she asked Renata if she didn't want an answer? Advising appointments should focus on the student's progress. Instead, they'd side-tracked to current events. Perchance, inevitable, she realized now.

The conversation replayed in Jacqueline's mind. Concerned how students were coping with the unexpected passing of a peer, she'd asked Renata if she and her friends were all right. The young woman raised her eyebrows as if puzzled.

Thrown off her stride, Jacqueline groped for delicate phrases without success. "I'm sure," she said, "you all must feel devastated about what happened… To Dorian, I mean."

"Oh, that." Brows relaxed, and the expression changed to eagerness. "Yeah, sure. Raised quite a shitstorm. A prof driving one of us to ending it all. Really sucks."

Jacqueline's efforts to instill reason by pointing out the danger of groundless accusations fell flat. Grasping at Agnes's straws, she asserted, "I am convinced Dorian's demise was a tragic accident, with no one to blame."

"Not what they say on Snapchat. You wouldn't believe the stuff posted all over social networks."

"One certainly shouldn't believe the rumors floating around," Jac had countered.

Eyes rolling, ruffling bristly hair with sinewy hands, Renata challenged her in an echo of Kalen's favorite line, "You profs got to stick up for each other no matter what."

Such low opinion of the ethics among academics appalled Jacqueline.

What on earth could one do to disprove the accusations against Herb? Unease filled her at the thought of Agnes getting involved with Timothy. Why did he have to barge in on their luncheon conversation? Agnes was trustworthy and discreet if left to work the case alone.

Here I go, Jac wryly interrupted her own train of thought. I am really thinking of Agnes as some sort of investigator.

The dratted Elliot, however, would turn it somehow to his own advantage. Though how investigating with Agnes could benefit Timothy, Jac couldn't imagine.

Or am I jealous of him—diverting Agnes's interest? Alienation of a friend's affection? Ridiculous—

A knock on the door cut off her introspection. She pivoted to face the door and called, "Come in," as she returned to her desk chair to check the advising schedule in the daily planner. The name next on the list triggered apprehension.

Before she could compose herself, the door had already opened to reveal a smirking Lester Kowalski.

Dressed in black, the long dark fringe falling well below the brows, he paused.

"Good to see you, Lester. Take a seat while I consult your file." Jac pointed toward the chair strategically angled sideway to avoid a confrontational position directly across from her desk.

Much aware of the psychological impacts of office setups, she'd requested her desk to be placed to the left of the door. Seated with her back to the bookshelves, she could welcome anyone entering from the hallway yet enjoy the ever-present panoramic vista outside. Though unavoidably, the desk presented a barrier, the angled visitor chair minimized the stance and enabled anyone who dropped by to admire the view. A second chair sat at the ready in front of the large window to be pulled up as needed.

To this one, Lester now veered despite her tacit invitation to sit closer. Backlit, his features lay in shadow even on this grayish day. For a second, Jacqueline considered flicking on the overhead fluorescents but resisted. Its harsh light would bother her more than reveal him, she suspected.

No word came from Lester, who hadn't returned her greeting. From below his fringe, his dark eyes watched her, biding his time, she sensed. His long, bony fingers plucked at loose strands of the frayed jeans, the torn black fabric framing a knobby pale knee.

Aware of her glance, his lips twisted into a sneer.

For Christ's sake, be professional, Jac ordered herself. He's not menacing—just different. Possibly suffers from mental health issues. As a coordinator, she knew he hadn't registered with accessible learning services for any accommodations.

Quite a number of students, she assumed, remained undiagnosed.

"Thanks for coming to see me, Lester. Before we review where you stand in program completion, how are things going for you? Any concerns or issues you might like to share?"

His staccato *hee-hee-hee* rattled Jac. The lips barely moved.

He's mimicking an insane character just to get a rise, she told herself. Ignore it.

"Well, if there's nothing on your mind, we can proceed—"

"To business as usual? Suit you fine, won't it?"

His head rose so abruptly it lifted the strands of hair to reveal glowering charcoal-colored eyes. Their penetrating stare caused Jac to sit back with a start.

"What...what do you mean?"

"Academic stupor. Things finally happen, and the lot of you pretend to remain comatose in your complaisant slumber."

"What on earth are you talking about?" Though she knew all too well. Unable to prevent sinking into pomposity, she hurried on. "We—faculty and administrators—are deeply concerned about recent events. The passing of—"

"Euphemisms. Nothing but empty platitudes to mask your inaptness in dealing with life at the raw. Stifle authentic emotions—sacrificed on the altar of prescriptivism."

With an effort, Jacqueline regained her poise. "I don't like your tone, Lester. Nor the sentiments expressed."

"Bet you don't—"

"Let's return to the subject of this meeting. Your academic progress and program requirements—"

"Then why did you ask about concerns and issues? Too disturbing, aren't they?"

"Could it be that Dorian's passing has upset you more than you care to show?"

"There you go again. 'Death' is the word. A good, wholesome, honest word. Why does everyone shy away from it? The 'grim reaper,' as you like to call *Thanatos*, gets you eventually."

Again, the pseudo-insane cackle to fray her nerve ends. "About our dead genius—frankly, I don't give a f—"

"It seems to me today is not a suitable time for—"

A light triple knock interrupted Jacqueline's attempt to reschedule Lester's advising session.

"Door's open," she responded and never was more relieved to see Martha's reassuringly comfortable face poke around the doorframe.

"So sorry to interrupt. Could I have a quick word, Jacqueline? Out here, if convenient?" To the student, she added, "Won't take a minute, Lester."

With alacrity, Jac emerged from behind her desk to join the AD in the hallway. They stepped out of hearing range, Jac cutting short Martha's apologies.

"I take it Lester is being his usual confrontational self? In the two years he's been with us, none of us has escaped his moods. If he weren't such a brilliant student…"

"This time, they all have reason to be upset," Jac ventured.

"None more than Dorian's parents. That's what I came to discuss. They're arriving within the hour from Florida. We'll meet this evening at their request." Martha's well-padded fingers stroked an errant silvery curl from her forehead. In her late fifties and not inclined to exercise, as Jac knew, the AD dressed in tweeds and sensible shoes, completely at ease with the extra pounds her sedate lifestyle packed on. Neat, effective, and reliable appeared coined for her.

Now, she hesitated before coming to the actual point of her errant. At length, she said, "They've asked me to connect them with faculty who knew their son well. Can I impose on you to visit them at their hotel tomorrow morning?"

"Of course, I'd be glad to," Jac said, feeling anything but.

"Though Timothy is not among our full-time faculty, he apparently befriended Dorian. They can meet with him after his last class in the afternoon—just checked his schedule."

The thought of Elliot imposing his personality on the

grieving parents rekindled Jacqueline's unease about the man's influence on people. It prompted her to suggest, "Agnes Taylor might want to accompany me. Dorian was in two of her classes. They spoke frequently. She knew him very well." An exaggeration, but still.

"By all means," agreed Martha. "Agnes strikes me as a very level-headed yet caring person."

"Students love her." Any opportunity to sing Agnes's praise appealed to Jac. The job posting would come out in a few weeks. Now was the time to pave the way for her friend to get hired. "She's a valuable addition to our faculty."

"Too true. She's spoken of well by colleagues and students alike. So, that's settled. Ten o'clock suit you? I'll reach out tonight to confirm and pass on the address."

They parted ways at Jac's door. Her peripheral vision caught Lester scurry back to his chair. Did he listen at the door? Or worse, get into her laptop? Did she close its lid to hibernate before stepping out?

Chapter 9

Drizzle pearled on the Gore-Tex of her marine blue jacket and dripped from the hood onto Agnes's nose. The backpack clunked against her lower rips as she sped down the rain-slick pavement toward the bagel caff. From afar, mellow lights glistened through the windows, inviting passers-by to seek its haven. The black-painted storefront of the Bagel Bar highlighted their effect. A huge, twisted, golden bagel dangled above the door. Together with the baking scents pumped out by the exhaust system, it enticed hungry students and faculty alike. Agnes' stomach gurgled in anticipation.

Then she saw her, half-hidden in an adjacent doorway. Skeins of long hair, its copper color dulled by heavy moisture, reached snake-like down the front and back of an oversized sweater that must have been light gray before its exposure to the elements. Cassandra stood Medusa-like as though expecting impending disaster, Agnes thought.

This impression intensified on close-up. By nature, Cass's ivory skin glowed faintly pink with a dusting of freckles around the nose. Today, red blotches marked her cheeks, shading into bluish rings below the eyes. She appeared feverish and, yes, diagnosed Agnes, distraught.

"Cass, let's get you inside. Have a hot drink," Agnes greeted her. "You got soaked through standing out here."

Only then did Cassandra seem to take in Agnes's arrival. The startlingly green eyes lost their manic stare and focus—but without losing their anxious expression.

"No! Please, let's go somewhere else. Anywhere." In answer to Agnes' surprised glance, she went on, "Kalen's in there. With Cleo and Joel." As if that explained the need to avoid the venue.

Maybe it does, Agnes figured. Not conducive to confidential talk if peers hang about. Reluctantly, she fell into step with Cass, who was already heading away from the inviting gleam of the windows. So much for toasted bagel dreams.

Fifty yards farther on, Cass pointed across the street at the tree-lined entrance to a parkette. Without waiting for Agnes's agreement, she stepped into the road, not looking right or left.

In a swift backward glance, Agnes caught sight of an oncoming car and grabbed Cass's sleeve to pull her back onto the sidewalk.

"Watch it," she cried out belatedly. "No need to get us killed."

Mutely, Cass waited until the vehicle had passed and, now checking both sides, led the way across.

What a dismal place for a conversation, Agnes commented to herself when they reached their apparent goal. Trees dripping, grass water-logged, rivulets burrowing through the graveled pathways, yikes. A deserted playground, bordered by graffiti-adorned benches where puddles pooled darkly. Only a red bucket lying abandoned on its side in the sandbox spoke of past pleasures.

"I don't understand, Cass. Why do we have to stand out here in this weather instead of meeting at my office or something? We'll both catch cold."

Just the thought sent shivers along Agnes's arms and back. She huddled deeper into the unlined rain jacket that provided neither warmth nor comfort. The weight cutting into her shoulders reminded her of her laptop, a rental issued by the college. Would the backpack's repellent coating hold up against a prolonged soaking?

The agonized expression on Cassandra's face pushed her own trivial worries into the background.

"What's wrong, Cass?" Well, of all the stupid questions. Of course, she's grieving; Agnes berated herself and hastened to amend, "Won't you tell me how I can help?"

The question didn't soothe the girl, who cast frantic glances in all directions as though looking for an escape route. Or expects spies lurking among the bushes, flashed through Agnes's mind, her afternoon's experience still a fresh memory.

Her voice dropped to an empathetic murmur to ease the girl's tension. "I know you must be terribly upset about losing a friend. It's hardest when it's someone so young with their whole life yet to live." Smacks of ageism, her mind commented in reflex. Before it could veer off into philosophical pondering, she added lamely, "Accidents happen."

While Agnes spoke, Cassandra's head shook in denial, her eyes losing their focus as if mesmerized by an inner vision. The words came as though from far away, "Evil took him. I feel it. Pure evil."

"Cass? What are you saying?" Unsure whether to touch the girl's arm to recenter her attention or if, like with sleepwalkers, it might startle her, Agnes stood still, an eerie foreboding creeping into her consciousness. She shook it off, impatient with herself.

The movement of her shudder brought Cass back to the present. But not to a calmer frame of mind. Now, she burst out, "No! No, that wasn't an accident. He—" Her hand went to her mouth, knuckles pressed against her lips as if to hold in whatever was about to escape.

"Are you saying it was intentional? Dorian actually—" Agnes stopped right there, faced with the girl's vehement headshaking, the coiled tresses slithering in agitated motion across the sweater.

"He had everything to live for," cried out Cassandra, leaving Agnes thoroughly perplexed about what was really going on in the student's mind. Perhaps Cass was confused and completely in denial.

So, she said, "A sudden passing shakes up everyone. None more than those close. A note may yet surface to explain—"

"There was no note. I looked everywhere," said Cass, almost too quiet for Agnes to hear.

"When? Maybe the first responders—"

"No. I found him on his bed. I still have a key. I searched before they came." The girl's mouth quivered. One hand went up to brush across her cheek as if in anticipation of tears.

"Oh, Cass. I'm so sorry. I didn't realize. How terrifying and upsetting for you." Her mind, however, added, shouldn't have touched anything. Only to tell herself there was no crime to require such precaution. If Cass searched for a note, suicide must have seemed likely.

Right now, the task was to calm the girl.

Aloud, Agnes said, "He might have written to his parents. An explanation may yet come forth."

Suicides, she assumed, would still post letters, even in a digital age, if they wanted to avoid their confidences found by the wrong person. Instant digital delivery may give the recipient time to interfere with their plans.

"He didn't kill himself," Cass interrupted her thought. The voice, now strong and insistent, she sought Agnes's eyes to ensure being believed. "Cerebral hemorrhage one guy said."

"Who?"

"The paramedic. When they saw the rat poison."

"What?" Agnes's voice had risen despite her aim to instill calmness. She reigned herself in yet quavered as she went on, "Are you saying he took poison?"

"No. The stuff he was on. Meds for his heart. A fib."

First, Agnes misunderstood Cass to refer to Dorian lying. Then it clicked.

"Oh, you mean he suffered from arterial fibrillation? Ah, I get it. Warfarin. A blood thinner, I believe. Originally conceived as a pesticide for rodent control, wasn't it?" She mulled over the implications.

"But then—" The inference she'd drawn remained unstated as Cass startled her by an outcry.

The girl's features went rigid. Wide-eyed. Her mouth partially open as if frozen in a cry, she stared past Agnes's head at the parkette entrance behind them. Before Agnes could turn to see what alarmed her, Cassandra swung around on her heels and ran off toward the opposite end of the green space.

"Hey! Wait up! Cassandra!" She made to follow but realized she was no match for the lithe and fit runner.

In frustration, her mouth twitched as her head gave an involuntary exasperated little shake. Resigned to have no choice but to await Cass contacting her at some point, she turned to leave by the way they'd come.

As she passed from among the trees at the narrow entrance into the street, she caught sight of the trio Cass evidently sought to avoid. Little Joel, Cleo, and Kalen were hastening around the corner onto the side street leading to the other end of the parkette.

Cassandra would be none too pleased if they caught up with her, mused Agnes. Did the sight of them prompt her to flee?

Chapter 10

"Just in time for dinner," Jac called out when she heard Agnes coming up the stairs. She lifted the lid to give the fish chowder a final stir and turned off the stove.

"Tea is on the table, and the soup won't take a minute. If you feel up to it," she added, giving Agnes an uncertain lopsided smile. "You haven't eaten yet, I hope?"

"Hey, are we celebrating or something? Not my usual homecoming to be greeted with a dinner invite. Hang on a sec while I change. Got soaked out there," said Agnes, deposited her backpack on the bench behind the kitchen table, and headed upstairs, not waiting for a response.

Dinner under control and no further chore to complete, Jac regarded the table, a retro 1950s Formica relict with a moss-green top. It stemmed from a yard sale together with two rather comfortable mismatched metal tube chairs. Spongy synthetic seats and backrests, one upholstered in light pink, the other in baby blue, they matched the ancient bulging fridge in powder-rose color. Back when she moved in, Jacqueline considered carrying the vintage vibe further but resisted. Instead, she'd opted for an uncluttered, clean look with white cotton drapes for the old casement windows giving on to the rear yard, which really was a parking lot. The few countertop appliances they owned were stainless steel. To enforce the 'Do not clutter' rule proved a constant trial to her patience.

By habit, everyone in the house catered to their own meals according to personal preference. Her male tenants rarely cooked and lived mostly on cheap take-outs, cans, and frozen dinners consumed at odd times. Weekends, Jac might make breakfast for two, and occasionally, she and Agnes prepared a joined dinner if their busy schedule allowed. Most days, however, each grabbed a solo meal on the fly.

Today, Jacqueline had a special reason to share her soup.

When Agnes returned in comfortable sweats, hair still moist around the temples, Jac placed filled bowls on the table. "It's just your lucky day," she joked and, pointing at the basket filled with fragrant slices, added, "Multigrain baguette fresh from that little bakery on Main Street."

They ate in silence for a few minutes. The only sound was Agnes's content sighing after the first spoonsful. Even if the cook said so herself, Jac felt the chowder turned out delicious. Chunks of haddock, cod, and some baby shrimps submersed in creamy broth, rich in vegetables.

Off and on, she stole a glance at Agnes to gauge her mood.

Before she could launch her appeal, Agnes sat back, raised her teacup and a quizzical eyebrow, and asked, "So, what game's afoot?"

Jac's rather insincere "Nothing much" received a friendly laugh and the comment, "C'mon. This uber-delicious soup comes at a price—admit it."

Further prevarication was pointless. "I plead guilty. Two things. One: Paul and Moshi invited friends over for this evening."

Agnes already started groaning, "Again?"

"Unfortunately, yes." Jacqueline glanced at her phone. "In roughly an hour. It's their buddy's birthday, and the intended venue fell through at the last minute. They are out stocking up on beer and other provisions. Expect a noisy, late night."

"Guess I'll better head right back to campus," said Agnes. "Got lots of grading and stuff to catch up on."

The tiredness in her friend's voice caused Jac a stab of compunction. "I thought you might. Hence, the quick dinner to provide sustenance for your midnight labors."

Though she aimed for a light tone, Jacqueline regretted the inconvenience. A constant juggling act to keep the three tenants happy, she thought. While Agnes was her best friend, whose comfort mattered most, fairness demanded to treat the males' tenancy on par.

Previous occasions showed how much the graduate students' boisterous company distracted Agnes. One couldn't tell if their lively conversation proved irresistible or if the incessant babble interfered with concentration. Either way, Agnes appeared unable to work once guests arrived. Jac herself simply withdrew to her private sanctuary, the small but cozy study, and donned noise-cancelling headphones.

"So?" Cup still aloft, Agnes broke into her reverie. "What's number two?"

"Ahem… More of a favor, really." Jac glanced down at their empty bowls and stood to move over to the stove. "More chowder?"

"Eating up's the favor? If so, any time," laughed Agnes and held out her bowl for a refill.

From the safe distance of the stove, Jac ventured, "Martha asked me to meet with Dorian's parents. Tomorrow at ten. They want to speak to the faculty who knew him. I…" Again, Jacqueline hesitated. Her friend's grin, however, reassured her. "I suggested—and Martha liked the idea—you should come along since you knew him quite well."

More chowder placed in front of her, Agnes chewed this over while ostensibly devoting her attention to the soup. After sipping more tea, she said, "Can't say I mind. Tough to talk to grieving loved ones. I don't relish the prospect. If it makes a difference to them, it's worth it." Upon Jac's relieved expression, she added, "From what Dorian mentioned about home, I'm curious what they're like. Come to think of it, they might shed light on this whole affair with Herb, don't you think? Um, could be awkward to mention, eh? You still want me to play sleuth?"

The reassurance of Agnes's easy agreement gave way to renewed apprehension. "Yes and no," Jacqueline temporized. "We need to quell the rumors before this malignant chatter harms the program. But—" She sat upright for emphasis, "I do not want Timothy involved."

"Why ever not?" A puzzled shake of her head dislodged Agnes's heavy hair she kept looped behind her ears. Both hands went up to tuck the strands back again. "I don't get it, Jac. He's been here a lot longer than me. Knows everyone, including Herb, of course, and was a sort of friend to Dorian."

Disagreements made Jac anxious, none worse than any with Agnes, who could run logical circles around her. She trusted her friend's judgment implicitly—unless it came to men. Perhaps growing up without a father made Agnes susceptible to males, or at least to the more forceful specimens of the breed.

Instead of voicing her thoughts, Jac took a stab at reasoning. "Prior knowledge won't influence you. At least you don't have any axes to grind and will be objective."

"And TC has axes lined up? Can't see why he'd be more— hey, why are you rolling your eyes at me? What is it with you and TC?"

For a moment, Jac hesitated what to do. Back in the day, she'd never shared, not even with her friend, how Timothy had attempted a come-on only to sabotage her during the hiring process. Through hints from a couple of colleagues and a few students, she'd heard about innuendos dropped strategically. By the time she gave her sample lecture and fielded a discussion, he'd been out of the running and undermined her credibility by bombarding her with unfair questions and comments, as it seemed to her. At the time, Agnes had her own woes and worked as a sessional instructor at a university too distant for them to meet, making it malapropos to rehash the episode in their infrequent emails or rare phone calls. They'd texted to cheer each other on and some minor griping, not anything requiring lengthy explanations.

Now, Jacqueline's role as program coordinator—with aspirations to climb the admin ladder—gave her pause for thought. Though she trusted Agnes implicitly, sharing the dirty linen about a colleague might ultimately backfire.

Since Agnes continued to regard her expectantly, Jac aimed for diplomacy, "Look at it this way: you and Timothy will compete for the same full-time position once the job is posted. He's shown himself to be fiercely competitive during hiring processes. If you get too familiar, you might end up giving him leverage he'll turn to his advantage."

"Like what?" asked Agnes. "Didn't you say my PhD is a clear advantage? How could closer acquaintance harm me? If advantage is to be had, wouldn't it go both ways?" The momentary grin, as though pleased with her reasoning, faded when she concluded, "Or do you assume he's smarter than me?"

"Not smarter, but more egotistical. Your sense of ethics would never allow you to be unscrupulous."

"So, he's unethical and lacks scruples?"

Flustered, Jacqueline backpedaled. "I asserted nothing of the kind. My point is, I'm certain of your integrity."

"Then you know more than I'd like to claim for myself. How can any of us be sure what we might or mightn't do if push comes to shove?"

"Oh, Agnes. You would never act seriously unethical. Not even mildly, I wager."

"Neither you nor I—and I think you're less likely," she smiled warmly, "set out to do wrong. The same, I take it, goes for most people. In our own mind, we'd judge what we do as the right thing to do. At least while we act. Take Herb, for example."

When Jac nodded, Agnes studied her speculatively. "Say I'd find out he indeed and intentionally misappropriated Dorian's work—hard to imagine what proof might consist of—would you suppress the evidence to save your program?"

Caught unawares, Jacqueline fidgeted. Her mind anticipated Agnes to make a point about Herb's potential wrongdoing, not pose a moral dilemma for Jac. While her hands lined up a milk pitcher and teapot, her heart accelerated. Would she?

"Hey, no need to answer. Was merely rhetorical, just to make a point." Agnes aimed to reassure her.

It only increased the need to confess. "I hope I wouldn't." With a shy smile, she admitted, "My Catholic upbringing might save me. I'd feel dreadfully guilty if I did."

"Oh, I remember. The old fire and brimstone priest back in Quebec."

"You can't shed childhood indoctrination. My dad always told me not to worry. Back then, I had nightmares of purgatory after *Père* Mártin's sermons. He taught religion at my school, too. Like a gigantic crow spreading its wings, he used to hurry through the hallways in his billowing black cassock, always ready to pounce on hapless pupils." In memory, Jacqueline shivered.

"Whew, what a scare for kids. Still, maybe you're lucky. For most of us, life's circumstances interfere with the best of intentions. They drive people to deeds their sober mind neither anticipates—nor condones. As the saying goes, the way to hell is paved with good intensions."

"Don't you believe some persons or personality types are prone to unethical—even criminal—actions?"

"Psychological and biological determinism? Can't say I buy into that. Or, at least, not prenatally determined. Certain psychological and character developments, together with nurture and circumstances over time, may prepare the ground for unethical seeds to flourish. Ultimately, however, it's still a choice to succumb to temptation—or not."

"Aren't you contradicting yourself? Didn't you say no one knows what they might do in a crunch?"

"Exactly. None of us can be sure what their choice will be when temptation is strong enough. It's just some develop a more fertile ground for choices which push them over the edge to the wrong side."

A wide grin split Agnes's face and turned into a spontaneous laugh. "Listen to me waffle on in cliched phraseology. The ancient philosopher Aristotle puts it most succinctly: it's all about habituation to virtuous actions. According to him, humans are not moral or immoral by nature but become so through how we act."

She heaved herself up and grabbed their bowls to carry to the dishwasher. Over her shoulder, she said, "Speaking of which, I'd better head back to campus for a bout of virtuous grading."

Still sitting at the table, Jac realized they'd effectively side-tracked each other from discussing Timothy.

Chapter 11

"Oh shoot!" Startled by her own voice, Agnes's head jerked up. No one was there to hear her.

No sign of life. Humanity might as well have abandoned ship.

The basement office lay deserted. Only the hissing, gurgling, and humming of the exposed air exchange pipes overhead kept her company. For over two hours, she'd graded non-stop, eyes glued to the screen, oblivious to her surroundings. An occasional click of her mouse when opening yet another file did not interrupt the monotony.

Then it hit her. She'd totally forgotten to drop off the paperwork for the cheating case. What with rushing about all day, no wonder her memory bank ran on empty.

No time like the present to remedy her omission. A good excuse to stretch her sore muscles, crammed from hunching over the laptop, by running up to the admin office. Leave the docs on Fraser's desk. As chief of support staff, he'd be in early the next morning and could process them.

While thinking it through, Agnes rummaged in her backpack for the fat envelope that held the completed forms and documentation for the integrity breach. Quickest, going up the backstairs, she figured. They opened onto the far end of the hallway, across from the admin office space upstairs.

Out in the dingy basement corridor, her steps echoed off the blistering institutional-gray walls and ceiling. A steel door with a quick-release push bar led to a utilitarian stairway with treads of stark metal grid. At every step, a clanging resounded in the narrow stairwell of exposed concrete. Designed not for aesthetics but for fire safety.

Not fond of elevators to begin with, Agnes never took them at night, too worried about getting stuck with no one around on campus to notice. Silly, of course, she realized. Security was on duty 24/7. The emergency intercom would work. One would hope.

As she pushed open the fire door to the upper floor, the hallway there proved just as devoid of life. Several yards across, dim light illuminated the milk glass of the admin entrance from inside. Just the nightlight. Agnes swiped the access card dangling from a black ribbon around her neck. A click and a tiny, flashing green light announced she was free to enter.

Envelope tucked under her left arm, she nudged the door open. No one around here either.

Straight ahead, the partition around Fraser's workspace, roughly chest-height, impressed tidy as ever. On the ledge, he'd stacked promotional and informative material for the programs they offered. A box of tissues and hand sanitizer completed the ensemble.

Agnes's eyes veered to the right to the minute kitchenette. Should she treat herself to a coffee while up here? Someone on staff stocked a delectable array of pods in assorted flavors.

She took a step in that direction, intending to dump the envelope on Fraser's desk along the way when a sound behind her caught her off-guard. In reflex, she swung around to see the door to AD Muller's office inch open. A long black stick pumped in and out in rhythmical motion, accompanied by metallic creaking and rattling. In the dim half-light, it threw an ominous shadow onto the other wall.

Mesmerized, Agnes stood still. Envelope raised like a shield as if it could ward off an attack, she watched. The rear end of someone in washed-out blue trousers emerged. A curved back in navy blue followed suit. Finally, a head of sparse whitish hair protruded, moving back and forth in sync with the stick, now identifiable as a fat wooden mop handle.

Agnes was about to speak to make her presence known when a grating screech interrupted. A large zinc pail on metal castors scooted out into the reception area, evidently pulled along by the elderly gent. So deeply enrapt in his cleaning, he'd lost awareness of the world around him, she figured and opted for a gentle cough. No reaction.

Should she just sneak out, closing the door softly so as not to spook him? Just then, he straightened up, turned, and offered a wrinkled smile. The name tag on his chest read Giuseppe.

"Good evening, miss."

"Hi. I'm Agnes Taylor. I teach here. Sorry if I startled you."

"Not me. *Professori* work late. They come in here. Get mail. Bring mail. Lots of things."

Something clicked in Agnes's mind. "You mind me asking, Giuseppe, do students drop off papers," waving her envelope, "or stuff—at night, I mean?"

He looked at her, frowning as if she'd suggested some nocturnal drug racket going on under his nose.

She hastened to set the record straight. "You know, when they forget to hand in their assignments in class. Or are late. Do they leave them here on the staff's desk?" Demonstrating her point, she dropped her envelope with a satisfying thud onto the immaculate surface.

"No, miss. The students can't come in. At five, it is closed."

Agnes's face fell. Countless deep creases on his face crinkled all over as he added, "Happens many times. I open the door and see paper on the floor and big brown..." The mop handle stabbed toward Fraser's desk.

"You mean envelopes like mine?"

"*Si.*"

"They'd be in your way when cleaning. You don't just leave them there, do you?"

"No, miss. I put all things on the table." He emphasized with his mop pointer. Agnes hadn't noticed the small side table half hidden by the partition surrounding the workstation. Now she saw a lonely glove and a reusable water bottle in pink plastic.

About to ask whether he recalled any drop-off for Herb, she realized it to be a ridiculous question given the time lapse and number of students and profs. The clicking of the door release from behind interrupted. A glance over her shoulder brought on a smile of sheer pleasure. It turned into a grin when TC looked pointedly from her to Giuseppe and back, his eyebrows going up in mock wonder.

"A clandestine meeting? Or colloquium on mopping techniques?" His eyes pointed to the mop the cleaner's chin rested on, cushioned by knobby hands cupping the stick handle.

"Just enjoying a chat while I drop off some stuff for Fraser," said Agnes. Better to avoid drawing Giuseppe's attention to her real purpose. "You picking up your mail?" she asked to make innocuous conversation.

"Yeah—and borrowing our wizard's sharp scissors." He stepped forward and, coming very close to Agnes, leaned over the partition to grab a pair from a plastic holder on the desk. When he straightened up, their eyes met. "Catch you later downstairs, Agnes."

His neutral tone struck Agnes like a dismissal. A slow blush crept up her throat to her cheeks. "Right," she mumbled. Head lowered, she turned and caught sight of the mop pail. The presence of the cleaner cramped TC's style. The buoying thought made her smile at its owner, who reciprocated like a sweet-natured granddad.

"So nice talking to you. See you around. Have a great evening, Giuseppe."

"You too," the elderly man's eyes sparkled knowingly but kindly.

Outside, Agnes figured she might as well stroll down to the main stairs. More grading didn't seem enticing. Not even a coffee to sweeten the task. To go back now would be awkward.

Just then, halfway toward the staircase, she noticed a door a few inches ajar. Another nocturnal laborer. As she came abreast with it, a sob stifled by a gasping intake of breath made her stop dead. Unsure what to make of it, she hesitated. Invade a private moment? The person might need help or resent the intrusion. Her eyes fell on the nameplate next to the doorframe. Herbert Nessbit.

A wrenching sob decided for her. She inched open the door to see if help might be welcome. Cast in the candescent light of a shaded desk lamp, Herb's scalp shone through his scanty hair. Elbows splayed on the desk, his face buried in both hands, he moaned. Wrapped up in his own emotions, he didn't notice her.

About to speak, she took in a liquor bottle. Three-quarters empty. Next to it a glass with dredges of an amber-colored drink. Whiskey or something, she judged by the boozy smell that hit her nostrils. Relegated to the outer edge sat the fedora, like a silent observer of its wearer's agony.

Appalled at witnessing such a private moment of distress, Agnes took a step back. Make a run for it? What if security came by? A report filed just when Herb's two-year probationary period as full-time faculty came up for review at the end of this term, as Jac had mentioned, would kill his chances. Leave and shut the door tightly to prevent discovery? Another look at the almost empty bottle—how much of it did he drink tonight? What if he passes out? Sickens up and chokes. Some drunks do.

As if to confirm her worry, a retching shook Herb's body— followed by a resounding belch. Its violence jerked up Herb's head. Weepy eyes pointed unfocused in her general direction.

The scanty hair stuck out, disheveled by the grasping hands, cheeks blotchy and wet.

Agnes cringed, seeing the man in such a pitiful state. How embarrassed he must be, she empathized.

Herb, however, seemed beyond caring. For a second, the bleary eyes sharpened. He slurred, "Who t' hell're ya?"

Behind her, Agnes heard a sound from the hallway. In reflex, she nudged the door closed with her foot—only to feel trapped. Unaware of her action to save him from further exposure, his right hand blindly groped for the glass. His left came to its aid to bring it up to his lips. Both hands shook. The dredges left in the glass trickled down his chin. With an oath, he banged it back on the desk and reached for the bottle.

"Herb, if drink you must, wouldn't it be better to go home to do it in privacy and in peace?"

"In *peace*?" The voice rose on the last word and cracked. His shoulders shook in what sounded to Agnes like a high-pitched giggle mixed with burps. The bottle, still held in his right hand, waved at her. "She'll lock it away. Me with it—if she could," he enunciated carefully.

"Who's 'she'?" Agnes interjected into renewed giggles.

"The old witch."

Taken aback by the venom in his voice, Agnes realized she'd no idea Herb might be married and not happily.

"I'm sure your spouse understands—"

"No wife—no child—no home of my own," he chanted in theatrical pathos. The voice tipped into screeching, "My bloody mother! The wicked witch."

Sightless eyes appeared to turn inward, his small mouth pursed before it opened to utter, "Herbert, drink is the road to perdition. Think of your father, God rest his poor soul." Herb's mimicry of an upper-class female voice was so authentic Agnes almost expected an elderly woman to have materialized next to them.

"Maybe some coffee, Herb. I'll make you some," Agnes said, eager to escape.

"No! … Don't go," he pleaded after the outburst. Another belch shook him. He blinked and straightened up. In an effort at conversational tone, he asked, "Do I know you?" Then he enunciated overcarefully, "Herbert Nessbit. Writer in residence. Soon to be thrown to the wolves," he ended.

"Agnes Taylor. Philosophy." Conscious of imitating him, albeit unintentionally, she added, "Just started on a one-year contract. Nice meeting you." Once out, it sounded ludicrous to her own ears.

Herb didn't notice but carried on, "Hounded out by bloody students." A cunning glance at her seemed to sober him. "Never fear. Know thy enemy. A conspiracy fueled by my Nemesis, the self-styled genius." His torso shook with another high-pitched giggle before he added flatly, "A very dead genius."

To Agnes's dismay, he broke out in raucous laughter. Loud enough to raise security alarm bells, she feared.

"Herb, I don't think you want to—"

"You've no idea what Herb Nessbit wants," he hissed at her. "None of you pathetic academics has a clue. I know my fate. One day, my name will attach to something stupendous."

He leered at her. Agnes wasn't sure he'd been aware of quoting the German philosopher Friedrich Nietzsche. He certainly had stopped short of ending with the famous phrase, 'I'm dynamite.'

Time to bring him back to earth and lesser mortals. "Right now, the more pressing issue is security might pop by and find you the worse for drink. Granted, the best mothers are provoking at times. Still, you'd be better off at home."

The advice prompted him to raise the bottle, right hand clutching its neck, his left aided by grasping the bottom. The rim clanked against his teeth when he gulped down the entire contents until he had to tilt his head way back onto his neck to catch the last trickle. Imagines he's defying his mother, Agnes figured.

Tears ran down his cheeks. If from emotion or the bite of his booze, Agnes couldn't tell.

Her patience with the man was running out fast. Since she wasn't prepared to abandon him, she might harness the unpleasant encounter to uncover the truth. The man's too drunk to invent a lie, she trusted.

"Herbert, you said students are hounding you. Let me ask you, is it about Dorian's submission? Is it true Dorian submitted his story assignment to you, and you withheld it without a grade?"

For a moment, he stared at her uncomprehendingly. He sat down the bottle with great care. One hand went up to the gray scarf slung loosely around his neck and used it to wipe his face. She noticed now how the light gray of the wool contrasted with the black of his collarless sweater.

Each word punctuated, he said, "Mr. Gables did not submit. There was nothing to grade."

The effort appeared to exhaust Herb, who fell forward. His face hit the desk with a dull thud.

Alarmed, Agnes sprang into action. The distance to the surface could not have harmed his head on impact. Yet, she wasn't sure what the right procedure was. Herb's groan reassured her somewhat. Not unconscious, then. His head lolled sideways to come to rest on his outstretched arm.

Agnes scanned the room for something soft to ease his position while she went for help. The tweed jacket slung over the back of his chair should do. She moved behind him to retrieve it. Bunched up into a rough pillow shape, she sought to insert it gently between his arm and cheek.

"Hold tight for a few minutes. I'll take care of things," she assured him with more confidence than she felt.

Cautiously, she poked her head out into the hallway. Who should she get? Call Jac to ask where Herb lived? Call security?

Just the things she'd wanted to avoid. After all, as coordinator, Jac would be on Herb's probation review committee.

The answer appeared simultaneously to her eyes and mind. TC—of course! He just entered the hallway from a door farther to the end. Men's loo, she judged. Without closing Herb's door, concerned it might lock automatically, she rushed down the corridor, softly calling out, "TC, wait up."

His hearing must be acute, for he stopped to look over his shoulder, then came to meet her.

"What's up? You still hanging out here? I was going to be by later," he said.

"It's not that. Been talking to Herb," Agnes assured him. The startled expression quite satisfied her. He must feel caught slacking on the sleuthing job, she figured.

"Did you find out anything?"

"Not really. Nessbit claims Dorian made no submission."

"Why, of course, he'd say that. Did you expect a confession?"

"Guess not. Listen, the problem is I caught him stone drunk—"

"What else is new?" TC rolled his eyes.

"Well, this time, he's nearly passed out. We need to get him home before security finds him."

"Might serve him right. Guilty conscience catching up with him."

"C'mon, be fair. We're still in the dark. If he did nothing wrong…I mean, seriously wrong, it would be a shame for him to ruin his career chances. Jac told me about his probationary period review later this term. The decision to make his position permanent would be a moot point if this leaks out."

TC didn't look overly concerned. So, she pleaded on Herb's behalf, "Can you help? Any idea where he lives?"

"Sure. Lives at his mother's place, like mom's good little boy. Best part of town. She's inherited the family mansion when dad bit the bullet."

"How do you know?" Curiosity momentarily overrode Agnes's concern.

"Everyone here does. Lady Nessbit gives her monthly soiree to exhibit her poet in residence. Problem is, lately, the poet is unproductive. Thus, no private readings. Embarrassing lack of consideration for the lady."

"Is she really titled?" asked Agnes, somewhat incredulously.

"No, of course not. Feels to the manner born and expects to be deferred to like a grand dame. By her son, too. The great Herbert strikes me as hen-pecked."

"Interesting... He's not a favorite with you, is he? More to the point, how do we get him home now?"

"Leave it to me. I'll ferry him out to my car and deliver him safe and sound to his mommy. If somewhat worse for wear, I gather."

"Thanks, TC. So kind of you."

"Think nothing of it."

"If you come back after, let me know how it went."

His eyes searched her face. She returned his gaze, acutely aware of how attractive he was. Dark, tousled hair contrasted with violet-blue eyes under long lashes over high cheekbones. The three-day stubble rendered his looks endearingly rumbled.

A captivating smile slowly moved up from his lips to generate fine lines.

To defuse the moment, she hastened to explain herself, "I mean, we want to discuss how to sort this rumor, don't we?"

"Not to worry. I'm on to it."

He tapped her shoulder lightly and moved on to Herb's door.

Reluctantly, Agnes made for the stairs to descend to the dungeon.

Chapter 12

It was ten AM on the dot on Wednesday when Jacqueline cast a nervous glance at the old-fashioned dial above the hotel's reception desk, wishing they had discussed their approach to this meeting with the bereaved parents. She and Agnes met outside the hotel a moment ago, Agnes coming straight from home and Jac from campus. The night before, Jacqueline had been so exhausted she didn't wait up to talk to Agnes. Instead, she resorted to earplugs to shut out any party noises and slept like a dormouse until the shrieking alarm cut short her hibernation.

Now she asked the staff at the hotel's reception where they'd find the Gables. The clerk, a young female in a crisp uniform, took their names and walked them over to a small meeting room, its privacy indicated by a 'Reserved' sign.

"Professor Xavier and Dr. Taylor to see you," their guide announced upon opening the door for them.

The unadorned room struck Jacqueline as too austere for meeting the grieving parents. Or, she wondered, would a business-like setting keep emotions at bay?

Jac stepped forward, her right hand stretched out, to extend her condolences. Both parents, who'd been standing at the window rather than sitting at the conference table for eight or twelve, came forward. AD Martha Muller had texted their names last night: Emma and Gordon Gable.

The mother, even more petite than Jacqueline's 5'2" in her high-heeled Oxfords, appeared frail and drawn. It spoke of longer-term health issues beyond the recent shock. At Jac's guess, in her fifties, Mrs. Gable's paper-thin facial skin and hands showed grayish-blue over the veins underneath. Ash-blond hair hung limply to chin length. Arms wrapped tightly around the skinny torso, the shoulders hunched forward as though she was freezing cold in her pale-blue angora sweater and stylish ebony wool trousers despite the overheated room.

When they shook hands, the most striking feature was the woman's large gray eyes, red-rimmed now but regarding the visitors kindly. A brave effort to hide the palpable pain. Faced with such heartbreak, Jac felt her condolences inadequate.

The husband's handshake was brief but firm. In a cream-colored, light sweater over a pinstriped shirt and navy dress pants, Jac guessed him to be only 5'10". The dark hair, cut no-nonsense short, shone silvery around the temples. His tanned, clean-shaven face glowed from the Florida sun and, perhaps, time spent golfing. He appeared fit, healthy, and business-like, clearly used to hosting guests. While he pulled out chairs around the table end, closest to where they stood, he asked their preference for refreshments. A carafe of water sat ready with glasses, which he now distributed and filled.

As Gordon Gable phoned in their order of tea and coffee from the room's extension, Agnes talked softly to his wife. Jacqueline didn't catch what she said, but it touched a chord because Emma Gable leaned over to pat Agnes's hand and then clasped it with both her own.

Concerned to leave the seat on Emma's other side to the husband, Jac opted for the chair across the table from Agnes. When Gordon joined them a moment later, Emma turned to him eagerly.

"Remember the philosophy course Dorian was so excited about, darling? Dr. Taylor teaches it."

"Ah, so you're Agnes," Gordon said, reaching over to shake hands again. "Our son's favorite prof." When Agnes demurred, blushing fiercely, Gordon assured her, "No, he really meant it. Said you took him seriously and never begrudged time spent discussing 'deeply philosophical questions.' His words."

"We're so grateful to you, Dr. Taylor," Emma said, laying her hand over Agnes's.

"Please, it's Agnes. I enjoyed every minute. Dorian's an outstanding student and a wonderful person." Agnes's eyes moved from the mother's face to the dad's, expressing helpless concern. "We can't begin to feel what you must be going through. For parents, it's the worst." Her voice petered out.

An emotional meltdown was averted by the entry of a waiter. Jac bit her lower lip and took a large sip of water to lessen the stinging in her eyes. The waiter's efficient distribution of their order gave a welcome respite.

They thanked him and busied themselves with their beverages.

To introduce an innocuous topic, Jacqueline asked the couple, "Have you moved to Florida more recently? The climate is year-round quite agreeable compared to ours up here, isn't it?"

"Three years ago," Emma said. "We waited until Dorian started college. Gordon was so pleased our son followed in his footsteps and enrolled as a business major. Then he fell in love with creative writing, and that was it."

"Kissed by the muses," said the dad. "Either way, we were happy he stood on his own feet. The doctors thought it best for Emma's health to move south. She wouldn't budge until her baby finished high school." His arm reached over to pull his wife in for a hug.

"Oh, Gordon," murmured Emma. Then she turned to Jac, "I must plead guilty to being a helicopter parent—at least by some people's standard. Our son always was the center of our life." Her voice cracked as she teared up. "That's why I can't understand what happened to him. He'd never do this to himself. Dorian knew he could turn to us—night and day." Softly, she added, "We saw no alarm signs."

"Nor did we," affirmed Agnes. "The Dorian I knew embraced life."

"A tragic accident," Jac said. "Entirely unintended." She stopped, uncertain why Mrs. Gable shook her head rather impatiently.

"Dorian would not make a mistake with his medication. He was too aware of the risks."

"The rat poison," Jac heard Agnes mutter.

"What?" Jac cried out in horror at the idea.

But Emma's features softened into a smile. "Ah, he told you his little joke."

"No, Cass did," said Agnes, and then hesitantly, "You know Cassandra? Dorian's friend?"

The mother's face tightened into a mask of disapproval. Jac shot Agnes a glance. Her friend's cheeks were aflame. The rat poison comment offended the parent despite the effort to pass it off as a joke, thought Jac and determined to ask Agnes later about the inappropriate remark.

Gordon wrapped his left arm around his wife's bony shoulders again. Mrs. Gable's fingers reached for a napkin. She dabbed her eyes. They could barely make out her words. "She broke his heart."

"Come, come now." Gordon hugged her close. "Not that dramatic. Happens all the time. A young guy needs to get experience. In love, just as in life."

"I know Dorian," Emma insisted. Her voice grew stronger, buoyed by conviction. "It devastated him when this girl broke off their relationship."

"Might it not have been the reason he—" Jacqueline broke off, shocked at her own words.

But it was already too late. Both parents had understood and immediately went into denial. They protested Dorian would never have used this ultimate escape from reality, as Emma put it.

"See," Dorian's dad said. "Just what I told you. Experience in romance is what writers thrive on. Think of D. H. Lawrence."

The literary reference distracted Jac enough from her embarrassment to make a mental note not to jump to conclusions about people she met.

The spouse, however, shook her head in wistful exasperation. Then she admitted, "You might have a point, darling. A mother's perspective is one thing. I often forget he's grown up." Her eyes took on a faraway look. "Yes, I can see him sublimating it into writing the grand, tragic romance."

"Was that Dorian's literary genre?" asked Agnes. "Like the story that was lost somehow? Sorry, just realized you might not know about the incident."

"Oh, I do," said Emma. "Dorian's trouble with Professor Nessbit?" When Agnes nodded, she went on, "My son told me shortly after it happened. We talked every other week and texted in between. Such a caring boy. Our chats meant the world to me."

Dismayed, Jac watched tears trickle down the mother's hollow cheeks. She wanted to signal Agnes to stop probing. This whole meeting was too much for the grieving parents.

Too late. For Agnes already asked, "Was he very upset about it?"

Mr. Gable, who'd stayed very calm throughout, handed his wife a fresh napkin and squeezed the tiny hand gently. She swiped at her cheeks, murmuring apologies that prompted Agnes to say how sorry she was for badgering them with questions.

"No, no. I am quite alright." Mrs. Gable pulled herself up

and attempted another of her brave smiles. "It helps to talk."
Gordon nodded in agreement.

"Let me think," continued Emma. Again, the glance lost
focus, as though she was visualizing the past. "You know," she
began hesitantly, "I believe, at first, he was angry with himself.
About being late again, I mean."

The dad chipped in, "Perfectionist from when he was a little
nipper. Wanted to do everything just so. Lost track of time." He
turned sideways to his wife. "How many times did we tell him, 'You
need to learn to let go,' didn't we? 'Just hand the damn thing in.'"

"Well," Emma smiled. "That was you speaking. You're right,
though. I tried to teach him time management skills—which
wasn't the actual issue."

"She's a schoolteacher. A darn good one," said the husband
and leaned in for a peck on her cheek.

"Do you teach high school?" Jac asked to give the conversation an innocuous direction.

"Primary. Mostly Grade Four," explained Emma. "I took
early retirement and now volunteer in literacy programs at local
schools."

"When you said, 'at first,' Dorian blamed himself, do you
mean his opinion changed later on?"

Jac frowned at her friend for harking back yet again to an
emotional minefield.

Emma, however, responded readily. "How astute of you,
Agnes. Yes, over the next weeks, Dorian became convinced that
Professor Nessbit received his novella but pretended he didn't."

"Now, sweetheart, his friends influenced him and spread
things on Snapchat." Gordon looked at Jac and then Agnes.
"The old story—kids like to blame the teacher. I don't hold with
that. Take responsibility for what you do, is what I say. If you
mess up or miss a deadline, you've only got yourself to blame."

"Oh, I'm sure, from what I've seen of your son, he was a
highly responsible person," Agnes assured him. Jac echoed this,

though they both were more than aware of Dorian's habitual tardiness.

To Emma, Agnes said, "Did you get the impression Dorian truly believed Herb, I mean, Professor Nessbit withheld the… 'Novella,' did you say? I thought it was only a short story."

"A 'novelette' would be most accurate," said Emma. "Much longer and more developed than a short story but shorter than a novella and, of course, far shorter than a novel."

"Ah, he must have put in lots of time writing it. A significant loss," said Agnes. "I heard he never kept copies and submitted hand-written originals when he wrote fiction."

"Yes, tempting fate, I used to tell him. When I scolded him for such recklessness, he—quite rightly—pointed out humans hand-wrote for thousands of years since the invention of writing." The mother's lips softened into a smile while her eyes lost their focus as if the past was more present to her.

"When she says, 'scolded,'" interjected the dad with a loving gaze at his spouse, "think, 'gentlest of remonstrations.'"

While she listened to them, Jac's professional mind pondered the question of effort in writing short stories *versus* novelettes and concluded the former, if of literary merit, might be more challenging. Either way, she thought, for a writer—and Dorian deserved that appellation—the loss of a creative piece hurt. A forceful realization dawned. If he'd explicitly told his mom that he submitted this piece, then either Herb indeed received it, or it disappeared after Dorian handed it in. Unless carelessly submitted, the latter appeared unlikely. They needed to find out. But how?

"I'm sure you've been wonderful parents," Agnes said. "Your son spoke most fondly of you and loved you dearly. Though a slight consolation, the happy memories you shared may eventually lessen the pain of—" Helplessly, Agnes reached out to touch Emma's skinny arm.

The mother teared up as she covered Agnes's hand with her own. "Every moment, I still expect to wake up, and it's all just a nightmare," Emma confessed quietly. "My baby would never have put us through this agony. He did not kill himself. And he wouldn't mess around with his medication. He loved life so intensely."

"But," murmured Agnes, oblivious of voicing a thought, it seemed to Jac, "if you rule out both, what killed him?"

Chapter 13

Back at her desk in the basement office, Agnes checked the time on her laptop. Fifteen minutes to spare before the first cheater appointment. She and Jac had rushed to campus without dissecting their meeting with the Gables. Too many commitments awaiting them. They'd catch up later over coffee at Starbucks. At the hotel, none of them had finished even their first cup. The encounter had been that tense.

The memory of her own contributions made Agnes grind her teeth. Why couldn't she leave well enough alone? Jac's frowns spoke volumes when she kept on questioning the poor couple. The Gables had been incredibly kind about it when she apologized for her inquisitiveness before they parted. Both kept on assuring her it was cathartic and helped them verbalize their own misgivings.

Toward the end, their talk skirted the possibility of an autopsy to establish the cause of death. Of course, no one used such a blatant word. Gordon implied it when he said neither Emma nor he could contemplate the ultimate indignity visited upon their son. They'd have to appeal the coroner's decision, who, based on Dorian's medical history, saw no reason for further steps and issued a death certificate.

Why the Gables questioned the verdict of death from natural causes puzzled Agnes. Emma worried someone slipped something into Dorian's drink—saying how often one hears nowadays of kids doing it for a joke at a party. For Dorian, many substances could prove fatal.

Yet, no one mentioned any party the night Dorian died. The idea was a non-starter to Agnes, but she didn't voice an objection. The paramedics who found him on his bed treated it as a medical emergency. The Warfarin prescription made the underlying medical condition obvious to them.

Still, Dorian's mom spoke of 'a mother's intuition' to which Gordon had nodded assent. The memory of Emma's pronouncement sent a shudder through Agnes's body. Someone's walking over my grave, she thought ruefully. Why it should conjure up Cass's Medusa image, she couldn't fathom.

A red dot on the email icon on her laptop's status bar caught her attention now. Instead of letting her mind drift, she should clear her inbox.

The call of duty triggered awareness of her surroundings. A sessional instructor passed by her desk with a quick 'hello.' Two colleagues kept busy pecking at laptops. The fluorescent glare of the overhead tubes—who had turned them on?—showed the windowless place at its shabbiest. The harsh white light mercilessly exposed the blistering and peeling walls and banged up rejects furnishing their office. She must ask TC how he'd wrangled a workspace upstairs.

Her eyes wandered to the laptop screen. Like sirens luring passing seafarers, her thoughts netted an email from the man himself. 'Timothy Charles Elliot' read the 'from' line. Brief as it was, the message lifted her mood.

'Sorry about last night. Too late after safe delivery. Catch up today? – Chuck'

Well, they weren't on chucking terms yet, grinned Agnes to herself. Her fingers busily replied.

'Sure, why not? Join us at Starbucks. 12:30ish.'

The night before, she'd been miffed. Hung around until security returned pointedly at brief intervals after ten. When she got home, Jac had been sound asleep. Agnes had joined the last remaining revelers in the living room for a bit of pseudo-philosophical waffling, political gripping, and warmed-up pizza. She'd greatly enjoyed herself but was dead beat when everyone left around one or so.

A voice next to her caught her by surprise. She'd forgotten all about the cheater. Now, a petulant Cherry regarded her with disdain.

"You insisted we meet, miss," the girl said accusingly.

"I did, indeed. Hi, Cherry. Have a seat. Give me a sec to pull up your file."

In a quick sideway glance, Agnes noticed the girl slumped back in the rickety visitor chair. Only the way she clutched a bulging backpack to her chest—knuckles of all fingers showing white—betrayed tension. Or anger.

"You've received and read the forms setting out the case, have you? Was it all clear? We don't ask students for their admission of a breach. But if you like to comment, you can do so now or enter written comments on the form later."

Cherry pouted. Her golden-blond curls framed a rather pretty face now distorted by fiery patches and potent emotions.

A storm is brewing, thought Agnes, and aimed for a soothing tone. "Let's see. Would you like me to explain the breach the form outlines? Did you read our Academic Integrity policy attached to the email?"

"You profs are such hypocrites," the girl sputtered. "All you do is preach at us and wait for a chance to punish us. And then you do it yourselves."

As Cherry's voice rose, Agnes glanced around the room. So far, no one was paying them any heed. Across, at the far end of the space, she saw a part-timer talk earnestly to a student. Two other instructors sat bent over their laptops, hacking away, oblivious or pretending to be.

In measured tones, she said, "Do what? I don't follow what you are trying to say, Cherry. Let's keep our voice down—this is a public space."

"I didn't steal from anyone like the prof did. All me and my friend did was help each other with the essay. The college always preaches peer support. Now you say it's cheating!"

"Whoa, Cherry. Let's unpack all this. First, no one said you stole anything. Collaboration on an assignment requires permission to pair or group work. Otherwise, it's considered cheating. Remember the academic honesty module early on this term?"

The student avoided Agnes's questioning glance and scowled.

Nothing for it but to carry on. "Second, as you can see from the document properties and the revision history, your friend wrote the original piece a few days before you selectively revised it. Then, you handed it in as your own work, which makes it 'plagiarism.' The impermissible collaboration between two or more people is called 'cheating.' Do you follow?"

"Whatever." Cherry's glance remained glued to a phone she toyed with.

Agnes hesitated for a moment, unsure whether to tackle the Herb issue. Maybe students didn't realize what their rumors amounted to. So, she carried on, "Now as to your remark about professors stealing from someone. Unless you have proof of such action—in which case you ought to report it to admin—making groundless accusations is slander. Not a good idea."

"Yeah, you guys stick together. Just get on social media if you want proof. Everyone says he did it. I mean the writer guy. The prof."

"Unproven accusations in written format are libel," Agnes said without thinking. "The point is," she hastened to clarify, "people repeating slanderous or libelous remarks does not amount to proof. Did anyone put forward actual evidence?" While she spoke, Agnes realized she shouldn't be discussing this with the student.

The girl merely shrugged, one side of her lip twitching up in response.

"Anyway. Sorry, Cherry, I was digressing. We're here to talk about your own case. Unless there's something pertinent to add, please sign the form. Your signature, as it says here, merely confirms you've read and understood the nature of the breach. We'll email you our decision about sanctions. Do you understand all this?"

The girl muttered, "I'm not stupid."

"No one says you are," Agnes assured her in a cheery tone. "Come with me to the printer over there, and you can sign."

Five minutes later, Agnes was alone at her desk. One of the laptop-hunching colleagues had given her a commiserating smile as she and Cherry walked by. No teacher remained a stranger to tense interviews with students. Agnes counted herself lucky. Unpleasant encounters were infrequent.

This, however, was different. The Herb issue was poisoning the well. Something needed to be done to stop this insidious campaign against Nessbit. Last night, she'd felt sorry for him. Admittedly, also repelled. Either the man was innocent and the victim of slander and libel and needed to be exonerated, or he was guilty. If so, the college must take a stand to regain the students' trust. She'd do her darndest to prove one of these hypotheses, Agnes vowed.

Chapter 14

Jacqueline placed a Matcha latte for Agnes and her own Americano on the tiny round of the tall table in a far corner of Starbucks. If Agnes didn't dawdle on her way from campus, her drink should still be hot, Jac thought.

The Starbucks' main street location, crowded at lunchtime, was noisy enough to mask the most confidential of chats. She was fortunate to snatch a table vacated the very moment the barista presented her order with a cheerful "Enjoy."

Perched on a barstool facing the entrance, legs in slim black slacks crossed at the knees, Jac took a sip of her coffee, deploring the barista's use of paper cups. It tainted the taste and added to the billions of disposables wasted every day. Most of them ended in trash bins, or worse, along roads or green spaces, she thought, exasperated with herself for not remembering to ask for proper cups when ordering.

The meeting with Dorian's parents left her drained and yearning for a quiet debriefing with her trusted friend. Upon leaving her office to head over here, she'd run into Herbert Nessbit. Deathly pale and hungover, he'd glared at her—malevolently, she thought. Why the man was out to alienate colleagues was beyond her comprehension. As program coordinator, she would serve on the committee for his probation review at the end of this term. Maybe that irked him into contrariety.

Just then, the door opened. The growing smile froze on Jacqueline's face. Above Agnes's glossy black-brown mane loomed Timothy Elliot's sardonic grin. Cheeks aglow, Agnes rushed over while Elliot joined the order queue. The hope his presence might be a coincidence died when her friend wriggled onto the other barstool with a broad grin.

After a deep draught from her latte, light-green foam circling her lips, Agnes said, "Ah, I needed that. Thanks, Jac." Over the rim of the cup lid, she asked, "Hey, what's this stern look for? You don't mind TC coming along, do you? He'll be such a help."

"In what?" Jacqueline's pretense of bafflement didn't prevent a curt tone. She relented. "Your chumming up with him worries me, Agnes. Befriending someone who competes for the same position is risky." Her own word choice surprised Jac. 'Chum' meant 'boyfriend' in francophone Quebec.

Oblivious to her *faux pas*, Agnes said, "Wait until I explain. We've got to clear up this Herb business once and for all. TC's the man for that."

"Don't say you actually invited him? I assumed you met by coincidence outside."

Guilt flickered in her friend's eyes. A clear admission. Anger welled up, acidic like her black coffee.

"Hear me out, Jac," pleaded Agnes. "Let's be objective and rational about this. It's your program and the college I'm concerned about."

A snarky retort remained unspoken as Timothy Elliot entered Jacqueline's line of vision. Serves him right. No place for him to sit, she thought—only to see a patron get up to leave the moment Elliot wove his way among the tables. Cup in his left, he dragged the stool along with his right hand.

His eyes challenged Jac as he drawled, "No objection to me joining the chick chat?"

"Of course not," Agnes butted in. "This is all important to Jacqueline."

"If looks could kill, eh?" muttered the intruder. "No worries, dear Jac. I'll be gone in no time. Got a class at one and a rendezvous with the Gables after."

The reminder of his meeting with the grieving parents made Jacqueline close her eyes in dismay. For their sake, she pleaded, "Please go easy and focus on positive memories. Dorian's parents are so vulnerable at present."

"Well, dear me. I'd never have realized, would I?"

"Don't be offended, TC," Agnes urged. "Jac's concerned because our meeting with them got so tense. All my fault for being insensitive and too inquisitive. Argh, I pestered them with questions. I could sense you worry about bothering them, didn't you, Jac?"

"Can't imagine you upsetting them," said Timothy, beaming his most charming smile at Agnes. "Would be only natural for them to be upset already."

"They certainly are," agreed Agnes. "Strange," she continued, slowly as if reexamining the scene in her mind, "they reject all reasonable explanations for their son's death." A puzzled headshake. "Wasn't it odd, Jac? What's left if you discount suicide, accident, and natural causes? And yet they didn't."

Not giving Jac a chance to caution Agnes about discretion, Timothy cut in. "What do you mean?"

"I really don't think, Agnes, we're at liberty—"

"Get real, Jac," he cut her off. "I'll be meeting the Gables later, anyway. If you expect me to hold off questioning, you'd better fill me in."

"He's right, Jac. Emma's bound to repeat her 'intuition,' as she calls it. After all, TC was her son's friend. They're more likely to confide in him than me as a total stranger."

For Agnes to side with this man... Defeated, Jac raised both hands and let them drop palms down on the tabletop. Her empty paper cup bounced and toppled over. Timothy reached

87

over to righten it. He grabbed an unbleached brown napkin to swipe at the thin rivulet seeping from her cup.

Like her old mongrel back home at her dad's lodge resort in Quebec, Timothy homed in on the most promising scent. "What's Emma's intuition, then?" he asked Agnes.

"Seems she believes someone spiked Dorian's drink at a party," said Agnes. To Timothy's startled, "What?" she replied, "Yeah, pretty unlikely. Or did you hear of any party going off that night?"

"Me? No idea," said Elliot.

Jacqueline guessed he was uncomfortable being caught clueless. The man always prided himself on his rapport with students. Or, at least, with the in-crowd.

Across from her, Agnes played with the empty latte cup, rolling it between her palms back and forth. Now, she muttered, eyes on the cup, the glossy dark curls falling forward to cover her face, "The way Dorian's mom said it... It freaked me out. Reminded me of Medusa in the rain."

"You've lost me, Agnes," said Timothy. He sat back on his stool as if to distance himself. "You're speaking in riddles."

"Oh, never mind me." Agnes pushed her hair back and hazarded a wry grin at him. "Cass spooked me a bit. What with her wet tresses snaking like Medusa's and dark utterings of evil. I'd only asked her about Dorian—"

"When did you see Cassandra?" Jac interrupted. As puzzled as Timothy, she needed a return to facts.

"Yesterday after class."

When Agnes avoided her eye, things clicked for Jac. "The rat poison," she blurted out before she could stop herself.

"Would someone care to enlighten me?" Fingers drumming a staccato on the scarred wood of the table, Elliot's voice dripped sarcasm.

With a minute headshake, Jac sought to forestall any further revelations in his presence. It annoyed her that Agnes had not mentioned anything at dinner—though, in fairness, her own news had distracted them. She needed to catch up with Agnes on all this in the evening. Her friend, however, ignored the signaling.

"It's actually not a blood thinner," she informed Jac. "Googled last night when I was wait—Never mind that." A quick glance at Timothy. "Anyway, Warfarin is a vitamin K inhibitor. Prescribed in cases of high risk for stroke and so on. The list of counter-indications, interactions with other meds and substances, is endless. Seems tons of stuff could trigger serious adverse reactions." She took a deep breath. "Hence, I don't see why the Gables won't accept an unintended side-effect triggering a fatal hemorrhage."

As if to herself, she added, "Of course, wouldn't rule out the spiking hypothesis."

"Ah, now I get it," Timothy said. "Brings back memories. Way back when Dorian joked about taking rat poison. Told us what he was on."

"Who's 'us'?" Agnes's nose twitched. "Who knew about this?"

"Don't ask me to recall what happened ages ago. The usual culprits, I guess. Let me think." His prominent forehead crimped. "Oh, yeah, I remember now. One of Lady Nessbit's dos."

In response to Agnes's, "Oh?" he explained, "Back when our poet laureate was still in good graces, the lady hosted literary soirees not only for the somebodies but also for the young, as she dubbed it. Herb invited students and a couple of us lowly instructors. Types like me, whom he doesn't perceive as a threat or competition."

Before Jacqueline could object to this scathing depiction of a colleague, Agnes asked, "Do you recall which students?"

"C'mon, Agnes. Be reasonable. I didn't keep an attendance list. Same group as now, I'd say. Kalen and his buddies. The girls, like Renata and Cleo. Cass, of course, with Dorian. Oh, and Lester was around, too. Early on, he and Herb hit it off. Until Lester pissed him off with some diatribe."

The mention of Lester made Jacqueline flinch. A reaction observed by Agnes, whose brows shot up in questioning concern. Jac mouthed, 'later.'

Right now, it fell to her to redirect the conversation. The implications of this drift into suspicious causes for Dorian's passing unnerved her. Things like that just didn't happen in this peaceful town. Unlike Montreal or Toronto, there weren't any raves or drug gangs here, she felt sure. The use of cannabis, of course, proliferated since its recent legalization. But one didn't die of that, or did one?

On an impulse, she said, "On my way over, I happened upon Herbert in the hallway. He looked far from well. Quite under the weather—" She broke off when she intercepted a furtive glance pass between her companions. The intimacy of it hurt her to the core. It left her feeling excluded.

"Anything going on with Kafka…I mean, Lester?" Agnes's attempt to reroute to a topic Jac was loath to entertain raised Jac's hackles.

In fairness, Jacqueline told herself, Agnes couldn't know she'd be asking Jac as coordinator to share something from a confidential advising session. The realization calmed her enough to give a general—if pompous, she feared—reply. "My impression is that Lester, like other students, feels dissatisfied with admin and faculty for not investigating the allegations students make against Nessbit. They fail to understand that we cannot act in the absence of an official complaint."

"Tell me about it," burst out Agnes. "A cheat—A student I talked to earlier was incredibly vindictive about it. The whole thing is poisoning the well." She leaned in to lock eyes with Jac. "We need to find out the truth. TC and I should join forces."

Jac sighed. There was no way to avoid involving the man. To do him justice, she mused, Timothy's long-standing closeness to the students worked as an advantage. With him, they might be unguarded enough to let slip who was fueling the rumor mill.

Resigned to being stuck with the eternal ABD as Agnes's sidekick, Jac said, "What are you suggesting as your course of action?" Even as she spoke, she realized how vulnerable it would make her to be party to any unauthorized scheme to investigate a colleague. What if Timothy used this against her at some point? Logic kicked in. He couldn't do so without jeopardizing his own standing if he was the one doing any investigating.

Into the ensuing silence that did not bode well for the investigators' resourcefulness, she pointed out, "For all we know, Dorian's fateful submission simply disappeared."

"At least, it's clear he handed it in," said Agnes.

Timothy's eyebrow shot up in an exaggerated question mark. "Oh? How do you make that out?"

"Elementary." Agnes grinned. "He explicitly told his mom he submitted it. Not something he'd bother lying about talking to his mother a thousand miles away."

"Still," Jac said. "If he dropped it off after hours—"

"Precisely," Agnes cut in. "Found out last night from Giuseppe—the guy who cleans the office—students often push stuff under the door. He collects it from the floor and puts it on a table for Fraser to deal with in the morning. Anything dropped off after Giuseppe cleans remains where it's shoved in until someone stumbles over it. Presumably, not before morning."

"How careless to submit assignments in this manner. I always insist on digital or in-class submissions or in-person drop-off during office hours if needs be," commented Jac. "After all this time, no one will recall finding a specific submission. There's no way to trace it to Herbert. Or discover what happened to it."

"Put so bleakly, one feels kind of stumped," agreed Agnes.

"Never say die." Elliot's superior smirk met their puzzled frowns. "Help is near. I've got an idea."

"Hey. Go on. Tell us."

"Not so fast, Agnes. Duty calls. Got to run to class now."

"Arrrgh," growled Agnes. Jac felt like joining in. She'd eagerly have grabbed any lifeline. Even if thrown by Timothy Charles Elliot, MA.

Ignoring Jac entirely, Timothy leaned over to Agnes. "Tell you what. If you're working on campus tonight, I'll swing by. Deal?"

A fraction of a hesitation before a firm answer came. "OK. What time?"

"Hmm… I'm tied up 'til nine-thirtyish. Sorry. Too late for you?"

"No shortage of grading and lecture prep to keep me amused until the wee hours."

The conspiratorial smile her friend favored the man with disturbed Jac. Sidelined, resentment welled up from low in her chest. Prickles of jealousy disquieted her. Impatiently, she chided herself for such an unworthy reaction. All her friend wanted was to help kill the malignant rumors. If the task involved Jacqueline's old foe, so be it.

In the end, it might be better for them to work in tandem than for Mr. Self-serving Elliot to strike out on his own and reap all the glory for himself. If he proved successful in unravelling this mysterious conundrum in the first place, she figured.

Wasn't it Sun Tzu, Jac thought wryly, who said, 'Keep your friends close; keep your enemies closer?'

Chapter 15

"No! Stop! We can't do this," hissed Agnes at TC's back.

She grabbed his coat tail to pull him back as he inched open Herb's office door.

He grinned over his shoulder and raised a forefinger to his lips to shush her. As he entered, she'd no choice but to turn tail or follow. A quick glance around, and she slipped in. TC closed the door softly. Instead of switching on the overhead fluorescent, he dug into the bulging pocket of his greenish-beige, unbuttoned trench coat to withdraw a tube-shaped small flashlight. Its LED beam penetrated the gloom.

"Here, take this. I've got another one. Shield it with your hand.—Hey, don't point it at the window."

"TC, what on earth do you think we're doing? This is B&E. You'll get us both fired. How the heck did you unlock the door, anyway?"

"Questions, questions. Easy as pie." The dimmed light from two torches, shaded by their hands, showed Agnes his disarming boyish grin. Clearly proud of himself, he told her, "I chatted up Herb when he was leaving. Held the door open for him, reached in while he was busy straightening his mascot fedora, and set the knob in the unlocked position. Smart, *eh?*"

Agnes rolled her eyes.

"You women are never satisfied. Here I go out of my way to help, and what's the thanks I get?" A little irritation swung in the flirty tone. "Remember, you insisted we need to unearth the truth. So, here we are."

"I don't get it. Where does his office enter the equation?"

"C'mon, Agnes. Think. Office? Files? Work in progress? Ring a bell?"

"A weak inference. For all we know, he might work at home."

"No, he doesn't. Lady Nessbit's too nosey and interfering. He constantly gripes about her. Told me once she filched a draft of a poem and read it to the sycophants at her soiree. He blew his stack."

"Didn't move out, though," said Agnes.

"Can't afford to. Not with his pricey habits. No, he locks himself in here at night to wield his pen—or booze most days."

"Oh, no! Then he might come in any moment and catch us."

"Calm down. He won't. Her Ladyship commanded his company tonight for a vernissage at a downtown gallery. He'll be guzzling bubbly as we speak."

While Agnes remained frozen, her back against the door, she watched TC walking around, aimlessly picking up stuff and flicking through the scanty number of books on the shelves.

Now, he stopped in the middle of the small room. Outstretched arm, palm flat on the desktop, he leaned casually as though they'd come for a cozy chat. The tone offhand, as if it was the most natural suggestion in the world, he said, "Let's get cracking. You take the filing cabinet." He pointed to a gunmetal-colored two-drawer unit next to her. She hadn't even noticed it up to now.

"Are you nuts? We can't rifle through the man's files with confidential stuff and all?"

"Keep your voice down. You don't want to sic security on

us." In a step, he was distractingly close to her. His voice dropped to a fake-hoarse whisper. "The walls have ears."

Agnes grinned despite herself. This cloak-and-dagger act was as ridiculous as it was unnerving. What was it with the folks at this college?

"With—not B&E, but—trespassing to our name, we might as well find something to show for it," he said.

"In for a penny, in for a dime." Her bravado surprised Agnes. Maybe she wanted to postpone someone catching them leaving. Or her innate curiosity kicked in. To reassure herself, she said, "Okay. Just a peek. Anything confidential, I'll shut my eyes."

"That's the spirit. I'll start on the desk."

"Should don gloves," said Agnes, only half joking. "Any blockhead would nowadays."

"Here. Catch. Almost forgot."

The missile turned out to be balled-up, light-blue surgical gloves.

"Are you serious? You came thoroughly prepared." A creepy sensation stole over Agnes as the realization and its implications sank in. They'd irrevocably crossed a line. One thing to seize a chance opportunity to manipulate the lock, but quite another—

"Just get a move on. We don't want to be here all night."

For several minutes, they carried on, the silence punctuated by stealthy opening of desk drawers and creaking of metal on metal when hangers of file folders scraped along drawer rods.

The longer she searched, the more conscious Agnes grew of her awkward position. Raiding a colleague's office was not the done thing anywhere. Sweat broke out on her upper lip and forehead. She felt trickles down her armpits. Her hands were clammy inside the latex gloves. Not cut out for a cat burglar career, she thought in a futile attempt at levity.

Most of the folders contained admin notices, memos, and official documents she quickly stuffed back. Her fingers flipped through drafts of poetry and prose—machine-typed with tons of hand-written notations, strikethroughs, and blackened-out passages where a felt pen had wrought havoc.

She skimmed bits and pieces and failed to be impressed.

"What am I looking for?" Hand raised, she waved a sheet in TC's direction.

He barely glanced up from whatever held his attention in a bottom drawer. 'Porn stash,' flitted through Agnes's mind.

If so, TC was not ratting on their target. Instead, he said absentmindedly, "Hell, how do I know? Something incriminating?"

"Well, you *should* know. It was your idea to raid the man's office."

"Just keep on looking. I'm almost done here."

Stifled by the stuffy air in the cubbyhole of an office, Agnes eyeballed the lower file drawer with distaste. In a flash, disgust at what she was doing hit her stomach. Sour saliva filled the back of her mouth. This is insane, her mind shrieked. What if we get caught? Invading Herb's privacy—"Ouch!"

All thought ground to an abrupt halt. Her fingers, fumbling among the files of their own accord, got caught in a loose staple. Its tip grazed the index finger of her right hand.

"What?"

"Nothing. Pricked my finger."

"Don't leave a blood trail."

Despite the light tone, Agnes wasn't sure her accomplice was kidding. She sucked her finger just the same and tasted rubber in reward. The torch beam confirmed no red oozing from the minuscule puncture. Better check the file for blood, she figured. And then I'm out of here.

With her left hand, she pulled out the folder. It fell open without prompting as a bunch of notepad paper expanded. Held together precariously at one folded corner by the infamous staple, the sheets appeared crammed with hand-written text.

Her heart skipped and caught up with accelerating thumps

against her chest. The narrow beam of the flashlight pointed at the stapled corner, and a header sprang out at her.

The Betrayal
A Novelette by Dorian Gable
Capstone Project for H. Nessbit

No date, she noted automatically. Stunned, she held her breath. Her head rose in slow motion to seek TC. He'd moved on to rifle through the shelf next to the desk.

Her pallet felt dry, like crumbling parchment. She cleared her throat. Unsure if her vocal cords would forsake her, she tried to articulate the jumble of thoughts cluttering her mind. A weak, questioning, "TC?"

"*Eh?* What—" A glance over his shoulder must have told him something was amiss. He pushed a book back onto the shelf and strode over to join her.

"Found something?" His tone betrayed incredulity.

Agnes proffered her find and pointed the beam at the dogeared corner.

"Well, well … I'll be damned!"

His shoulder brushed Agnes's upper arm as he leaned in close. The masculine scent of whatever body products he used hit her nose agreeably. Pheromones. Impatiently, she shook off the thought. Get a grip!

She collected her wits to say, "What do we do now?"

"Take it, of course. Evidence of Herb's shady—"

"No way. Only if it remains *in situ* does it prove he received it and suppressed the fact. We got to think of something. Have it found officially, so to speak."

She stuffed the pile back in the folder, slipped that into its place, and shut the drawer firmly but with as little squeaking as possible.

"Right now, all I want is to get out of here. Safely." Her hand rubbed her midriff. "I feel sick to my stomach."

"Okay, okay," soothed TC.

He swept the room with his light shaded by his hand, carefully avoiding the window. Then he shut it off. Agnes followed suit. On impulse, she pulled a navy beanie from the pocket of her black jacket, twisted her long hair, and squished it under the hat. Despite her anxiety about the imminent exit into dangerous territory, she grinned ruefully, glad of her black-blue garb from head to toe.

"Fire escape," he said under his breath as he moved to crack the door open a few inches. No sound from the corridor. TC poked his head around the doorframe and exited. Heart in her mouth, Agnes slipped out in pursuit.

The hallway lay dimly lit and deserted. Her breath escaped with a tiny whistle. Startled, she craned her neck to glance behind. Against the stronger light at the far end, she thought she caught a movement. A shadow played against the wall of the main staircase.

In a panic, Agnes hastened after her accomplice. Her only consolation was to have changed into noiseless sneakers before returning to campus.

Chapter 16

The door to Jaqueline's study opened behind her. Not again, thought Jac. Half an hour ago, Moshi had interrupted her to borrow her MacBook's charger because his was toast, as he said.

No sound came from the intruder. With a sigh, Jac took her eyes off her laptop's screen and swiveled around in her creaking wooden desk chair.

Framed by the door jambs stood Agnes, dressed all in black, jacket hanging open over a turtleneck stuffed into jeans. Crimson cheeks contrasted with the creamy white forehead and chin framed by a dark blue toque entirely hiding the profusion of Agnes's hair.

Neither of them spoke. Jac, startled by the silence and wild expression in her friend's eyes, remained immobile. A sense of dread crept into her consciousness. Thoughts chased each other in fragmented snatches. Campus deserted at night–alone–the basement–Timothy—

Mon Dieu. He tried—

"Agnes! What is it? Are you hurt?"

Her own frantic voice spurned her into action. In one swift movement, she jumped up and advanced upon her friend, hands stretched out.

The agitation shook Agnes out of the freeze. Before Jac reached to embrace her, Agnes stepped forward and pushed the door shut. Her voice hoarse, she said, "We've got to talk, Jac. There's something I need to tell you."

"It is Timothy, isn't it? He—" Her tremulous words ceased shy of the unspeakable.

"No. Yes. Part of it," said Agnes and moved to the small settee by the curtained window.

Jacqueline followed and crouched on the edge of her favorite armchair. The soft forest-green velvet of its upholstery, usually so comforting, failed to relax her.

"Speak to me," she urged Agnes, who'd relapsed into brooding silence. Then, realizing her friend's state of nerves, Jacqueline chattered on, unable to stop herself, "Do you want some water? A glass of wine? Are you in shock?"

Without waiting for an answer, she hastened back to her desk. An almost full bottle of Beaujolais set next to her empty glass from earlier tonight. She refilled it and brought it over, cautious not to spill the dark red liquid, her hands were so aquiver.

"Wine will steady you." The French remedy for all ills. *À votre santé* wasn't an empty phrase. Her dad's often repeated words steadied Jac a little as she dispensed the cure-all.

Agnes took a few sips, then breathed in to exhale with a heart-wrenching sigh. Watching her, Jacqueline sank down on her perch again, afraid of what revelation to expect.

A tiny smile played on her friend's lips when she leaned forward to offer the last third of the wine to Jac. "Looks like you need it too." Jac downed the rest.

"Okay," said Agnes, her tone determined. "Here goes. You won't like this one bit."

"Please! Get to the point, Agnes. I'm sick with worry. You look so strange."

Her friend fiddled with the hem of the black jacket, not

meeting Jac's eyes. Then, she burst out, "TC and I raided Herb's office."

"You did what?" shrieked Jac and clasped her hand over her mouth.

"Wait. Hear me out. Herb's hiding Dorian's piece. I found it."

"Where?"

"In his filing cabinet."

A vision of metal filing drawers in Nessbit's dismal cubby flashed into Jac's mind. "He's not hiding it then," she voiced her somewhat irrelevant thought. "I don't understand. What on earth were you doing in the man's office?"

"Just told you. Promise not to interrupt?"

Jacqueline merely nodded, too perplexed for more.

"So, okay. TC got us into Herb's office and—"

"You mean tonight? Does he have a key to it?"

"You're cutting me off again. Not like you at all." A stubborn expression grew on Agnes's face.

"Continue, please. I'll shut my mouth … for now."

"Right. Before you ask, I did not know TC's intentions beforehand." Pensively, she added, "Followed him like a lamb. Couldn't chicken out." Agnes scratched at her cheekbone, the pressure of her fingers turning the skin white.

Mixed animal metaphors, commented the teacher in Jac's mind.

"TC searched the desk and told me to dig through the files. —Hey, I didn't read any confidential stuff."

Agnes's eyes pleaded to believe her. Jacqueline nodded.

"Just when I was ready to call it quits—Jac, I felt so disgusted with myself. Can't believe I did this."

A mixture of helpless anger and compassion churned Jac's insides. She sighed but avoided her friend's troubled gaze. Instead, she watched her own nails plucking the knees of her pearl-colored leggings. The sight invoked something unpleasant that eluded her consciousness.

"I pricked my finger on a loose staple," said Agnes, as though a minute detail explained everything. In response to Jac's knitted brows, she went on, "Worth mentioning because it led me to check the folder. And there it was. Dorian called the novelette *Betrayal*," she ended lamely.

Speechless, Jac gaped at Agnes. For what seemed a small eternity, but Jac realized, merely lasted a couple of minutes, they sat still. Agnes broke the spell by reaching for the wineglass resting on the side table between them. Now, she rolled the empty goblet between the palms of her hands.

"Say something," she implored Jac. "Tell me I did wrong. Anything. Just don't look so … horror-stricken. You make me afraid."

For friendship's sake, Jacqueline fought for self-control. Wearied, she said, "You realize he tempted you into putting your career on the line. I warned you he'd try to undermine your chances, did I not?"

"Come off it, Jac. We're in the same boat. TC and I."

Somehow, the expression hurt Jacqueline even more. She shook off the specter of jealousy to focus on what mattered most.

"What do we do about Herb?" asked Agnes. "Heck, we can't let him get away with this!"

"Nor can we use what you found out. They'd fire the three of us. You two for breaking into Herb's office—"

"Trespassing. Didn't pick a lock, or something."

"Whatever. And I for condoning—no, instigating this illicit snooping." Aware of how contemptuous the last word came out, Jac felt mortified at her blame-shifting. She squeezed her eyes shut and lengthened her exhale.

Afraid they might do serious damage to their friendship if they continued tonight, she leaned over to touch Agnes's knee. "I know you just wanted to help me. Your raid is a *fait accompli* we can't undo. Let's get some sleep and revisit things tomorrow. You look worn out."

A wry smile rose to her friend's lips. "Not exactly spry either, are you? Off into Morpheus's arms we go."

"Hot chocolate? Cognac? Or Sleepy Time tea?"

"Nah, I'm OK." Agnes pushed herself up and pulled off the toque. Masses of dark curls escaped their confinement and cascaded onto Agnes's shoulders. "See you in the morning." She bent down to peck Jac's cheek, murmuring softly, "Sorry."

For several minutes, after the door closed, Jac remained immobile, arched forward on the edge of her seat, her mind as frozen as her body. How in the world to extricate themselves from this terrible muddle? An insuppressible whimpering moan made her cover her face with both hands. If Martha found out—

She jumped up, grabbed the glass, and rushed to refill it from the bottle on the desk. In three gulps, she downed the contents. Her left arm went up to wipe her mouth on the soft fabric of the powder blue tunic sleeve, for once careless of red wine stains. The glass refilled; she went back to the refuge of the armchair.

Exhausted, she sat down, goblet on the little table beside her. Her slender foot in tan fleece-lined mules angled for the footstool. She kicked off the mules and, both feet resting on the stool, leaned back. A chill from spent emotions made her teeth chatter. Her hand reached for the pure wool throw draped over the armrest. Shaking it out, she covered herself from chin to toes.

Time to think this out. Sleep wouldn't come tonight, anyway.

Chapter 17

On Thursday morning, Agnes checked the time on her mobile. 9:30 AM. Students filed into the classroom on their return from the midway break. She stifled a yawn.

Too much excitement the night before and too little sleep. Rudely awakened from a wild dream around 1:30 AM by clanging sounds on the steel patio outside her room, she'd jumped out of bed and turned all lights on. Hasty footsteps banged down the fire escape. Sure to have disturbed burglars, she'd woken up Jac, only to hear that the inmates from the halfway house next door sometimes snuck up to use the tiny patio for a smoke.

Despite being dead tired for the ungodly early eight o'clock start, her lecture on Immanuel Kant's moral theory had gone very well. His eighteenth-century deontological or duty ethics were challenging and often misunderstood by students and others alike. It had nothing to do with obeying any authority—other than the authority of moral absolutes recognized by reason itself. In the end, her students seemed to grasp the concepts. Now, they were about to discuss it.

As students settled back into their seats, Agnes marveled at the sense of confidence she felt this morning despite physical exhaustion from lack of rest. After Jac's explanation of the rumpus, she'd fallen into a deep slumber and awoke certain she could fix the mess of the reckless raid on Herb's office and clear up the whole Herb-Dorian issue. If she could cling to the certainty and let no self-doubts sneak in.

The class's noisy chattering brought her back to earth. Time to unleash the debate.

"Okay, everyone." Her upbeat tone caught their attention and settled them. "Let's discuss what I asked you to consider during the break. To recap, the German philosopher Immanuel Kant argues for moral absolutes permitting no exceptions. For example, stealing is wrong, no ifs ands or buts.

"Your task was to consider Kant's view and what it implies in practical examples. Now, let's hear what you think of his position on theft." With feigned horror, she added, "Hey, I hope none of you put the idea of stealing to the test and ran off without paying for your coffee."

Into the class's laughter, a few students shouted their views to be heard first.

Agnes overrode the clamor. "Guys—mind the neighbors. We're not alone on this floor. You know the drill. Raise your hand and wait your turn."

A girl who'd politely raised her hand from the start had caught her attention already. "Sam, you go first."

Though Agnes, after years of teaching ethics courses, could have predicted many of the standard responses, she still enjoyed these discussions. In rare instances, she interfered to avoid serious clashes yet preferred students critically examining ideas and forming their own views.

"My friends and I thought Kant is wrong," Sam explained. The almond-shaped eyes sparkled under the glossy black fringe of a chin-length bob. Several of her peers nodded eagerly. "If someone is starving, we think it's not morally wrong for them to steal."

"Thanks, Sam, for leading the way," said Agnes. "Jasmeet, you're next."

The student sat poised, arms crossed. His black-bearded face under the rose-colored turban always impressed Agnes with its calm assurance. Now he said, "In my religion, stealing is wrong. Stealing, like lying, comes from greed. We—"

"But what if someone is starving, like what Sam said just now?" broke in a girl in the back row.

"We help and feed the poor. Not let them starve and become desperate," Jasmeet replied with dignity.

"Besides," added another student, "there are food banks and shelters."

"Good. Thanks, guys," Agnes said. "Lester, you had your hand up earlier."

Lester, just like Melanie, took not only her existentialism but also her ethics course. As so often was the case, they also sat in the exact spot they veered toward in the other classroom, a twin of this room one floor below. Mel shyly kept to the window seat while Lester opted for the center of the first row, smack in front of the podium.

Nor did Lester, aka Kafka, vary in his habit to address only Agnes and ignore the class behind him. Repeatedly, she urged him to speak up when he fell into his usual mutterings. When he uttered his most controversial views, his voice grew strong enough. Whether he played devil's advocate to rile his peers or truly believed what he said, Agnes could never be sure.

Now, his almost black eyes shot her a glance from under the stringy dark fringe. The whitish tapered fingers twirled a sharp pencil. His low voice struck her as filled with contempt. "Moral absolutes and Kant's duty ethics are for the weak. Give me Nietzsche's will to power and Ayn Rand's egoist ethics any time."

"Well," Agnes pointed out mildly, "we'll learn about their philosophies in later modules. For now, stick to Kant on stealing. I gather you don't think it's always morally wrong?"

"Of course not," said Lester, his didactic tone preparing

Agnes for a longer argument. Since his reasoning often proved interesting, she let him take the reign.

"If you accept the common example of the starving poor as a valid exception, then by implication, stealing for survival is permissible. Take everyone's favorite current topic, stealing intellectual property."

Oh no, Agnes almost groaned out loud. But Lester was unstoppable.

"If a guy," he went on, "steals someone's manuscript because his own survival as a writer is at stake, the stealing is justified."

A quick retort flitted through Agnes's mind. She held back and turned to the class. "What do others think of Lester's example? Do you agree?"

Lots of headshaking in response. No one wanted to cross swords with the outspoken peer, as unpopular in this class as in the other. Lester gloated. He realized, she was sure, most students—other than Kalen and Renata, who weren't in this class—feared to take him on. They left the task to her. Sneers aside, she sensed that Kafka, aka Lester, appeared to like her in his own way, or so it often seemed to her when they engaged in debate.

After waiting a few moments, Agnes sighed. She couldn't let such an opinion go unchallenged. "Well," she said offhandedly, "it seems to me there are lots of other options for one's survival if stuck as an author. Seek advice. Change career if needs be."

"So, you would cave in and give up your job as a professor rather than lie or steal, Dr. Taylor?" An insolent sneer from below emphasized her title. "Perhaps you're not passionate about your job. Writers live for their passion and are defined by it." Head bowed, he muttered, "We'd kill to court the muses."

Agnes could only hope others hadn't caught the last bit. To divert attention, she aimed for a cheerful, brisk cadence. "As much as I love my profession, I'd rather go waitressing than stealing or—" Thoughts of last night flashed into her mind. She finished vaguely, "Or whatever."

Then she realized her remark was open to misunderstanding. "Oh, and this is not denigrating servers, by any means. I quite enjoyed my job as a waitress during my undergrad years." No need to mention she was well-endowed with scholarships and the usual teaching assistantships during her graduate years to live comfortably—by her frugal standards.

Time to change topics. "Okay, everyone. For the rest of class time, we do some group work," she said. "Topic and instructions coming up. Hang on a moment. Get together in your assigned groups while I pull it up."

Some students groaned or grumbled. Most, however, joined their groups, quite eager for a chat. While fiddling with her laptop, she noticed Mel texting frantically, the youthful face puckered and stressed out. Instead of moving to her group, Mel stuffed her belongings into a shoulder bag and made for the door. Highly unusual for a dedicated student like her to run off, Agnes figured. Melanie's mien struck Agnes as stressed out or anguished.

Concerned, she came out from behind the podium and met the student before she could exit. "Is something wrong, Melanie? Are you not feeling well?"

"I'm so sorry, Dr. Taylor, but I need to leave." The expression changed to a timid questioning one. In a sudden rush, she uttered, "Please, can we talk outside? Just quickly?"

"Of course, Melanie." Agnes turned to the class. There was no need to say anything. Groups dotted throughout the room huddled in animated talk. Somehow, she doubted their chats focused on the assigned topic on the screen. Only Lester remained isolated in the front row. Biding time and watching her intently.

Agnes held the door for Melanie and followed her into the deserted hallway. A sense of déjà vu took hold of her.

"It's Cass," said Mel, confirming Agnes's foreboding. Tears

glittered in her light blue eyes. The face was taut, maybe from the low ponytail which pulled back the ash-blonde hair. "She's … She's in hospital … Her roommate texted me."

"What?" The vehemence of her involuntary exclamation startled Agnes. With forced calm, she said, "Sorry. Any idea what happened?"

"They think she took something—" As the voice broke, tears flowed freely.

Agnes reached out to put an arm around Melanie's shoulder but didn't—too aware of rules of conduct. "That's so distressing." To put it mildly, she added in her own head. Horrific! "Can I call anyone to come and get you? Drive you home?"

"Thank you, professor. It's okay. Cass's roommate is waiting for me outside. We'll go to the hospital." Tremulously, she added. "Cass is all alone. Her parents are on a cruise. They live out in BC, anyway."

"I'm so glad you look out for your friend. Please, Melanie, let me know as soon as you find out more. You can count on my help. Just tell me how I can assist."

"I will. Thanks, Dr. Taylor, for caring so much about us." Like a scared hare, Mel rushed down the corridor.

Bemused and somewhat stunned, Agnes's eyes followed her. The image became overlaid with that of Medusa in the rain. If only I'd gotten in touch with Cass—Guilt flooded in.

Dejectedly, she returned to her unsuspecting class.

Chapter 18

All morning, Jacqueline had checked the time congealing like lard in a cooling frying pan. Half an hour before the official end of her contemporary Canadian literature class, she couldn't take any more. Exhausted from a sleepless night and nail-biting worries, her favorite novelists held no appeal. In a sudden decision, she'd dismissed the class early. The last students leaving tossed her cheery goodbyes, exuberant like little kids playing truant.

Ten-twenty-five read the display on her mobile as she stuffed it into a side pocket of her bag. The unscheduled break gave her time now for a caffeine boost to see her through the admin meeting at eleven. Throughout the night, she'd fretted over the potential fallout from Agnes's reckless action. The morning brought no relief. She'd rushed to her eight o'clock class without speaking to Agnes, only to find herself scatterbrained during her lecture and the follow-up discussion. Distracted by anxiety over losing Martha's goodwill and the career she'd been so careful to build—

About to pack up the paperbacks of today's novelist, Jacqueline froze, paralyzed by another thought. Herb might already have discovered traces of last night's intrusion. Her hand went up to her mouth, stifling a moan. What was she to do?

Even if Elliot kept his big mouth shut for now out of pure self-interest, he'd whistle-blow if Agnes scored the full-time position they'd both be competing for. He'd shown his vindictive streak, Jac thought, during her own hiring process. The public kudos for her program initiative she'd received after her probation hearing six months ago must have irked him.

Jacqueline stared at the paperback in her hand. Margaret Atwood's *The Heart Goes Last* stared back, the exchangeable orange-clad male and female springing out against the turquoise backdrop of its cover.

An image of her own former lover—fiancé of five years—flashed into her mind. Steve had exchanged her for another, neither younger nor particularly good-looking woman. It had been Agnes who helped her through the harrowing experience of being ... dumped overnight with a curt text message. Night and day, Agnes stood by. Ready to empathize, listen, or offer rationally sound advice, she always sensed what Jac needed most.

While her dad urged patience and womanly wiles to win her man back, and her brother Phil was ready to "beat the hell out of the bastard," his words, Agnes worked to restore Jac's self-esteem.

A few months later, Jac had landed her current professorship in the Humanities department of Bowman College. And thought life was wonderful...

Until now. Maybe, she mused as she banned Atwood to the depth of her bag and zipped it up impatiently. Some distrust of males still lingered after the Steve episode. Surely Elliot would not be so stupid to sabotage his own future for the doubtful pleasure of revenge? Owning up to the raid would mark the end of his pipe dreams of any permanent professorship or any academic employment. After all, it was he who instigated the illicit search.

As she walked out of the classroom, another mental flash made her stop. Agnes's word against his. No proof for Timothy Charles Elliot being the instigator. Worse, Jac herself couldn't deny urging Agnes to disprove the rumor.

Horrified and frustrated at herself for being the true cause of all her troubles, Jacqueline headed down the corridor toward the main staircase. An extra potent brew might restore her for the admin meeting. The Second Cup outlet would serve the purpose.

Wedged into the outside perimeter of the wide third-story hall which bridged the classroom and office wings of their building, the coffee counter was a popular spot for break-time or to grab a quick bite for lunch without having to descent to the food court in the far reaches of the ground floor. One couldn't help but pass it since it faced the grand staircase to the foyer two stories below.

Now, only one customer preceded Jac at the counter. Aimlessly, she eyed the glassed-in display of sumptuous pastries and sandwiches wrapped in clear plastic. On top of the counter, bell-shaped glass domes covered piled up brownies and nut-studded or chocolate glazed biscotti.

Today, they failed to tempt Jac. She ordered a double shot expresso and, cup in hand, made for one of the few counter stools off to the side. A cloth partition divided the narrow ledge for patrons in a hurry or simply fond of bar-style seating from the more popular tables and chairs fronting the outside window wall behind it. For, on that side, the unobstructed view from the third floor over the campus grounds and adjacent park toward the picturesque town and river was stunning.

Right now, however, Jacqueline contemplated the mottled pewter of the high room divider. It mirrored the twilight in her soul this morning. 10, 15 minutes' quiet time to still her monkey brain before the admin meeting that would require her full concentration was all she sought.

The first few sips of the extra dark roast perked her up sufficiently to register the steady flow of voices behind the partition. With a smile, she identified the dominant bass as Kalen's, recognizable even when not booming loudly. Safe from being drawn into any conversation, she didn't mind the chatty ebbing and flowing suited to distract her from the now fainter voices clamoring in her own mind.

The problem was, once your subconscious tuned into other people's talk, it proved difficult to tune out again. Snatches caught her attention.

"…met his folks before and…" Clearly, Kalen.

"Why you? We're…" A female voice rising, then falling. It sounded familiar, but Jac couldn't quite place it.

"Yeah. Why not Cass?" Eye-rolling, Jac recognized Renata's strident tone.

"*Duh?*" Kalen now boomed. "Gotta be kiddin', right? After she ditched him?"

The image of Emma flickered into Jac's consciousness. Kalen must have met with the Gables. No surprise there. They'd want to connect with Dorian's friends, not only with his professors.

Petulant, the other female complained, "AD Muller didn't ask me and Renata—"

"Yeah, right, Cleo." Oh, of course, thought Jac. The girl always formed part of their clique. Kalen went on with a boisterous laugh, "You hated his guts from way back when he won the first-year story competition."

"I did not!"

"C'mon, Cleo. Admit your sins. You shouted blue murder when you didn't get the prize, and our genius snared it. You and Lester had your hopes up. Sucked up to our Herb, the resident poet. Did you bribe him to vote for your story?"

"That is so not true," an outraged Cleo shouted back.

"Dr. Muller wouldn't know," squeaked the unmistakable voice of Joel.

The entire clique, noted Jac wryly. To eavesdrop was not her style. Yet, something kept her glued to the spot, staring at the black and beige logo on her empty espresso cup.

"What's that got to do with—"

Renata's voice interrupted Kalen's impatient question with yet another one. "Did his parents say what happened to Dorie?"

"Don't know more than us." Kalen sounded dismissive, but then added, "Weird. His mom asked about parties. Not sure if she meant popping knock-out pills or—"

"What?" shrieked Renata. "He wasn't—"

"Nah. Don't think so," Kalen asserted. "They'd have reacted quite differently then." In a pensive tone, he continued, "Reminds me, though. Cleo, didn't you tell us about the queen at your high school prom? A guy spiked her champers to make her pass out?"

"Yeah? I don't get it. It wasn't Dorian. Or anyone we know here." Louder, Cleo asked, "You said nothing to his mom, did you?"

"*Eh?*—Don't be stupid—"

"What I can't figure out," cut in Renata, "Who's Cass's new mystery lover? Any idea?"

Kalen's rumbling laughter startled Jac. She really ought to leave.

"Your guess is as good as mine," he said. "Seen her with old man Nessbit—"

"So what?" hooted Cleo. "She's in his poetry class, dodo."

"Night class at the Riverside Pub? Yeah, right. Saw them a couple of weeks ago. Me and a mate popped in before closing, and there they were. Cass yakking away and him ogling her."

"Doesn't mean they're dating," countered Cleo. "Her and Chuck hang out too."

"Hey, she plays the field. What a laugh. Our miss prissy about town," shouted Renata.

"You guys don't understand." Joel's high-pitched squeak cut across excitedly. "TC is sussing out things. He rumbled Nessbit's game, I tell you."

"Oh, Joel. You and your spy stuff. You're such a hoot," gurgled Renata.

"I saw him!" Joel sounded genuinely hurt. "With my own eyes—go into Nessbit's office—at night!"

"So what?" Cleo's rejoinder dripped sarcasm. "They're friends, aren't they?"

"Sort of," boomed Kalen. "Our Herbert *works* late with Johnnie Walker—if you get my meaning."

"Professor Nessbit was not there when I saw TC," insisted Joel, his voice rising over the riotous laughter.

"So? Maybe he picked up some stuff," Renata said, still spluttering with laughter. "Or went to fetch empties?"

Joel sounded deflated when he said, "He had—"

The insistent ring of her phone startled not only Jacqueline, who scrambled to fish it out of the side pocket of her bag. Conversation ceased behind the partition.

The time display lit up and Jac groaned to herself. Oh my God, I'll be late.

'Agnes' appeared on caller ID. One hand grabbing her bag, Jac swiped the green 'answer' and made to leave.

"Sorry, Agnes. Can't talk now. I've got to run to my meeting," she said without giving her friend a chance to speak.

In an afterthought, she tucked the phone between shoulder and ear and turned back to grab the empty cup.

Three heads poked around the partition, mustering her accusingly.

"Well, well," droned Kalen. "Big Sister is watching—nah—listening to you."

An impatient shake of her head and Jacqueline hurried off toward the office wing, leaving the cup to make its own way to the counter.

"Pardon? I didn't catch what you were saying, Agnes."

Her friend's distress was palpable in the shout, "Listen to me!" Then more quietly, "I said, Cass is in hospital. Mel emailed just now. They think Cass tried to kill herself. She's in a coma."

"Oh–my–God." Jac staggered with each word—her world crumbling as she spoke.

Chapter 19

Agnes stared up at the sky. It ought to be weeping. For Cass. For Dorian. For wasted youth. Lives thrown away in the moment's despair. Instead, the sun shone brilliantly from a crisp blue sky.

In the wake of Mel's email from hospital, Agnes couldn't bear hanging around campus to wait for Jac's meeting to end. The thought of bumping into Herb—or even TC—after last night's exploits was cringe-worthy. Notes posted online and outside the basement office informed students of her canceled office hour. Students didn't mind. Emailing or stopping her after class was handier, anyway.

For the past half hour, she'd tramped through town, aimlessly popping into a store or two to distract herself from worrying.

In summer, leafy streets and flower containers, now barren, along sidewalks studded with vintage lamp posts would attract tourists and day-trippers. Quaint storefronts abounded, inviting passersby into one-of-a-kind boutiques, second-hand bookstores, crafts and pottery shops, and assorted coffee shops and tearooms.

None of these captured Agnes's attention today. Her mind churned over the same questions as she moved restlessly along.

What did it all mean? From what Mel said, they—presumably the doctors—thought Cass took something. Sounded intentional, but why would Cass attempt to kill herself?

A chain reaction? How doubly horrible if Cass believed herself to have caused Dorian's death when Herb's theft of the manuscript might be the true cause.

Or maybe Emma's intuition was right, against all odds, and someone spiked Dorian's drink for a laugh. But the night Dorian died, there was no party—at least, no one mentioned one.

Agnes shook herself out of her reverie. Her steps had taken her down a narrow street, lined with meticulously kept front yards leading up to dwellings equally well-tended in a medley of traditional Ontario residential styles. Painted clapboard with shutters and trims visually offset, red or brown brick, and mellow classic Fieldstone dominated. The steepish incline led down to the river.

Jac's SMS twenty minutes ago suggested meeting at the Riverside Pub. Unsure why down there, Agnes figured Jac wanted to get away for a while. The place was far enough out of the way to be quiet off-season at lunchtime.

Close to noon, the day turned unseasonably warm. Climate change came unbidden to her mind as Agnes left behind straggling houses along the river road and veered onto an unpaved lane, the coarse gravel crunching underfoot. Trees lined both sides. Leafless now, they gave unobstructed access on her left to the lazily flowing river. Churned up by recent rains, the water appeared murky along the shoreline.

In summer, the grassy slopes would invite picnics and sunbathing. Transported for a brief moment, she imagined canoes punting by—if punt they did—while stretched out on a blanket on the banks, lulled by the fragrant scent of grass and wildflowers. Next summer. If all went well.

The lane followed a bend in the river. From her one and only visit to the pub early on this term, she seemed to recall a lookout resting place in the vicinity. Maybe she'd wait there for

Jac to come down the footpath, which connected to the park much farther uphill. A shortcut for anyone venturing to the pub from campus. The incline was rather steep and rugged, but fitness junkie Jac kept her running gear at the office.

As soon as she reached the junction, Agnes stopped short. Someone descended the narrow trail. Not Jac, but the very man she'd tried to avoid all morning.

Fedora, tweed jacket, and black scarf slung over one shoulder were dead giveaways. No concession made to today's unseasonable temperature.

About to dodge among the trees, she realized how furtive and futile it would be. The barren brush provided no cover. The aborted movement must have alerted him. For Herb's head tilted back. Only ten yards away now, he raised a reluctant hand in a half-hearted greeting.

What could she do but wait? She must forewarn Jac, though. Change the venue in case Mr. Nessbit aimed at a midday pub crawl. A step closer towards the lookout, and she dug out her phone, pretending a mere midday stroll was the goal all along.

Instead of moving on toward the pub, Herb joined her. "Beautiful day, isn't it?" The almost friendly timbre of his gravelly voice took her by surprise. A smile might lurk among the bristles and creases. If so, it didn't reach the eyes scrutinizing her.

"Sure is," mumbled Agnes. "Phew, quite warm for a walk," she added to cover up for her flaming cheeks. How embarrassing, she thought, not even sure he recognized her. For all she knew, the guy habitually chatted up women on lonely lanes. The creep. The idea made her skin crawl.

His bloodshot eyes still ogled her. Agnes's hand went up to grab at the lapels of her jacket gaping wide to cool her skin during the sunny walk. The top buttons of her blouse were undone to aid ventilation. With an effort of will, she forced herself not to look down to see how much she was revealing, mentally cursing her over-generous cleavage.

"You're the new hire, aren't you? Didn't you tell me about teaching?" His eyes strayed toward the pub, barely visible two hundred yards in the distance. An ugly crimson spread on his cheekbones.

To refresh his hazy recollection, she reminded him. "Yes, indeed. I'm Agnes Taylor, philosophy. We spoke the other night." If talk we did, her snarky mind commented. Only to recall last night's raid and cringe.

Nessbit's right hand reached into the pocket of his corduroy slacks to bring out a white cotton handkerchief and dab his brow.

Agnes stared in disbelief. I swear it's starched and ironed. Is this guy real?

"Well," she said aloud, "I'd better let you go. Don't want to hold you up when you were on your way to—"

"Ahem…I fear I owe you an explanation, Dr. Taylor. About the other night. A most unusual—"

"Oh, please. No worries. You don't have to explain," she interrupted, eager to get away from his unbearably miserable expression. Guilt about intruding welled up.

"No, no. I insist. Wouldn't do for you to think… Not for the world." Hanky fluttering in the breeze, he pointed to the bench. "Won't you sit down for a moment? If you're not in a rush, that is."

His reddish eyes regarded her earnestly—pleading. Resigned, Agnes shrugged. She let him lead her the few steps to the bench roughly hewn from weathered half-logs.

The view over the river onto the distant rolling hills, so typical of southern Ontario, was pleasing. Two months ago, lush after late summer rains, it had been breathtaking. Now, it provided an excuse for not facing the man at the other end of the bench. Yet, she sensed his gaze.

Politely, she turned a fraction to signal her willingness to listen.

"You see," he began, only to clear his throat without altering the hoarseness of his voice. "I'd received bad news that afternoon."

"Oh, yes, of course. We all heard of Dorian's—"

"No. I wasn't referring to—Of course, you are right. Terrible news, indeed. Dreadful. And so young. No, I fear, it wasn't all that happened."

Agnes swiveled to face him. What worse thing could have happened to him that day?

"You see," he said again, "I received a letter from my publisher—Isn't it worse when it's on paper? They declined to publish my novel. I'd poured my lifeblood into this truly cutting-edge literary piece! I was devastated." Headshaking, the voice petered out, overcome by emotion.

Stunned, Agnes confronted him. He regarded her mournfully, reminding her of an unhappy wrinkle dog.

Her face must have mirrored her outrage at this narcissism. A rejection letter on par, nay, worse news than the death of their student?

His hands flapped up, reddish palms seeking to placate. "Don't get me wrong. I understand. To you, this must sound trivial. For a writer, however…" He mopped his face with the hanky still clutched in his right hand. "Alas, enough of me," he added gruffly.

Disgusted, Agnes made to get up. "Thanks for sharing," she said, not caring how facetious it came out.

Then, an idea hit her. "Too bad about your novel. What kind of story is it?"

The puce color of his face deepened. "I never discuss rejects. It's back to the drawing board."

"Oh, sorry I asked. Well, then, enjoy your walk."

Herb wasn't ready to let her go. He leaned in, perhaps eager to soften the rebuff. "Can I interest you in our literary soiree? The mater is hosting her Thursday at Home tonight. It's just a little get-together. Some of our local 'big wigs.'" His fingers tapped scare quotes in the air between them. The hanky fluttered intact, amusing Agnes against her will. "And lesser mortals like me," he ended ruefully.

Lost for a reply to this unexpected invitation apropos of nothing, Agnes regarded him, mouth slightly agape.

"You'll find the mater and some of her intellectually endowed regulars philosophically stimulating. If you're planning to extend your sojourn at this admittedly humble institution," he pointed vaguely uphill in direction of the college, "it will be to your advantage to mingle with the right people."

What in the world have I done to deserve this? Sarcasm and censor seeped in when she replied, "Well, thanks a lot for thinking of me. I'm not sure I feel up to such diversion at present."

How callous, she fumed, to even consider it while Cass— Does he realize how this looks? Here, the lives of two young people destroyed, for all we know by his senseless action, and all he seeks are distractions from his literary woes.

Anger bubbled up. Without preamble, rather self-righteously to her own mind, she hissed, "I, for one, am too anxious about Cass to contemplate partying."

"Oh, mater's soirees are not parties. They are quite low-key and dignified." Then it seemed to hit him. "Cass? You mean the student Cassandra? Oh, yes, she was a friend of Dorian Gable, wasn't she? Yes, I see. She must be rather upset."

Was this feigned ignorance on top of blatant insensitivity? she wondered.

"Surely, another suicide is more than an upset."

Now, Nessbit appeared stunned. The crushed handkerchief shot up to cover his mouth.

A quaver distorting the voice, he murmured, "She survived?"

"Barely. She's in a coma. I don't know more than that." Nor do I wish to discuss it with you of all people, she added silently.

"We can only hope—and pray if we could," he said under his breath.

"Listen," Agnes said decisively, "I don't want to be rude, but I've got to go."

She rose before he could reply and walked in the direction of the pub. Damn the man. If he followed suit, she'd just keep on walking and text Jac to meet farther down the lane. It looped back toward the outskirts of town, she recalled. Her next class began at three. Tons of time until then.

With her back already turned to him, she tossed a curt "See you around" over her shoulder.

The man had the nerve to respond, "I'll email you the invite to the mater's soiree later this afternoon. We hope to see you there."

Not on your life! Agnes vowed.

Chapter 20

Jacqueline stared at the fingers of her right hand. Of their own accord, they brushed the edge of the notepad in front of her, endlessly flicking its pages in a twitchy movement. It was all she could do to prevent them from drumming the table.

For the past forty minutes, she'd struggled to focus on the various issues under discussion. Against her usual habit, she offered no contributions, barely responding when asked for her opinion. AD Martha Muller, who chaired the policy and strategic planning committee, shot her concerned glances when no insight on key points was forthcoming.

Her sights set on reaching the pinnacle of executive management positions, Jacqueline had devoted years to self-improvement. Yet, the sterling qualities of patience, attentiveness, and leadership deserted her today. The news about Cassandra, the uncertainties, and implications crowded out any point of policy tabled during the meeting.

Certain committee members' habitual repetitiveness, harking back to questions or objections long addressed, ground on her nerves to a breaking point. Any mantra to stay positive and charitable forgotten, she allowed herself to dwell on the inescapable fact meetings comprised stereotypical attendees. The nay-sayers, the grumblers, the enthusiasts, the pacifiers, the bores, and the ramblers. The silent majority in larger meetings harbored the nodders, the distracted, the meek, the disapproving, and so on.

No matter how hard Jacqueline tried to reign in her errant mind, once it zeroed in on negativity, the mood persisted. I'm just out of sorts, is all, she figured.

A volume increase in AD's resonant, kindly voice made Jac look up. Relief flooded her. The chair embarked on closing remarks.

"Thank you all for your most valuable input," said Martha. "I think we can all agree it was a most profitable session, with much achieved. Fraser will distribute the minutes as usual. We shall reconvene in two weeks, as per schedule."

Hands flat on the table, Martha pushed herself up. As the final sign of closure, she stacked the various papers and hand-outs spread in front of her. Colleagues, according to tempera-ment and personality, said their cheery or frowning goodbyes. A few jumped up to be first in line to have a word with the chair. Some filed out in haste, evidently glad to be shot of another meeting. Others lingered to chat.

Jacqueline remained seated at the end of the long table closest to the exit. Her late arrival had prevented opting for a midway spot, which she preferred. Bent forward, ostensively preoccupied with her notes and her mobile, she bided her time for a quiet word with the AD once everyone was gone. Several colleagues stopped to chat, but her monosyllabic responses discouraged their attempts. Puzzled at such unaccustomed aloofness, they let her be.

From her end of the table, Jac furtively watched Martha collecting the stack of paper and tucking it under one arm while the other hand grabbed the water bottle. A clear sign of impending departure.

"Certainly, a good point, Clark," Jac heard the AD say to

the last straggler. "We'll revisit it during our next meeting. Drop me a line if you wish."

Clark, a traditionalist who taught history electives, never failed to cite his thirty-plus years of college experience. There always was a precedent to draw on for any occasion. In Martha, he'd found his match. She dealt kindly, yet effectively, with his administrative anecdotes.

When he began to reiterate his point, she excused herself, saying, "Absolutely. I fully understand. We'll consider your objection. Let me have a quick word with Jacqueline before I must dash to my next meeting. You and I, Clark, can chat at more leisure at your convenience. Fraser will schedule you in if you reach out to him."

With that, Clark had to be satisfied. Accompanied by the AD's friendly smile, he turned to leave, stroking his grizzled goatee while clutching a scuffed leather satchel in his other hand. The once dapper three-piece suit, the vest correctly buttoned over a well-worn light blue shirt, sagged at the knees and elbows. Despite garrulous tendencies, Jac knew him to be a kind-hearted and supportive colleague, much beloved by students for his unexpected bursts of witticisms and understated humor.

As he passed her, he smiled sweetly. "Cheer up, Jacqueline. History has shown there's always another sunny day in the offing."

Martha waited until he was well out of earshot before shutting the door with care.

"You're not quite yourself today, I noted, Jacqueline. Is there anything I can help with?"

"Sorry, I was late." Jac began, uncertain how to convey her news.

"I'm sure something unavoidable came up. Your punctuality is legend and a good example to us all. Not to worry. The way you slipped in unobtrusively and took a seat by the door could hardly disturb anyone."

The lengthy speech, Jac realized, aimed to calm her.

The older woman placed her paraphernalia on the table. When Jac half rose, Martha eased herself into a chair. "No, no. Don't get up. I sense there's more you'd like to say."

"I don't want to detain you, but, yes, something terrible happened. Sorry to be so blunt. Difficult to put it gently."

Martha's face turned grave as if preparing for the worst. Her soft, dimpled hand reached out to Jac. "Just tell me straight."

"It's Cass—perhaps you already know?" When a fleeting shake of the gray curls negated, Jac took a deep breath to steady herself. "Cassandra is in hospital. A suicide attempt, they think. She's in a coma, they say."

For a moment, the AD remained immobile. Shock-widened pupils met Jac's before Martha's lids closed to shut out the raw moment.

"What in the world is going on here?" the AD murmured. A slight shake as if to regain control, and she faced Jac. "Go on. Tell me what happened."

"It's all I know. Agnes called—that's what made me late." The now irrelevant detail ground to a halt.

"Why didn't Agnes notify me? How did she hear about Cassandra?" For once, AD Muller sounded reproachful.

"Agnes was aware of our meeting and hoped this was the fastest way to convey the news to you." A fib. Agnes didn't mention Martha. "This is the first chance to talk to you. We received no further detail than the bare fact."

"Who told Agnes?"

Fingering her notepad nervously under Martha's observant eye, Jac played for time. A moral conundrum. Jac shot the older woman a quick glance.

"A student. To pass on their name would breach confidentiality, don't you agree? They only trust us—or Agnes, in this case—if we honor their confidences. Of course," she added in response to Martha's raised eyebrow, "when a student is in acute danger, there's an obligation to disclose. Here, the information stems from a third party, imparted after the fact."

"Quite right. I see your point. A tightrope walk as we all realize. Will Agnes's—shall we say, 'source'?" she queried with a flash of humor, "pass on further details once available?"

"I'd expect so. Sorry, we lacked time to discuss it." Somewhat surprised at Martha's tacit request for second-hand information, Jacqueline asked, "Won't you contact the hospital?"

The town's sole hospital, Jac assumed, admitted Cassandra.

"Privacy policies prevent our interference. The student has the right to decide whether to inform us of her hospitalization or any reason for it."

"How can she—she's in a coma," interjected Jac, more emphatically than intended.

"Allow me to elaborate. The next of kin are the decision-makers in cases of incapacity. One would assume this to be the parents. We must wait for them to reach out."

In response to Jac's obvious frustration with their forced inactivity, Martha's hand tapped her sleeve lightly. A gesture among friends, oddly comforting when dispensed by a motherly figure like Martha, Jac felt.

"Meanwhile, please pass on—informally, as you will—anything conducive to our helping the student. Presumably, Agnes feels at ease sharing with you as her close friend. Talk it over with her and share with me—as your friend—whatever you can without breaching confidentiality."

After this marvel of circumspection, Martha grabbed her papers and tapped the ends on the faux wood of the tabletop to align them. "I'll be tied up in meetings all afternoon. Send me an SMS to my private number if anything transpires."

The kindly smile reassured Jac somewhat. Yet, anxiety churned her insides.

"Oh, on another note," said Martha, perhaps sensing a distraction might help, "I've been meaning to ask. Any news from Paris? Is a decision forthcoming?"

The questions came so out of nowhere Jac had to regroup before answering. Months ago, she'd applied for a visiting professorship at the Sorbonne, where she'd spent a year during her doctoral studies and again as a post-doctoral fellow. A decision was imminent.

"Not yet, Martha. Their deliberations are a few days overdue."

"Well, we know you're among their three short-listed candidates. I'm rooting for you." A warm smile enveloped Jac. "Such a feather in your cap. And the program's—if the latter can be said to don a cap."

The infectious smile as they collected their belongings lightened Jacqueline's despondent mood.

"Keep me posted," said Martha when they parted at the door.

Back in her office a few minutes later, the darkness of anxiety descended again. Far from being a glimmer of hope, the prospect of a visiting professorship might be equally in jeopardy through the predicament engulfing her, thought Jac. Cassandra's suicide attempt—horrific in itself—could only add fuel to the firestorm if Elliot chose to light the fuse. Martha had no inkling of the maelstrom awaiting them.

Distracted for an instant by the trite metaphors her mind produced, a tiny grin pulled at the corners of her mouth. Then, the image of Martha's gentle face interceded, causing Jac to tear up. To disappoint her staunch friend and mentor—

Dismayed at getting emotional in her professional space, Jac locked the door and grabbed joggers and trainers from the bottom drawer of her desk. Away from the windows, she slipped off her pumps and charcoal pencil skirt. The comfort of the soft running gear soothed. A brisk jog through the park, followed by a hamstring-stretching descent to the river, would set her right.

All she really needed was a one-to-one with her best friend. A tentative smile played around her lips as she pulled off her blouse and replaced it with a running top and jacket from the drawer. She couldn't wait to flee campus for a couple of hours.

Chapter 21

From the raised entrance porch of the Riverside Pub, Agnes ostensibly admired the vista, no matter how unspectacular. A few cars dotted the graveled parking lot. The unkempt bush lot on the opposite side held little attraction. The lane widened from this point into a paved road. Her glance went back the way she'd come. No sign of Herb. If boozing he had in mind, he must have opted for another drinking hole.

So far, so good. Once Jac was free to join her, their chat would be undisturbed in this quiet place. Tons of time before her afternoon class, Agnes had replied to Jac's SMS about being delayed. She'd grab a tea while waiting inside.

Agnes pulled open the bleached oak door that blended in well with the sandblasted fieldstone of the one-story pub building. A strong smell of fried food, mixed with the unmistakable odor of draft ale accumulating in old taverns, hit her nostrils. Blinded by the dim interior lighting after the brilliant sunshine outside, she blinked and stood still.

Vision adjusted; she got her bearings. The rustic, solid wood bar on the left side sported vintage brass draft beer taps. A rack above the counter dangled beer mugs and wine glasses. Most impressive, however, was the backdrop of roughhewn shelves mounted on the exposed fieldstone wall storing a vast array of liquor bottles. The barmaid, busy at the sink, did not look up or greet the newcomer.

Custom, as expected, was slow. Through rows of latticed windows, Agnes glimpsed some people who'd opted for tables on the back patio, intent on soaking up the unseasonable warmth while enjoying the gorgeous river view onto the undulating hills beyond. Most of the cornflower blue umbrellas remained furled.

For a moment, Agnes felt tempted to join the sun worshippers. Inside, it would be easier to spot Jac coming in, she figured. Few tables were occupied in the taproom, mostly those she coveted along the window wall toward the river. On the lookout for a spot with a view, Agnes sauntered farther in.

Then she saw him. Backlit by a sunray that penetrated the dim interior at this end, she hadn't recognized him until she was level with his table. Nor did he notice her—too busy with his mobile. The chestnut hair glowed in the slanted beam of light. Stubble shadowed the hollow under prominent cheekbones and emphasized the strong jawline. Sleeves of his casual black shirt rolled up to the elbows, exposed muscular underarms. The soft collar gaped wide despite the coolness of the pub's interior.

Aware she was staring mesmerized at the man she'd wanted to avoid most today, Agnes stepped back in retreat—and promptly knocked into the chair behind her. The scraping sound drew TC's attention. His eyes rose from the screen as if reluctant to withdraw their focus. As they met her startled look, they sharpened. The jaw clenched. A frown contracted the dark eyebrows.

Like her, she realized, he'd hoped to avoid an encounter after last night's raid. How totally embarrassing. Better grin and bear, she told herself. No way now to beat a retreat.

"Sorry, TC. Didn't mean to disturb you. Just looking for a window table… I'm meeting Jac here. Plenty of other tables." Shocked at her own babbling, she ground to a halt.

What was it about this guy to disconcert her so? The way he flipped back the wayward curls, which so bewitchingly flopped forward after bending over his phone, made her want to reach out to touch him.

Get a grip, she ordered herself.

His lips curved upward as if, tuned into the recesses of her mind, he liked what he divined.

"Well, well. I sure did not expect to see you in this godforsaken tavern," he said and leaned back, tilting his chair onto two legs. Head angled, chin facing up, he regarded her along his aquiline nose.

"Gosh, I'm sorry. There you were, just as anxious to avoid me—"

"Me? Anxious?" he drawled and paused. "Why?"

A brave attempt, she thought, to appear unaffected.

"You know—feeling guilty. Last thing you'd want to see—" 'Your partner in crime,' she'd intended to say, half-jokingly. Something in his expression unnerved her. Not sure at all how to read it, she couldn't gauge his reaction.

"I've no idea what you're talking about." His attention wandered to the entrance door as if looking for a distraction to save them both further awkwardness.

"Well, I'd better go grab a table," she said. It didn't come out as upbeat as she'd intended.

"Why don't you stay for a bit?" The caressing tone surprised her as much as TC's suggestion. "You guys can opt for another table when Jacqueline arrives. Plenty to choose from in this cavern of a place." His long arm swept the room in an elegant, mocking gesture.

Agnes pulled out a round-topped bentwood chair and sat down, still mindful of his initial reticence. "Thanks, if you're sure I don't interrupt."

"Nothing to interrupt." He pointed to a half-empty pint glass. "So, tell me. Why should I want to avoid you? You're quite easy on—" A disarming grin transformed his features as he held her glance and amended, "easy to talk to."

A tiresome blush crept into Agnes's cheeks. Its heat annoyed her. Did he mean to say something about her looks? After the midday walk, she must appear disheveled. At least she'd buttoned up her blouse and straightened her jacket before coming in. Now, she wished she'd gone to the restroom to restore some order to her unruly hair.

"It's just because of last night." Honesty was best to clear the air, she decided. "We got ourselves into quite a mess. I know how guilty I feel. So, I assume—"

"Why the heck do you feel guilty? You did nothing wrong."

"Oh, sure, it was your idea, but I'm as much to blame." Her lips curved into a smile. "Partners in crime, eh?"

Instead of grinning in complicity, his eyes narrowed. A deep furrow appeared as his brows contracted. Anger colored his voice. "Not my meaning at all. Bloody hell, Agnes. Did you forget what we found? Neither I nor you did wrong. Our poet laureate is guilty, not us."

A waitress in jeans and a tight T-shirt, carrying a tray with used dishes, stopped by to take Agnes's order for tea. They waited until the server was out of earshot. TC's eyes followed her until she vanished through a doorway into the kitchen.

The brief distraction gave Agnes time to mull over Timothy's grumpiness today. In a flash, it hit her. Of course, he'd be upset about Cass. Much more than Agnes herself. How could she be so insensitive? He'd be friends with Cassandra, just like with Dorian. Didn't he mention all of them hanging out together? Worried about Cass now when he was grieving about the loss of a young friend. No wonder TC wasn't himself.

She tried to make up for her lapse in empathy. "I'm so sorry, TC. You must feel totally awful. You've known her so much longer. When I heard—"

"Agnes, you're talking in riddles. What are you going on about?" He eyed her warily.

"Cass, I mean. The poor girl being in hospital—so upsetting for you as a good friend."

"In hospital? Cassandra?" A stricken expression distorted his face, eyes wide, his mouth slightly open. He caught his breath. "I'd no idea," he murmured.

Oh my God. Not again! She'd blundered like a clod. After Herb, she ought to have foreseen this. On impulse, she reached out to touch the hand that clutched the pint glass so tightly the knuckles showed white.

"How stupid of me. I assumed Mel, or perhaps the room-mate or someone, would have told you first."

Absorbed, he stared at the glass. He lifted it to his lips, leaving her hand behind like a useless encumbrance. Self-consciously, she pulled it back down into her lap. Her left cradled it like a protective shield.

When he glanced up, the intense blue, almost violet, of the irises caught her by surprise.

"Tell me what happened," his tone neutral and controlled.

"She attempted to kill herself and is now in a coma, is all I heard. Can't say how sorry I am to spring this on you. God, you're a close friend of Cass and—"

"Let's get this straight, Agnes. Cassandra was Dorian's close friend. She's a student of mine, just as she's your student. No need for you to treat me with kid gloves."

He eyed the beer, took a sip, and rested the glass on the table.

The back of his hand wiped his mouth before he continued, "Jeez, Dorian's death must have unhinged her completely. These young kids are so fragile." Cheeks on both sides squeezed in the vice grip of fingers and thumb, his hand left marks when it dropped to grab his glass again. Instead of drinking, he slid it back and forth on the tabletop.

Torn by regret about Cass, Agnes watched the movement, unable to meet TC's eyes when she confided, "If only I'd followed up after talking to her. God, I feel so guilty. She was obviously distressed, and I—"

"When was that?"

"A couple of days ago. I told you yesterday. Of course, she'd be distraught the day after he died. Honestly, I intended to put her in touch with a grief counselor. She ran off before I'd a chance to suggest it."

With minute nods, TC commiserated. "Might have been too late anyway," he said. Yet Agnes didn't feel exonerated.

His earlier words echoed in her mind. "You said, 'unhinged completely.' Did you sense mental health issues before?"

His hand went up to stroke the stubble along his jawline, fingers on one side, thumb on the other, as though trying to elongate the chin. For a moment, it distracted Agnes. A spark gleamed in his eyes as he met hers. He's noticed, she thought, chagrined.

If so, his words showed no sign. "Not sure I should share this," he said hesitantly. "Fact is, I did wonder for a while. Unbalanced, I thought. A tendency to dramatize herself." He shook his head in recollection. "In fairness," he went on, "Dorian wasn't the easiest to get on with. High-strung, self-absorbed, abrasive if the mood took him." With a rueful chuckle, he added, "Like any true genius."

Agnes tried to square TC's impression with her own experience of Dorian and realized hers was different. Thoughtfulness marked the interactions. Then again, they'd only talked philosophy and existential questions.

"Not a desirable combination with Cassandra's key traits," continued TC, who'd watched her ruminate. "If it weren't such a cliché about women—thanks to Father Freud—I'd say, 'hysterical.'"

"Are you sure?" Agnes frowned, attempting to recall any signs of this. "Cass always struck me as quiet and calm in class."

"What about your Medea in the rain? My scanty memory of Greek myth tells me Medea stands for a ruthless and murderous mind. Something about Cassandra must have trig-gered such a Freudian association, don't you think?"

"Hah, no. You're getting things mixed up. Or misheard. Cass's wet curls reminded me of Medusa's snaking tresses. Plus, her truly tragic face as she stood there. Nothing to do with Medea, the poisoner."

Aware of falling into lecture mode, Agnes went on, "Born the only beauty among the hideous gorgon sisters, Medusa was turned into the most fearful one by the goddess Athena."

Since TC appeared interested in her digression, she risked a comment. "A gross miscarriage of justice, to my mind. Instead of punishing her fellow god Poseidon, who'd seduced Medusa in Athena's temple, the wrath of the goddess struck the innocent victim of the man's transgression. Figures—gods stick together. Well, not always in the ancient Olympian tradition," Agnes qualified in an afterthought.

"I stand corrected," said TC with a slight bow.

"Which reminds me. Something occurred to me on my walk. How awful if Cass attempted suicide believing their breakup caused Dorian to kill himself, when Herb's betrayal drove him to end his young life. If Dorian's death was self-inflicted, to begin with." She sighed. "What a waste of a promising future, no matter how you look at it."

Another thought resurfaced. "The weirdest thing. On the way here—you know where the footpath comes down from the park?"

TC nodded distractedly, his glance straying to the entrance again.

Was he hoping to see Jac to relieve him of his discursive company? Agnes wondered. She sped on in her narrative to recapture his attention, "Anyway, I ran into Herb, and you won't believe this. He had the nerve to invite me to his mother's soiree tonight. 'Thursday at Home.' What a pretentious appellation. After I told him about Cass, he still said he'd email me an invite." Agnes shook her head in disgust.

"Got mine already," commented TC, unperturbed by Herb's insensitivity. "Lady Nessbit graciously includes me off and on."

"Do you go? Sounds like you're snarky about the woman."

"Oh, she wines and dines—well, snacks—you to death. Likes to splurge, the good lady does." He regarded Agnes speculatively. "Why don't you join in tonight?"

"Hell, no. I couldn't. Kind of callous distraction, don't you agree? What with Cass's condition so uncertain."

"On the contrary. A brilliant opportunity to deep dive into Herbert's affairs. The man warrants watching, now more than ever after this second tragedy."

"You think he's involved with her? There's talk about a new lover after the breakup. An older guy, apparently."

"Worth looking into, I'd—" A frown creased his forehead as he broke off, his glance fixed over Agnes's head.

Agnes swiveled in her seat to face the entrance.

Clad in running gear, ice-blond hair pulled tight into a tiny ponytail, Jac stood in the doorway, immobile. Blinded by the dim interior, Agnes figured. To draw her attention, Agnes rose and waved.

The broad smile died on Jac's lips when she stepped close. Agnes saw the sweet features attempt a scowl that deepened upon TC's welcome.

"Ah, there's our champion runner. Dr. Xavier in the flesh. Will you grace us with your company, or is yours truly still *persona non grata*?"

Oh no, not again. Agnes could have kicked herself for losing track of time and not forewarning Jac. Unbelievably stupid after Jac's reaction last night. And TC's teasing didn't help.

Ignoring him, Jac said, "Smells bad in here. I'd rather be out in the sun. Do you want to stay, Agnes? Or—"

"Want to sit on the patio?" interrupted Agnes, taken aback by Jac's unaccustomed rudeness.

"Let's leave if you don't mind."

Agnes fished her wallet from her jacket pocket and pushed a five-dollar bill across to TC. "Pay for me, will you?" She got up to join Jac, who'd turned her back to them.

"See you tonight." The caress in TC's voice made Agnes seek his eyes, only to tear hers away when his lit up.

"Don't bet on it," she retorted with unnecessary force and hastened to fall in step with her friend.

Chapter 22

Jac sucked fresh air in greedy gulps. She sprinted down the porch steps into the parking lot. Too angry to speak, she veered toward the lane.

"Stop! Wait up," she heard Agnes shout. Annoyed, she spun around.

Already panting after a twenty-yard jog, Agnes drew near. "Not that way. Ran into Herb earlier at the lookout. Can't we get back to town by the road?" She wriggled her left hand into the opposite direction.

"Whatever. I don't care which way," snapped Jac. Then she relented. "There's a footpath by the river. About a mile out, it meets the trail along Water Street in town."

"Sounds perfect," said Agnes.

A nature walk might calm her frayed nerves, Jac figured as they crossed the pine grove adjacent to the pub and entered the narrow path. The quick jog from campus through the park brought temporary relief—shattered too soon by Timothy's smug and smirking visage. The memory still festered despite the beauty of the winding path.

On their right, conifers shielded from the road. No traffic sound penetrated the serene atmosphere. The pub, the only habitation at this end, drew visitors in larger numbers solely for special events like weddings or music gigs at this time of year.

The sloping bank on the left was sparsely treed. In summer, blooming bushes and wildflowers rioted with color, their scents perfuming the warm air, Jac remembered from walks in the past. Across the river, the vista of rolling hills reminded her pleasingly of Constable's pastoral paintings. Brilliant sunshine sparkled on the water and bathed the distant slopes in a glorious play of light and shadow.

The soothing calm of the setting fractured when Agnes, beside her, asked in a peeved tone, "If you find the pub smelly, why did you pick it in the first place? Sounded like an under-handed jibe at TC—pretty rude if you ask me."

Anger mounting again, Jac snapped back, "What was the 'see you tonight' all about? Are you two planning another B&E? Didn't Mr. T. C. Elliot create enough problems for us already?"

"Come off it, Jac. Remember, it was you who wanted me to figure out what was going on."

Incensed, Jac stood still to face Agnes. Her friend's features, heated both by the sun and annoyance, fell as their eyes met.

"Sorry, Jac. I didn't mean to—"

"No. You're right," admitted Jac, her temper evaporating. The hurt in the darkened eyes shamed her. "Timothy brings out the worst in me. Strange to find him at this pub," she muttered, more to herself.

"Well, you chose it too."

"Unthinkingly. After you told me about Cassandra, I was so in shock. When you asked where to meet, the Riverside Pub popped into my head because I heard it mentioned a moment before."

"You rarely go there, do you?" Agnes glanced at her and tucked her arm under Jac's. "Should we mosey on while we chat?"

A smile hovered on Jacqueline's lips. Exercise was not Agnes's favorite activity. They strolled on as Jac replied, "Mostly in summer. Last time was with you early on this term." She rearranged her thoughts. "An odd coincidence. When you called, I was at Second Cup and overheard—Okay, to be honest, I was eavesdropping—"

"You? Never!" Agnes burst out laughing.

"Seriously. Can you picture the partition which divides the counter from the seating area in front of the floor-to-ceiling windows?" Agnes nodded. "Well, Kalen and some others were talking on the window side. They couldn't see me but grew so noisy I couldn't help listening. The pub came up in conversation."

"Ah, I see. Hardly eavesdropping, though."

"Oh, it was. Something caught my attention and kept me glued to the spot. If you hadn't called, I'd have been even more delayed for my meeting."

"Look, there's a bench. Want to stop and tell me all about your spying?"

The rustic seat perched on a rise afforded a panoramic view of the river. Down below, the flowing stream bathed in the midday sun's rays.

Jacqueline heard Agnes breathe in deeply and exhale with a contented sigh.

Loath to disturb the peace, Jac hesitated. Her friend needed to know, she decided. "You won't like this. I think Joel spotted the two of you last night going into Herbert's office."

"What?" Agnes jerked upright from her laid-back posture.

"Sorry to startle you so," said Jac and placed a calming hand on her companion's sleeve. "Joel said he saw Timothy go in. My phone rang just then—your call—and stopped him mid-sentence." Jac rolled her eyes, remembering their faces. "They all crowded around the partition and caught me listening in."

"Well, if they yak in a public place, they can hardly complain if people hear them," said Agnes. "Don't let it worry you. More to the point, what exactly did Joel see?"

Put on the spot, Jac had to admit, "Good question. He

claimed to have seen Elliot. Renata—or was it Cleo? not sure—pointed out that Timothy is Herbert's friend and might have valid reasons for going into his office at night."

"Oh okay, if that's what they believe." A hint of relief swung in Agnes's voice.

Far from sure Joel thought anything of the kind, Jacqueline let it slip by.

"What on earth brought it up, anyway?" asked Agnes. "The little guy turns into a veritable snoop. 'Joel the Spy, at your service.'"

"They were chit-chatting about Cassandra's new boyfriend, completely unaware, I'm sure, of her hospitalization. I meant to ask: did you receive any updates?"

"Not yet. I'm waiting for Mel to get back to me."

"I figured you'd have mentioned it right away."

"Not to sound callous, but did any of them know who the boyfriend is?"

"Wild guesses, I'd say. Kalen saw Cassandra with Herbert down here at the pub one night. Ergo, the mentioning of the Riverside," Jac explained. "Cleo insisted it meant nothing since Cassandra also hangs out with Timothy."

Jac looped a strand of hair that had escaped her makeshift ponytail back behind her ear. "I'm surprised how much some faculty members mix with students off campus. A small town makes for proximity, I guess. On Friday nights, they all hang out at the HCC in town, including Herb, apparently."

"Oh? What's the HCC? I thought Herb wasn't on speaking terms with their gang."

"Hotel CAL Club, everyone's late-night hangout, I gather. No, but one of them mentioned Herb was ogling Cassandra while Dorian and Elliot avoided her last Friday. Anyway, just before you called, Joel dropped the bomb about Elliot spying on Herbert and—"

"Oh no! He actually said TC *spies* on Herb?" Agnes spun

around from contemplating the river to face Jac, alarm widening her eyes.

"Well, no. Perhaps he didn't use the word. Joel tends to use catchy phrases, like 'cottoned on' and such like. Quite frankly, it's difficult to recall." Something else, however, came back to her. She didn't receive an answer earlier on. Time to ask again. "What was the 'see you tonight' about?"

"*Eh?* Oh, you heard? You mean, what TC said?"

"Indeed, I do," said Jac, raising one eyebrow in mock sarcasm.

"It's the funniest thing," said Agnes. "Okay, not hahaha-funny, rather curious—which again, is so ambiguous—"

"Agnes. Don't red herring me."

"Hey, I was just about to explain. Anyway, I ran into Herb, as I'm sure I mentioned earlier. Out of the blue, he honored me with an invitation to his mom's soiree tonight. La-di-da."

"My goodness. I never was invited in the two years since he joined us. Whatever prompted him?" Aware this sounded wrong, Jac hastened on, "I mean, how did the topic arise?"

"No clue. Herb claims it would help me network with the movers and shakers in town and at the college."

"Hmm… Ordinarily, I would agree. People covet Mrs. Nessbit's Thursday invitations. Some well-known artists, literary and political figures are her guests of honor, Martha told me. She attends when it's someone who interests her."

"Not my kind of scene, is it?"

"You're used to such dos from uni. Visiting speaker receptions and so on? Same idea. There are benefits to mingling with town and gown in a social setting."

"Ha-ha. Yeah, I guess." Agnes stretched. "Should we trudge back to town and grab a bite? I'm famished."

They rose and sauntered along the footpath at Agnes's sedate pace.

"So," Jacqueline rebooted their conversation, "Timothy, I

take it, is invited too?" In retrospect, she regretted encouraging Agnes to attend if he was.

"Yeah, sure. Lady Nessbit invites him off and on as Herb's friend, TC says."

"Keeps him on her list of spares, more likely."

"*Meow.*"

They both laughed. Goodwill restored. Arms lightly touching at times, they strolled on. Jacqueline felt her muscles ease. A nature break from worries, sunshine, dear company, what more could one ask?

Not even five minutes later, vibrations transmitted from her companion's pocket.

Abruptly, Agnes wriggled her arm free and fumbled to withdraw the juddering mobile from a jacket pocket.

So much for any delusion of serenity, thought Jac as Agnes stopped, saying, "Sorry, got to check this. An email from Mel."

While Agnes read, Jacqueline cast a regretful glance over the river sparkling in reflected sunlight, preparing herself for bad news.

"They just got back from the hospital. No change, but the doctor questioned them."

Jaqueline's eyes swiveled back to Agnes, who looked up just then and asked, "Mel wants to talk rather than email what it's about. Do you mind, Jac? Can you please come with me?"

"If we make it brief—I have an appointment at two. Where about are they?"

"Hang on. I'll ask. Hope she'll respond right away."

Focused again on her phone, Agnes's thumbs hammered the screen, paused, went on again, and waited. Not even a minute later, Agnes said, "Okay. At Andrea's flat—she's the roommate. It's right behind the old brewery. Here. Check the map."

One glance at the screenshot of the map Melanie had included in her last email sufficed for Jac to say, "There's a shortcut a few hundred yards from here. Ten minutes altogether —if you speed up a little."

"Yikes," Agnes groaned. "Well, let's get a move on."

Chapter 23

By the time display on Jacqueline's mobile, it took them fifteen minutes to reach the drab apartment building. While the old brewery, a nineteenth-century red brick monstrosity converted into lofts, was now upmarket stylish, the mid-twentieth-century low-rise apartment complex behind it appeared depressingly uninspired.

Flat-roofed, worn concrete-walled with rusting balcony rails on the second and third floors—offering a view of assorted junk tenants stored outside—it wasn't a home Jac imagined looking forward to. For most students, such abode would likely be temporary. Those were the lucky ones.

They walked along the weed cracked sidewalk and found the correct number and make-shift name tag at the bottom of a long list of tenants. No buzzing sound followed to unlock the entry after Agnes pressed the bell button.

A minute or two later, the door burst open, and a breathless Melanie gasped, "I'm so sorry to keep you waiting. The automatic door opener never works, Andrea says. Please, do come in, Dr. Taylor. Oh, hi, Dr. Xavier. Just watch your step."

The girl's cheeks turned crimson as she prattled on, a sign of how shaken she must be, Jac noted with concern. A promising young student who delighted in writing romantic verse and prose, Melanie usually was the quiet, timid type. Though Agnes had joked at one point Mel would surprise them some day by publishing steamy romance thrillers. Still waters and all that, she'd laughed.

Now, babbling apologies about the dismal ground floor corridor, blistering with oil paint that might have been beige in its younger days, over cracked tile floors tripping the unwary, Melanie led them around several corners to the back of the building. Finally, they arrived at a narrow staircase down to the basement.

"The janitor's flat." The student pointed to an entry they were passing. "Over here is Andrea's," she explained while her arm stretched out to ease open a door which stood slightly ajar.

The young woman, who came to her aid from inside, greeted them. "Hi, I'm Andrea. Good of you to come." As they introduced themselves, she stepped aside to let them enter straight into a small room that obviously served as the living space. Melanie brought up the rear and closed the door softly.

"Have a seat, please, while I'll get tea," said their hostess. "I'm afraid the place may seem claustrophobic."

With the four of them standing, it felt crammed. Yet, Jac and Agnes murmured polite denials while they moved to the two-seater sofa to get out of the way for Melanie and Andrea to load tea things onto the crate serving as a coffee table. Maybe they needed the comfort of the familiar ritual.

From where she sat, Jacqueline surreptitiously studied Andrea busy in the kitchenette. It took up one side of the room and consisted only of a stove and fridge, separated by two cabinets and a sink. Minimalist by any standard. At a guess, in her late twenties, Andrea appeared competent and mature. The super-short pixie cut curling her black hair emphasized the intelligent nut-brown eyes. Her olive skin needed no makeup to glow with health. Dressed in loose-fitting gray sweats with a navy Queens University top, she padded back and forth in stocking feet, her movements deft and efficient.

No one broached the subject of their visit until tea was poured.

The young women, seated on round poufs in colorful Indian-style carpeting material on the opposite side of the makeshift coffee table, regarded the professors expectantly. Behind them stood two shelves crammed with books and stacks of paper. A scholarly environment noted Jac with approval.

To set them at ease, Jacqueline asked Andrea if her sweat-shirt stemmed from her alma mater. Andrea, they heard, did an internship at a local theatre while completing online coursework for a Master of Arts Management program at the university in eastern Ontario.

"I hate to rush things, but I need to be back at college by two," said Jacqueline, sensing Melanie's shyness prevented her from coming to the point of their visit.

"Same here. My work starts at two today," said Andrea.

"So, could you tell us about Cassandra, please?" Jac asked.

The young woman tensed. Both hands cradled her mug tightly when she turned to Agnes, "Mel told me she and Cass trust you explicitly. Will you treat what I say as confidential?"

Jac and Agnes exchanged a look before Jac spoke for both. "Yes—up to a point. If any of it affects the safety and well-being of our students, we—as no doubt you realize—must disclose it. I'm sure you yourself would feel the same obligation toward Cassandra."

Slight affirmative nods told Jac the graduate student agreed with her assessment. The younger girl, who watched them closely, sat primly upright on the small pouf next to Andrea, hands clasped in her lap, her head tilted downward. It struck Jac as an endearingly demure pose.

"Point well taken," said Andrea. Her resonant voice rang with determination. "I'll stick to the facts and flag any surmises I make. Interrupt me if you have questions."

Like them, Jac thought wryly, Andrea was no stranger to leading a class or audience.

"Normally, Cass comes in here to grab breakfast before her eight o'clock class. I'd been up since six-thirty, preparing for my online class. In passing, I wondered if she'd left by the back door. Her room has a separate entrance to the parking out back."

"Is that how she comes and goes?" asked Agnes.

"Never in the morning, as far as I can recall. I'm an early riser." Andrea smiled ruefully as if admitting to a bad habit. "Cass uses it if she returns late at night or brings company. Incredibly considerate. I was so lucky finding her as a roommate through a Kijiji ad before this term."

Melanie cast a shy sideway glance at Andrea. The pointed chin bobbing agreement while her delicate fingers plucked at the hem of the soft, lilac sweater she was wearing over skinny jeans. A nervous habit, thought Jac.

"Anyway," Andrea went on, "I figured I'd have heard her use the bathroom." She indicated the tiny hallway at the back of the room. "So, I knocked on her door and called out the time. Kind of awkward. If she had company, I'd rather not barge in. Yet, if she overslept—or worse, was ill—she'd want me to look in on her. Conscientious as she is, she'd hate to miss class."

"Was there any reason to worry about her health?" Agnes put in.

Again, Andrea hesitated and stared into her mug. After she'd brought it up to take a sip, she placed it with slow deliberation on the crate.

"Not about physical health," she said, looking straight at Agnes. "For a while now, Cass has been anxious or apprehensive about something. To me, it seemed related to the person she was dating." Andrea glanced at Melanie, whose fragile features expressed unspoken doubts.

A direct question might encourage her to share her

thoughts, Jac reckoned. "What was your impression, Melanie," she asked quietly.

The girl's fingers moved restlessly, and a blush brought color to her pale cheeks. In a timid voice, she admitted, "Andrea and I talked about this while we waited at the hospital." She turned to Agnes for corroboration, "I mentioned to you before I think Cass feels guilty because Dorian killed himself over their breakup."

Agnes nodded thoughtfully before she asked, "Could it be both? Her new relationship might suffer because of her feeling guilty about Dorian's death. Sorry, Andrea, please continue."

The young woman sucked in a deep breath through her nose, reluctant to go on, Jac noticed.

"I didn't want to butt in on Cass," she said, "in case there was a visitor. So, I cracked the door open just enough to see if she was alone. One look and I realized something was wrong. She was lying fully clothed on her back on top of the duvet. Somehow, it looked unnatural. No response when I called her name louder, which worried me enough to go right up to the bed and gently shake her shoulder."

Andrea stopped abruptly to gulp down some tea. Her voice sounded hoarse when she hastened on, "I saw the note on the pillow next to her head, felt for a pulse on the neck. So weak ... I raced in here for my phone and called 911. They said to wait for the paramedics."

Andrea's face turned greenish. Her hands shook uncontrollably. Either to still or to hide the shaking, she tucked them tightly into her armpits.

In a swift movement, Agnes got up, saying, "Here, I'll get some more hot tea. Mel, can you show me?"

While Melanie and Agnes prepared fresh tea, Jacqueline knelt next to Andrea and murmured soothing phrases.

It took a few minutes for the young woman to regain composure. When Jac suggested they should leave to give Andrea time to prepare for work, the graduate student assured them she'd rather finish her tale now. Telling it might be therapeutic, she said with a wry smile.

"The ambulance," she told them, "arrived in no time— seemed ages to me keeping watch at the bedside. They asked a few questions and then took her out by the back way I'd shown them. I followed in my car. Oh, and from hospital I contacted Mel, who's immensely supportive."

She reached out to touch the girl's shoulder, smiling her gratitude.

"Thanks so much for filling us in. It must have been a terrible ordeal for both of you," said Agnes. "Was there any sign of what Cass had taken?"

Once more, the young women exchanged glances. "That's the weirdest thing," Andrea responded. "Mel believes it confirms her view about the guilt motive. Right next to Cass, on a little side table, was her bag spilled wide open. An empty meds container—you know, the plastic type you get for prescriptions —lay on the flap, lid removed. Without touching it, I could see the label. A refill for Dorian Gable's Warfarin."

"*Mon Dieu.*" Shocked, Jac reverted to her native language. Agnes uttered a mild expletive.

"Now, don't misunderstand," interrupted Andrea. "It's unclear if she took the stuff. Would be crazy. Neither the paramedics nor the ER doctor confirmed—or denied—it. They would give such info only to the next of kin."

"The doctor questioned you, Mel said. Can you tell us the details?" Agnes asked.

Andrea waited for Melanie's nod before resuming. "A nurse came to get us. The ER doctor led us to a relatively quiet corner —on her way to the next case, I guess. Most questions were about Cass's state of mind. Early on, I'd already told admission I don't have the parents' contact info and mentioned they're on a cruise somewhere. Asked about any meds Cass takes, I could only tell the doctor I've seen herbal supplements on the counter here. No prescription drugs." Andrea pointed to the kitchen counter.

"Then she asked—out of the blue, I thought first—about Cass's connection to Dorian. Of course, the paramedics had bagged the Warfarin container, I realized, and the doc either knew about the death—it's a small hospital, after all—or had looked it up." Andrea turned sideways. "Mel?"

Fingers pulling threads from the elevated seams of the pouf, the girl paled even more. She cleared her throat painfully.

"Here, take a sip of your tea," said Agnes, leaning in. "Stone cold, but hey, imagine it's iced tea."

This elicited a tentative smile, transforming the fragile features. Irrelevantly, Jacqueline noticed freckles on the straight nose as the girl bent forward to drink obediently from the mug virtually untouched since their arrival.

Surreptitiously, Jac checked her phone's display. They'd have to leave soon for her to be on time for her appointment with the provost academic, a man no one would dare to keep waiting.

"I'm so sorry," said Melanie, and was promptly reassured by the others. "Did I do the wrong thing? Because I told the doctor about Cass and Dorian and how I think Cass feels guilty. The doctor was so understanding, no matter how busy they are at ER."

"She asked me for my thoughts—a frown might have given me away," admitted Andrea. "I shared my impression that Cass's current love interest causes her emotional turmoil. Asked directly, both of us had to admit we don't know whom she is dating. The doctor seemed puzzled."

"No educated guess who the boyfriend is?" Agnes asked, eyebrows raised.

"No clue." Andrea's palms went up to underline being mystified. "You?" she asked Melanie.

The girl shook her head without looking at anyone. Somehow, Jac suspected, they'd discussed this during their long wait at ER.

"My unsupported guess," said Andrea, perhaps to take the pressure off the younger woman fidgeting next to her, "the person is considerably older and wants to keep the affair quiet. Married? College faculty? Or both? No idea. Anyway, the doctor said she'd notify the authorities—police presumably—and we might hear from them."

The casual mention of police threw Jacqueline's stomach for a loop. Of course, she should have realized a second suicide would raise alarm bells, not only in her head. As though from far away, she heard Agnes say, "One more question, if you don't mind. Can you tell us about the note you found?"

"'Note' is perhaps an overstatement," said Andrea. "A cryptic message scrawled on a mere slip of paper, 'I'm so sorry' and below it, 'Cass.' She's very economical and cuts up used paper for study notes to insert into textbooks or to jot down ideas for novels and stuff."

Before Agnes could inquire any further, Jac interjected, "Sorry, everyone, but both Andrea and I have commitments at two."

"Oh, my—right you are," said the graduate student after quickly consulting the mobile resting on the crate.

In the bustle to leave, Jacqueline and Agnes thanked Andrea and Melanie, who assured them they could get in touch any time, whereupon Agnes exchanged phone numbers with Andrea.

Two minutes later, Jac parted from Agnes on the sidewalk to jog back to campus while Agnes announced she'd grab lunch in town. How Agnes could eat after the bomb dropped about police was beyond Jacqueline to fathom.

Chapter 24

A quarter after nine that evening, Agnes stood somewhat dazed at the fringes of Mrs. Nessbit's drawing room.

Her arrival at the stately Victorian in the residential 'old money' part of town went unnoticed, except for the maid decked out in black with a frilly white half-apron and matching hairpiece. For a second, Agnes thought she'd entered a sitcom. They exchanged a commiserating grin when the hired help took her coat as Agnes introduced herself. Sure to be a theatre program student employed for the occasion, she figured.

The soiree appeared to be in full swing, spread over two impressive rooms connected by broad double doors now wide open. High ornate plaster ceilings, flowing floor-length drapery in light gold tones, and elaborate chandeliers increased the impression of spaciousness. So did the casually clustered seating islands, gracious in period furniture. Agnes caught a glimpse of a huge marble fireplace at the far end, half hidden by a group of guests congregating, cocktail glasses in hand, immersed in animated conversation.

What startled Agnes were the contemporary abstract paintings displayed to striking effect where one would expect Victorian oils. Not seeing any familiar faces, Agnes sauntered over to admire a symphony in blue and red which dominated the opposite wall space. Her mom, Sera, a painter and fine arts professor, would love it, she thought. Though not an arts aficionado herself, Agnes felt irresistibly drawn in by a mesmerizing explosion of color.

Lost in admiration, the sudden tenor drawl behind her made her jump. "D a r ling," drawn out like a fake caress, "How marvelously exquisite. Too ineffable for words."

The philosopher in her wanted to point out the tautology of the latter statement, but she suppressed the pedantry. Instead, she agreed, "Yes, it's truly stunning. Who's the artist, do you know?"

"Not the daubs by poor Rita, darling. Your little black number I was applauding. Too delicious."

Now it clicked. The Canadian artist Rita Letendre was a household name Agnes recognized.

Rather than defending the accomplished painter or her own choice of couture, she mustered the speaker critically. A retro bohemian in paisley jacket over a fuchsia open-neck shirt, tight ripped jeans ending just above swede ankle boots with, at her guess, two-inch heels raised a wine glass in a mock toast.

Her gaze lingered over the Prussian blue barrette, crowning a profusion of mahogany curls. With a slow grin, she replied, "After all, the LBD is a girl's best friend." Nonetheless, she smoothed the skirt of the black dress, thinking it overemphasized her ample curves.

"Have we met before?"

"Jeez, a pretty lame line for a bohemian," she countered. "But, no, first time here," she added, glancing around the room. "Where's our hostess? I'd like to thank her for the invitation."

"Oh, darling, no rush. Let me introduce you to our illustrious fellow guests. Speaking of which, I'm Carlos."

She'd barely uttered her own name when she spotted Herb. No fancy evening attire for him. In his usual get-up, he lumbered in from the foyer and made a beeline for one of the drinks carts spaced along the perimeter. Before she had a chance to detach herself, Carlos hailed him.

"Sweetie, come and meet demure Agnes, our newest acquisition."

Simultaneously, Agnes and Herb assured him no introductions were needed. To judge by her colleague's scowl, neither Carlos nor she counted among his favs, Agnes thought wryly. Why on earth invite her? Or maybe he resented being interrupted on his booze run.

"My, are we glum today, sweetie. The muses still desert you? No more crumbs of genius to bestow on the *hoi polloi* gathered in these hallowed halls?"

To defuse the tension generated by Carlos's malicious glee, Agnes asked Herb, "Would you introduce me to your mom? I'd like to thank her."

Just then, a husky laugh attracted their attention.

"There's the mater now," said Herb, matter of fact.

A stately woman disengaged herself from the group around the fireplace and still in company of one of the males worked the room. On Herb's face, a mixture of exasperation and grudging admiration fought for dominance. When he made to walk toward his mom, Agnes fell in step. Carlos's snide remark about their hostess taking center stage followed them as they left him standing.

Taller than her son, coiffured silver hair swept back from the high forehead of a discreetly made-up face, an azure silk dress complimented Mrs. Nessbit's complexion and full figure. The only ornaments were a single string of moderate-sized pearls and matching pendant earrings. Carefully outlined deep-red lips drew attention away from the hooded gray eyes that seemed to miss nothing.

"Mater, meet Dr. Agnes Taylor. A colleague." With that, Herb left her stranded and departed for the next booze station.

Put on the spot, Agnes apologized for interrupting so rudely. His mother's gracious response made clear poor manners didn't stem from the maternal line. Instead of resenting the intrusion, the hostess skillfully included her in the conversation with a local painter about an upcoming vernissage of his newest work. When it turned out that Mrs. Nessbit was familiar with her mom Sera's watercolors, the ice was broken, and Agnes felt at ease with them.

Without losing a beat, Mrs. Nessbit foisted the young painter on a couple of art lovers who had joined in and drew Agnes aside.

"Would you like to see a little treasure I keep in my boudoir, as my dear friends love to call it?"

Agnes's expression engendered a throaty chuckle. "Oh my. Said by a man, we'd immediately suspect seduction or nefarious designs. Not to worry. My intentions are benign."

On Agnes's assurance that no such thought had crossed her mind, her hostess led her through a door half-hidden by drapery. They entered a lovely small sitting room reminiscent of pictures Agnes had seen of sunlit morning rooms despite the soft incandescent light shed by floor and table lamps. No LED bulbs here.

Mrs. Nessbit filled two wine glasses but from different decanters on a side table. She handed one glass over and appeared to be watching for Agnes's reaction to this deeply personal space.

"What a charming room," Agnes assured her.

"*Salute*," toasted Herb's mother and raised her glass. With a satisfied *aah*, she downed its whole content. And promptly burst into laughter at Agnes's open-mouthed astonishment.

Like mother like son, flitted through Agnes's mind.

"Don't look so shocked," said the lady. "It's only grape juice with sparkling water. Personal preference and high blood pressure prevent me from imbibing. Only my close friends realize I never touch alcohol." In a low voice, she added, "My late husband's fondness of liquor taught me sobriety."

Resolutely, her hostess turned and pointed to a framed

picture on the wall behind them. She flipped a switch to illuminate it by a light bar placed strategically above. An atmospheric seascape aquarelle emerged.

Without ever having seen it before or bending close to decipher the signature, Agnes guessed it must be one of her mom's artistic efforts. For years, she and her mom had barely seen each other. After a memorable summer vacation, Agnes had vowed to mend ways in the future. Shame-faced, she'd even googled Sera's artwork. Seeing the real thing deeply moved her. Surreptitiously, she wiped the corner of her eye that threatened to tear up.

"I often sit here to gaze at it," said her hostess. "Reliving fond memories is a sign of aging, they tell me." A soft chuckle. "You're fond of your mom, aren't you, Agnes?"

Surprised, Agnes realized the truth of the statement and confided to this virtual stranger that she'd been estranged from Sera for two decades but now hoped to grow closer again—even if they could never recover the closeness of childhood.

Perhaps thinking of her own offspring, Mrs. Nessbit agreed things changed once kids turned into teenagers. Then she startled Agnes by saying, "Now, why can't Herbert hitch up with a sensible person like you instead of that woman?"

Speechless, Agnes regarded her.

"Have I shocked you?"

The mischievous glint in the hooded eyes caused Agnes to smile in response. Here was the golden opportunity for some serious snoop—sleuthing, she amended her brainwave. No wonder Mrs. N. disapproved of Herb's relationship with a young student. Though, his mother could count herself lucky if he brought home someone as nice as Cass.

To probe where things stood, Agnes assumed guileless cheerfulness. "Oh, I'm sure your son found someone much better suited and more interesting."

The mater cocked a sardonic eyebrow. "Interesting she may

be. If you consider an affair with an older married woman suitable."

"I'd no idea."

"He doesn't advertise it. Quite the contrary, Herbert believes no one knows. In a small town like ours, I ask you?"

Even more surprising for his mom to blow his cover to a casual visitor associated with the college, thought Agnes. Or was she aware of Cass and wanted to mislead Herb's colleague?

"You're wondering why I'm telling you about my son's affair —so am I. Something about your face. No," she added while studying Agnes closely, "Your whole person invites confidences."

"Very nice of you to say so." A guilty blush crept up from her neck. "Don't think I deserve—"

"No reason to be modest. Never apologize, never justify, should be today's woman's credo." The deep voice lent authority to the pronouncement. "Herbert suffers from a mother complex. A hangover from being raised since early childhood by a widowed mother, I'm told. Though God knows, I tried to instill values of independence and self-sufficiency. Yet, he keeps coming back here like a homing pigeon—or the proverbial bad penny."

Her husky chuckle didn't quite take the sting out of the assessment. Agnes was lost for words.

"Well, never mind. We'd better get back to my guests, no matter how soothing I find our chat, Agnes. You must come for tea sometime."

With a lingering look at her mom's lovely watercolor, Agnes followed her hostess back into the fray. When they entered the drawing room, Mrs. Nessbit introduced Agnes to a group of her friends and moved on to others.

Minutes later, Agnes spotted TC across the room. Legs casually crossed at the ankles, thumbs hooked into jeans pockets, he leaned one shoulder against the frame of the connecting doors and surveyed the assembly. In a loose-fitting black sweater over faded jeans, his hair tousled, a mildly supercilious smile on his lips, he stood out from the well-dressed crowd—and looked darn attractive, Agnes admitted.

Their eyes met and locked despite the distance. As if pulled by Ariadne's string in King Minos's labyrinth, Agnes threaded her way among the scattered guests to reach her quarry.

"My goodness, we're on intimate footing already," the irrepressible Timothy drawled. Agnes's heightening color elicited an amused smile. After a few beats, he went on, "A private audience with the grand lady herself."

Annoyed at her initial wishful thinking, Agnes responded sharper than intended. "One of us got to do the job. While you dawdled God knows where, I grasped the opportunity to find out more."

"Good for you."

Neither tone nor expression conveyed the interest she'd hoped to generate. To ensure not being overheard, she leaned in and upped the ante, "Much has transpired since we parted."

A mocking twitch of his lips greeted her arch tone. "Your cheeks tell me you're burning to share."

"Ha-ha. You wish. This place is simply too hot with so many people, is all."

"Got just the remedy," he said, pushing his shoulder off the wall. "Follow me."

Curious, she weaved in his wake through the gathering to a French door on the far side. He pushed it open, and they entered a glass-domed conservatory at the back of the house.

Soft light from a few table lamps threw long shadows of countless potted plants and trees in various shapes and sizes. Wicker furniture with padded cushions dotted the remaining space. The scents of an abundance of blooming species mingled in an onslaught on one's olfactory sense akin to a cacophony assaulting the ear. The temperature would do nothing to cool her off, thought Agnes. No wonder other guests hadn't sought this refuge.

As though quite at home, TC led her to a couple of chairs at the far end, facing another set of French doors. An exterior lantern casts its beams outward onto a garden shrouded in darkness.

"If we crack it open a bit, we shouldn't suffocate in here," TC joked as he pushed down the handle.

A cooling breeze brought relief. The chairs sat close enough to speak softly and angled slightly for comfortable discourse. Agnes breathed a contented sigh, ready to relax. A short-lived illusion, she discovered.

"Now shoot, Holmes. What devilish doings have you uncovered?"

Her companion's question put her in a bind. Neither Angela nor Mrs. Nessbit would thank her for a breach of confidentiality. What's more, Jac would be livid if she broke their tacit promise to the grad student. Yet, without TC's help to sort this out... Or was it the fatal attraction he exercised which prompted this urge to unburden herself?

Aware of drumming fingers marking his waning patience, she groped for a strategy to avoid concrete revelations yet loop him in. She twirled a lock that had escaped the confines of the slide intended to tame the mass of unruly hair, pondering how to phrase her ideas.

"Since talking to you earlier," she began, "something's been bothering me. I've got the growing sense it's not adding up—I'm missing the vital point."

"Oh, Christ," groaned TC. "Could you be a bit more specific? Didn't you say new stuff came up?"

"Let me unpack my thoughts my way. Maybe thrashing out things and separating facts from surmises will illuminate what doesn't jive."

"Howsoever you want to play it."

Not the most gracious invitation, thought Agnes, as a neatly bulleted list formed before her mind's eye.

"Okay, here goes. Imagine it nicely ordered and indented."

She smiled, jabbing dots and stroking parentheses in the air between them.

Fact #1: Dorian died—either from

1. *Pseudo-natural causes (as per coroner's verdict)—his medical condition in conjunction with prescription drug complications.*
2. *Suicide (as per rumors)—upping his dosage or something.*
3. *Accident (my original hypothesis)—unintentional overdose.*
4. *Outside interference (Mrs. Gable's intuition)—someone slipped him something fatal for his medical condition.*

"Wouldn't you expect the coroner to get it right? Aren't they trained for the business?" TC crossed his legs and slouched back more comfortably.

"For sure. Googled around after we met the Gables. Ontario coroners are physicians trained for death investigation. In Dorian's case, the medical history apparently made it look straightforward. If it weren't for the rumors, together with the next item on my mental list, I'd buy it.

Fact #2: Dorian's missing manuscript is in Herb's filing cabinet.

Surely, an indication there's some truth to the rumors."

"To play devil's advocate, #2 may well be unrelated to your Fact #1."

"Admitted. Yet, since the rumors have a foundation in fact as far as absconding the manuscript goes, #1 (b), the suicide hypothesis may also gain support." Something about her own reasoning nagged at Agnes. If only she could pinpoint—

"Granted. So, what else?"

Reluctantly, Agnes abandoned her search for the elusive flaw and refocused.

"Fact #3: Cass attempted suicide:

1. *because she feels guilty of causing Dorian's suicide through ending their relationship,*
2. *and/or*

3. *because her new relationship puts her under intolerable mental strain."*

"How did you come up with 3(b)? Is it the new info you alluded to?"

The scrutinizing glance caused Agnes to wriggle in her seat. "Oh, that," she said, waving a careless hand. "Rather an obvious inference, don't you think? It hit me today. Everyone agrees Cass left Dorian for a new boyfriend, though no one's certain who the mystery lover is. They even cast you in that role, TC." Her attempt to laugh if off sounded uneasy to her own ears. "Of course, you've already told me you weren't close—"

"The last thing I need, become the butt of another rumor," growled TC. "My money's still on our poet laureate. You should've seen how the wanna-be writers flocked to him when he swanned in a couple of years ago in all his awards glory. Girls like Cassandra swooned over the brooding wordsmith, drank in his verse like nectar. Hard to think so now, but back then, he had quite a presence." Lost in reminiscence, TC's brows furrowed.

"Frankly—no, I can't picture Cass with Herb. Nor can his mom—" She broke off. Too late.

"Ah, a juicy tidbit you ferreted out tonight. Did you ask Lady Nessbit point-blank?"

"What do you take me for? No, she mentioned Herb's current partner in passing. An older woman, I gather. *Ergo*, Herb's not Cass's mystery man."

"Has the old girl met his lover?"

"No. I got the impression Herb's too secretive about his affairs."

"There you are, then. More grist for the rumor mill. Mothers are the last to know and the first to toss around wild, unsupported accusations."

The bitter tone and sour expression had Agnes wonder if he spoke from personal experience.

"Herb's our culprit," TC went on, jaw set and voice exuding

certainty. "He stole the damn novelette. The rest follows of necessity."

Weren't they jumping to hasty conclusions? mused Agnes. Aloud she said, "Yeah, it's in his possession. Doesn't mean he's consciously aware of it. Accidentally stuffed it into the drawer. No," she corrected herself, "in a folder by itself. Hmm ... Might, however, have received it like that and filed it by mistake."

"Why the heck are you grasping at straws to salvage the rotter's reputation? Under his poetic spell, are you?"

"Don't be ridiculous. I don't even like—Well, okay, I kind of feel sorry for him." She scanned TC's features, even more alluring when he scowled. A paradigmatic Heathcliff. No mad wife in his attic, she thought, amused by her own fancy.

"Why do you hate him so?" she asked softly.

"Whatever gives you such an absurd idea? He's merely a colleague among many now. Not the most prepossessing, I grant you."

On a hunch, she asked, "Oh, so you go back a while. Didn't meet him at Bowman College?"

"Nah, we grew up in this one-horse town. Same high school. He's a few years senior. Lady Nessbit condescends to an acquaintance with my mom, a mere store clerk."

"Ah, which store? Maybe I've met your mom."

"At Rexall. Nothing to do with anything. Let's stick to the topic here," TC said testily.

A sore spot, Agnes diagnosed as a few pieces slotted into place. Mrs. N.'s remark about the bad penny... TC was peeved at his former peer riding into town as a lauded poet and swoop up a position where Timothy's own long-standing efforts failed to secure a full-time job. Soirees designed to celebrate and foster the homecoming poet's literary endeavors might understandably sting TC's ego.

Why then attend them? Perhaps, Agnes reflected, it was a human, all too human, desire to partake in the lauded poet's fall from grace. Not nice. Then again, academia bred cutthroat sentiments.

To draw her brooding companion out of the moody silence her probing had caused, she reverted to what really mattered. "So, what do you think happened? Are the three facts correlated, or merely coincidental?"

"Sounds like a no-brainer to me. The connection is obvious. First off, Nessbit stole the manuscript. Second, Dorian killed himself. Third, Cass tried ditto."

"Renumbering hardly explains the 'why.' You've got to do better than reiterate."

"Aren't you the master sleuth here?"

When she rolled her eyes, he sighed as if explanations were redundant.

"Ever wondered what Dorian's tale was about? You saw the title. *The Betrayal.* What if it's autobiographic? The story of poet Herb the Great stealing genius DG's girlfriend. A double betrayal by prof and lover. *Eh?*" Relaxed, TC sat back and regarded her expectantly down his aquiline nose.

On the verge of calling the hypothesis fanciful, Agnes paused. Hadn't Emma Gable suggested something along those lines? Dorian sublimating disappointed love by writing a grand romance? She nodded thoughtfully.

"Go on. Spin it out."

"Elementary. Herb, the villain of Dorian's piece, filches the incriminating manuscript—"

"Hold on. Doesn't make—"

"Patience—not done yet." TC leaned in to command her compliance. "Anyone tell you of Bishop Berkeley's lost manuscript?"

"Where the heck does he come in?" said Agnes, unable to fit in the eighteenth-century idealist philosopher, famous for his *esse est percipi*—'to be is to be perceived.'

"Early on this term—before any of this happened—I regaled my class with the anecdote of the bishop's rationale for refusing to rewrite a lost manuscript. Said it would feel like a dog chewing over its own vomit."

"Yuck! How gross."

"Well, yeah. My students thought so, too. They'll never forget Berkeley, though." He laughed. "The point is, Dorian empathized strongly with the good bishop's attitude and agreed it would be unbearable to write a story twice. Once a final draft is lost, it's dead forever, he said. The rest of the class told him to back up his files. Dorian claimed typing stifles uniqueness."

"Yes, Mrs. Gables mentioned his argument for sticking to handwritten originals. So, why this rigmarole?"

"Self-explanatory, isn't it? High-strung genius that he was, he couldn't cope with the loss of a manuscript he'd literally poured his heart in, coming on top of the double betrayal by a revered prof and his beloved. He chose a dramatic exit. Followed in the footsteps of the great who'd gone before him. Think Hemingway and Virginia Woolf."

"Hmm—makes a devastating sort of sense," admitted Agnes. "Not how Dorian seemed to me. But a friend like you has far better insight into the workings of his mind. So would Cass. You figure it drove her to try to end it all?"

"Sure. Your Fact #3 holds on both counts. Guilt and falling out with Herb."

"Kind of hangs together." Still, something bothered Agnes.

"Wait," she said, "Why would Herb assume withholding the story would kill it? Could he count on Dorian not rewriting it? Or telling others about it? Like his mom? Emma Gable, I mean. Or even tell Cass in revenge for the betrayal? Would take a lot more to ensure the story remains untold."

"You mean make sure the teller told no more tales?" The raised eyebrow might have questioned the implications she herself had not consciously drawn. Or was he amused by his own alliteration?

Distraction didn't help. Her mind could no longer veil what

was hovering in the background. Too unbelievable for small-town Ontario.

"Foul play," she stated, matter of fact.

The words hung between them, spoken louder than intended.

"C'mon," said TC, sitting bolt upright. "You're kidding me, right? Ridiculous."

"A girl as bright as Cass could've figured it out. She had all the pieces. Was she next? If so, he screwed up there. The police are investigating—"

"Says who?" TC's voice rang loudly in the damp warmth of the conservatory.

"Heard of it today through the grapevine." She gazed meaningfully at him. He, too, must realize what this meant. "If they question us, we must tell them about the raid and what we surmise."

"Are you nuts? We'd lose our jobs." TC stared at her. His expression unreadable. Then he shook his head. "You got me all wound up there for a moment. Of course, the whole idea is absurd. Herb's a wimp." His eyes searched her face as if looking for confirmation. Not finding it, they grew distant as he muttered, "Worms do turn ... eventually."

They both brooded on that.

Footsteps on the flagstone floor cut into a momentary silence. Their wicker chairs creaked in protest as they swung around.

There stood the worm.

How long had he been near enough to listen? Agnes sucked in a breath between clenched teeth. Argh, how stupid can you get? Their voices, she realized, had reverted to normal conversation volume once they got too involved in their mulling to notice.

Nothing in Herb's expression betrayed him. If anything, he appeared abstracted, lost in a world of his own making. He glanced up in apparent surprise.

"The mater is drumming together the troupes. Her star of the day will delight us with a sound poem." Though spoken without emphasis, Agnes detected a gleam of irony when he added, "Too rare a treat to be missed."

TC groaned without restraint.

Next to the luscious palm tree, Herb remained motionless, either in contemplation or waiting for them to get up. When Agnes rose, he led the way through the jungle of greenery that stifled her breathing. Was she following a merciless killer?

As soon as they rejoined the gathering crowded in one room now, Herbert excused himself and veered for a beverage cart. Only two people took a stand in front of the fireplace. Mrs. Nessbit towered over a skinny young man in a dark green velvety vest over a blousy white shirt. Evidently, the sound poet about to perform, Agnes surmised. Amused despite her worries, she turned to share the moment with her conspirator.

But TC was nowhere in sight. Escaped in the nick of time, she figured, wisely foregoing the dubious pleasure of today's chief attraction. Or did her foul play hypothesis scare him off?

Chapter 25

Jacqueline sat in the cozy armchair in her study. A weighty hardcover edition of selected works by George Sand lay wide open on her lab.

For the past hour, she tried to reconnect with her favorite pieces by the 19th-century cross-dressing French novelist who'd been miles ahead of her time on women's and gender issues.

Instead, stuck in a playback loop, Jac's mind churned over the same worries, only punctuated by checking the time in fretful anticipation of Agnes's return.

She must have dozed off when the door burst open behind her. With a jolt, she craned her neck around the padded high backrest. The tomb slid over her knees and tumbled onto the floor with a thud.

"I'm back."

The cheery announcement struck Jac as redundant as the belated knuckle rap on the wide-open door.

"So I see," she said flatly, eyeing Agnes's flushed face and sparkling expression.

"Hey, what's the sarcasm for? Peeved they didn't invite you?"

"Not in the least. I have no wish to attend the soirees."

"Well, let me tell you. You've no idea what you're missing."

Agnes laughed good-naturedly. "A sound poet delighted us with a phonetic feast. *Gibri dibri gambi*," intoned Agnes.

"Glad you enjoyed yourself."

"By the sound of it, you didn't," said Agnes as she sashayed over. She slid sideways onto Jac's ottoman, shedding her coat carelessly onto the rug. The black dress Jacqueline picked out for Agnes on one of their rare shopping trips to Toronto accentuated Agnes's curvy figure in just the right places.

Now, Agnes's hands gently nudged Jac's feet a few inches towards the edge to make room for herself. She regarded Jac soberly and asked, "What's wrong?"

The caring tone broke Jacqueline's reserve. "Everything. I'm worried sick. How can you even ask? Two suicides. The police are about to descend on us. My life's falling apart—"

"Whoa. Take it easy." Agnes rubbed Jac's icy feet. "We can handle this. Don't you worry."

"How can you say—" Unable to control her rising voice, Jac broke off.

"Listen. TC and I talked it over. He's got such a plausible hypothesis." At the mention of Timothy, Jac groaned, which caused Agnes to pat her feet soothingly. "Hear me out. After TC took off—"

"Oh?" interjected Jac hopefully.

"Escaped the crowning poetry act of the evening, smart man. Anyway, I figured it out. To avoid police digging in, we need Herb's confession."

"Confess stealing a student's manuscript? If he did, it would go viral and drag college intern misconduct into the public sphere. A sure way to blow the scandal out of proportion."

"Wait until I tell you TC's theory. He made a strong case for Herb having driven Dorian into suicide. Then Herb tried to kill Cass because—"

"Completely insane!" The shock propelled Jac's body upright. "Have you lost your mind? There was no attempted murder."

"Are you so sure of that?" Agnes's soft and reasonable voice contrasted painfully with her own shriek.

"Of course I am," she countered with a confidence she didn't feel. "Absurd. Why would Herbert kill anyone? Least of all, our students."

"What if the novelette Herb stole was autobiographic? A fictionalized account of Herb betraying his students' trust. He seduced Cass, thus not only stealing Dorian's manuscript but also the student's girlfriend. Think about it. The piece is called *The Betrayal*."

"None of it means he sought to kill Cassandra. It provides a motive for taking her own life out of guilt. To concoct a wild and damaging murder hypothesis is inexcusably sensationalist and offensive of Timothy."

"Oh, no, it's me who suspects foul play. TC thinks Cass and Herb fell out over what Dorian wrote in *The Betrayal*. Cass's mental health issues then drove her to attempt suicide."

Jacqueline, too stunned to speak immediately, now exploded. "*You* invented this ridiculous murder idea? Pure lunacy to vent such slanderous claims. I thought you wanted to help disprove the corrosive rumors. Instead, you spin out lies for Timothy to broadcast."

Incensed, Jacqueline pulled her feet out of Agnes's reach and planted them firmly on the ground in preparation for jumping up. She glared at her friend, feeling utterly—betrayed.

"Whoa, Jac. Don't blow your stack. At least let me explain before you throw me out."

As though they were about to discuss a sticky point of scholarly interest, Agnes reached for Jac's half-full wineglass on the side table and sipped thoughtfully. Her soft, dark eyes no longer held their earlier, almost feverish, sparkle. They focused on Jac's midriff as she remarked, "You'll ruin that nice top if you keep on twisting the hem."

A vague memory stirred in Jac's mind as she followed her friend's glance to see her own fingers wringing the bottom of the velvety lounge tunic, one of her favorites. To revert in stress to the same nervous habit as the twenty-year-old student she'd watched this very afternoon deeply disturbed her. Perhaps Agnes was right. She needed to cool it.

With forced control, she said, "Okay. I'll listen."

"Mind, it's merely circumstantial. You'll call it pure speculation. Here goes. Since the ER doctor has called in police, she obviously suspects Cass's case is not straightforward. Best to assume the worst-case scenario and nail the culprit before police deep-dives into everyone's affairs. Hey, I'm sounding like some hackneyed private eye," Agnes added ruefully with a lopsided grin before she asked, "Or do you want to wait for the cops to dissect us?"

While Agnes spoke, Jacqueline made a conscious effort not to fidget. Her hands clenched the ends of the armrests. She inhaled deeply through her nose, down to her diaphragm to calm herself sufficiently for a rational response.

"I don't see how anyone can prevent a police investigation. They are probably already questioning people. We're powerless."

"Don't be so defeatist, Dr. Jacqueline Xavier. Not at all like you to cave in. Think of all you've achieved and conquered in the past."

"My so-called past achievements and hopes for the future are exactly what I fear for. To see it all come crashing down—" Her lips trembled uncontrollably. The hands holding onto the armrests lost their grip and flew up to her face to cradle her cheeks.

Agnes reached out to stroke her knees.

"Come, have a sip of wine. Please, don't despair, Jac. I promise I'll do everything I can to protect you."

"I'm sorry to be so selfish," murmured Jac. She took the proffered glass and emptied it. Agnes rose and refilled it from the bottle on Jacqueline's desk.

"Why don't I explain my ideas how TC and I can get quick

results to preempt a lengthy police investigation? None of it will involve you."

"Where Mr. T. C. Elliot is concerned, no one is safe from the fall-out. He can't be trusted."

"C'mon, Jac. Be reasonable. Don't be so down on the guy. Besides, I won't tell him you and I discussed any of this." Agnes's expression suddenly changed. "You do trust me, don't you?" The small voice and uncertain, anxious look on her dear face tugged at Jac's heartstrings.

She squeezed Agnes's hand gently. "You are my best friend. I never doubt you," she said and meant it.

Agnes's face lit up in a wicked grin. "Yeah, right, Jac. You doubt me plenty. Still, deep down, you know I want to do my best for you. Okay," she added in self-mockery, "I've screwed up at times."

"We all do," sighed Jac. "Never mind. Tell me why you believe Herbert tried to eliminate Cassandra. The man doesn't strike me as a murderer. He's conceited—but honestly, he's all bluster and no bite."

"In short, a wimp. My sentiments, exactly—until TC reminded me worms turn, eventually. Don't roll your eyes at me. Yeah, trite for sure. But often true."

"What do worms have to do with anything? None of this explains your wild claims." Jac's legs twitched and quivered restlessly, causing Agnes to wrap a hand around her foot to still at least the one closest on the ottoman.

"In a nutshell, I'm assuming Cass became a liability for Herb." Shifting her weight, Agnes straightened her back as if preparing to lecture. "Presumably, Cass realized her lover withheld Dorian's manuscript because its content, if made public, would have lost him his job. Say, admin found out Herb seduced a student. Would he get tenure at his probationary hearing? Or would he get fired? Canadian legislation on harassment in the workplace may apply. The one in a position of power taking advantage of someone under his supervision?"

"The probation committee certainly would weigh it against him," agreed Jac. For a few moments, she considered before saying, "I don't get it. If the novelette is about Herbert and Cassandra, he couldn't hope suppressing the manuscript would kill the story and protect him from exposure. Students let others read their pieces prior to submitting. Dorian could just write it again after it disappeared."

"Good points. From what TC told me, Dorian was adamant about never rewriting creative pieces—tons of people heard him say so. Remember, not even Emma had a glimpse of the novelette's content. Yet, she guessed Dorian might sublimate his disappointment in love and turn it into a grand romance piece."

Agnes stopped to regard Jacqueline keenly.

Perhaps taking Jac's nods as agreement, she continued to expound. "At the risk of shocking you again, I've got a hunch Herb prevented Dorian from spreading the story. Emma's intuition triggered it. What if Herb spiked Dorian's drink, so to speak?"

Jac almost jumped out of her seat. "That's crazy! How can you sit there calmly suggesting such mad schemes? A double murder—atrocious! Such things just don't happen around here." At the same time, her mind's eye conjured an image of Nessbit in his heyday when he joined the department. A clear case of megalomania and narcissism. His self-aggrandizement back then was legendary around college. Lately, he'd taken to brooding with bouts of antagonism...and drinking. Not a stable character by any means.

Her friend gazed at her with interest, as so often, tuning into Jac's mind with ease. "Insane, yes. Not too farfetched, though, is it?" Agnes said quietly.

Unable to voice the unspeakable, Jac nodded. Her hand clenched around the wineglass and tipped it against her lips to swallow the remnant.

"Tell me your plan," she said, resigned to hear the worst.

Agnes avoided her eyes. "Better not spell it out. What you don't know can't be held against you."

"Don't treat me like a child. Your risks are my risks. Friendship goes both ways."

"No, Jac. If things go haywire, I'll pay for my stupidity and mistaken ideas. I simply refuse to put you in harm's way. Besides," she added airily. "What do I have to lose? A hypothetical chance at a full-time job? Negligible stakes compared to yours."

"Never mind your job prospects. It's your life I fear for, Agnes. If the man killed before, as you allege, or tried to kill two young people, he might try again if threatened."

"Oh, I'll be super cautious. No worries, I'll plan my approach very carefully."

Such assurance coming from someone who colluded in a nighttime raid on a colleague's office hardly satisfied, thought Jac. Aloud, she said. "We must agree on some safety net. I won't have you endangered—"

"Okay, okay." Agnes held up both hands to curb Jac's growing agitation. "Fine. Here's what we do. In case of real danger, I'll text you, say, 'SOS,' plus the GPS location, and you dial 911. Sounds good?"

Before Jacqueline could say anything, Agnes got up with a groan. "God, I'm stiff." On one leg in stocking feet, she nudged the ottoman with her toe. This thing is not meant for comfy sitting. Let's call it a night. I'm bushed."

She bent down for a peck on Jac's cheek. "Stop worrying. All will be well."

Yeah right, thought Jac. Her eyes on Agnes's retreating back, she said, "Wait. In case I don't see you in the morning, I need to leave early tomorrow for Toronto. A whole day of meetings. Do nothing until I'm back. We must discuss this when we are both wide awake. Promise?"

"Yeah, sure. Not to worry," Agnes mumbled, sounding half asleep.

Left alone, Jac pulled the wool throw over and shrouded herself up to her chin. Dead tired now, she wanted nothing more than to be in bed and sink into oblivion. Yet, her body refused to muster the energy to leave her armchair. Bits and pieces of their talk floated around her mind.

If someone wanted to spike Dorian's drink in the first place, students had far better opportunities than Nessbit ... Like Cleo ... hated Dorian ... jealous cat. Lester...

A pinched, sneering face under a dark fringe manifested behind her closed lids.

She shuddered. Need to warn Agnes.

Her brain sent words. No action followed. Limbs, mushy with exhausted tension, refused to obey the dictates of a benumbed brain.

Chapter 26

Half an hour later, readying for bed, Agnes hit the third puffy pillow with her palm to plump it up. Two of them already cushioned the headrest of her bed. She sank onto the mattress and swung up her pajama-clad legs to burrow under the duvet.

Dead beat when she left Jac's study, all she wanted was to lose herself in dreams—only to snap back into wakefulness as soon as she got ready in the bathroom. Nothing for it but traipse back to the kitchen for hot milk and honey, which now sat steaming on the nightstand next to her.

Staring into the darkened room, dimly illuminated by a battery-powered candle on the nightstand, her mind chewed over possibilities to prod Herb into a confession. Agatha Christie's Poirot does it often enough, she mused. Gather the suspects and tease out their secrets. Confront each with the evidence against them until the killer gets antsy and unnerved when Poirot eliminates one after the other. Finally, twirling his mustache to a fine point, he hits the culprit with the ultimate trump, goading the murderer into a fateful admission or crushing confession.

Agnes slurped her milk thoughtfully. She'd need to reread Hercule's most effective showdowns. Did she need an assembly of suspects when she knew the perpetrator? Yet so did Poirot, even if no one else had figured it out.

Empty mug back on the table, Agnes extinguished the candle with a twist and slid farther down into her pillow nest. Ridiculous, she grinned under the cover. Never works in real life. Maybe TC has a better plan. His last scheme wasn't so hot…

———

Metallic clanging ricocheted from steel-gritted stairs leading nowhere. Doridi dunido daisie chanting faces leaned over railings. A thatcheresque face, hallowed by silvery sweeping curls, lowered from above. 'Oh, my blood pressure,' mouthed carmine lips. 'Take your rat poison!' Sharp clattering drowned the shout—

With a snort, Agnes awoke. Her eyes searched the darkness. Across from her bed, the contours of the window showed dimly around the ill-fitting blackout blind. Had she bolted the fire escape door? No recollection surfaced.

A sudden clanging outside spurred her into action. She jumped up. This was going too far, the guys from the halfway house robbing her sleep. To use her patio in the middle of the night, simply outrageous. She'll teach them to startle her to death.

Agnes reached for her phone and covertly checked the display. 1:18 AM. She'd slept for less than an hour.

Without turning on any light, she slipped into her felted Birkenstocks and groped for a fleece sweater to cover her PJ top. Phone clasped in her left, she padded soundlessly to the backdoor. Her finger shielded the lens on her mobile as she swiped its flashlight to 'on.' The bolt was not shot into the sturdy steel bracket.

She took a steadying breath, her right hand on the door handle.

With sudden force, she yanked the heavy door open. Her left pointed the unshielded flash out onto the little patio. "What are you doing up here?" she hissed in anger, yet concerned about waking other neighbors. "You're trespassing."

As she swept the light in a half-circle, it caught a dark figure about to descend the metal stairs. The rusted railing shrieked when the intruder swung around to face her. Pale, peaky features stared into the beam. Eyes scrunched up as in pain. Stringy hair, black against the white brow, stuck sweaty to the skin.

"Lester! What in hell are you doing on my patio?" Agnes heard herself screech.

No word came from the trespasser, immobile like a fawn caught in headlights. Agnes's mind raced. Was not Herb the killer—A deranged student—Rip the genius. Spike Dorian's drink. Easy for a mate…

What nonsense. Her rational mind kicked in. Peers lack motive. No student stole the manuscript. Herb did—But students were hyperemotional. Jealousies. Resentment. Anxieties. Mental health issues. Or a prank gone wrong?

Thoughts rattled around her brain, tumbling over each other in split seconds.

About to jump back into her room and bolt the steel door, she froze. A darker shape rose above Lester's head, towering a foot above him. Bulky and unrecognizable.

The flash of her mobile shot up to illuminate the new menace.

Two white eyeballs with black pinpoint centers, as if suspended in the night, made her yelp. Her heart pounded.

A sonorous voice murmured soothing sounds flowing out between two rows of sparkling white teeth.

How stupid of me. Not a balaclava at all. The guy's black and wears a hoody. Chagrined, Agnes's anger dissipated.

"You know you shouldn't be up here. The noise woke me," she said more reasonably, yet still puzzled by Lester's presence.

"Sorry, ma'am," the newcomer said contritely. "It's my fault. I got him to come out with me."

"Do you live next door, Lester?" Agnes lowered the light to shine onto the floor between them.

The guy, huge like a well-muscled footballer, broke into a deep, musical laugh. "No way. Works his ass off in the kitchen." He patted the other on the shoulder in noisy little slaps. "Lester here volunteers three nights a week. Talked him into playing cards after his shift. We came out for a quiet smoke. For me. Not Lester."

"I see," said Agnes, aware of how lame it sounded. "Much better, though, if you had some chairs out in a back corner of the yard. Under the trees back there." She pointed into the unlit parking lot, which comprises the so-called yard. "The fire escape rattles so when anyone comes up."

"They'd chase us off the premises if we'd made ourselves at home down there." His deep laugh took the sting out of his remark.

Lester had not said a word. In the dim light, his face still seemed tense and pinched.

"If you want, I can talk it over with Jac Xavier. She's the main tenant. Pick up some used lounge chairs from Value Village or something. I'm sure if you keep the noise down, no one will mind." She crossed her fingers behind her back.

To the silent Lester, she said, "See you in class." That garnered her a brief nod.

Huddled into her fleece sweater, she watched them clang down the steps into the darkness below. A "good night, ma'am" floated up to her.

Back in bed, the duvet swaddled around her chilled body, the mental carousel rebooted of its own accord. Word snatches and fractured images bubbled to awareness. The majestic visage of her hostess from earlier tonight morphed into Herb's bloated face. Surely, a vague family likeness. Minus the broken blood vessels and bloodshot eyes. The mater didn't imbibe. Other than sparkling grape juice. All that blood ... blood pressure—

Agnes shot bolt upright. A dream image mingled with boudoir memories. That's it. The means. Possibly, at least.

Mrs. N. suffered from high blood pressure—which increased the risk of stroke. Warfarin was commonly used in patients with high stroke risk. Chances are she took the stuff and keeps it somewhere in her house. Accessible to her son.

Pleased with her deductions, Agnes sank back onto her pillows.

Another thought hit her. She reached over and grabbed her iPad from the shelf below the nightstand.

For a few minutes, she typed furiously. Then, she sent off the email to her acquaintance in the US. Maybe by morning she'll have a clearer idea about the means.

She'd barely composed herself for sleep and counted sheep when the phone's vibration rattled the nightstand. The answer to her inquiry stared at her.

'Lucky you. Night shift in ER. Yes, sometimes high blood pressure in overweight patients warrants Warfarin. Effects of overdose show in 48-72 hours.'

Entire flocks of sheep wouldn't bring sleep now.

Chapter 27

Jacqueline's tiny Yaris inched forward, wedged in by a dump truck in front and an oversized SUV in the rear. Frustrated, Jac's fingers drummed the steering wheel. The dashboard clock read 5:18 PM. She'd been stuck in Friday afternoon rush hour traffic on the 401, outbound from Toronto, for fifty minutes. No end in sight.

When she left her alma mater, York U, after meeting her counterpart in their creative writing program, Google Maps urged her to switch to the 407 ETR. The express toll route snaked along the northern perimeter of the mega city conglomerate. Jac refused to pay the exorbitant toll charges and paid the price in time and frustration.

The rear brake lights of the truck faded. For a few minutes, they crawled forward, only to grind to another halt. The miniature Toyota her dad gifted her three years ago was hemmed in on both sides by vision-blocking giants. A Go commuter bus on the right and a Purolator truck on her left. Not that the concrete-scape along the highway would yield any aesthetic pleasure.

Jac's eyes veered to her mobile on the passenger seat. A notification lit up the screen. In defiance of the 'no hand-held devices' rule, Jacqueline reached over to pull the phone onto her lap. The snippet displayed was in French. A Sorbonne address.

Her fingers grew stone cold. To check or not to check? A rejection would be crushing. Acceptance was bound to throw her into a frenzy of worry. The shame of an offer being revoked if the Herb scandal hit the fan. Unthinkable. Horrendous. How much preferable an honest rejection now—

Someone honked behind her. Flustered, she fumbled for the shifter to put the car in gear. Nothing happened. She bit the nails of her right hand and swore in French. The honking grew in intensity. Her brain gave the right impulse to her thumb to press in the button on the shifter. In fitful bumps the Yaris caught up to the dump truck, whose brake lights flashed. Its driver let the engine howl in anger as they all stopped yet again.

Disgusted with her own weakness, Jacqueline's thumb unlocked the phone. The dreaded email opened. Her heart leapt and raced to make up for the lost beat. Accepted.

A cry of triumph escaped her lips. She'd done it!

For a moment, all fear of consequences retreated in the face of success. She'd beat the stiff competition. The prestigious visiting professorship was hers for the coming year.

Wait until I tell Agnes—and Martha, her mind gloated.

Then, black depression descended again.

She must stop Agnes. Any rash action now would be fatal to Jacqueline's prospects. She checked the time. Agnes's afternoon class finished at six, phone turned off or in flight mode. Better call her later.

Ten minutes and about two or three kilometers farther west, Jac's thumbs itched to text Martha the good news from Paris. They'd meet after the weekend to debrief Jac's meetings with heads of creative writing programs at the University of Toronto's satellite campuses and at York U. An eternity to wait. Jac caved in and thumbed her phone.

An answering SMS from Martha flashed on the screen minutes later.

'Congratulations!! If congenial, let's celebrate tonight. 8 PM at Le Bistro?'

Despite her anxious mood, Jac smiled.

The tiny French restaurant was her favorite in town. How lovely of Martha to suggest dinner. Jac thanked her with two emojis.

"Herb be damned," she muttered and hit the innocent steering wheel.

Chapter 28

Agnes stopped to catch her breath and calm her nerves on the second-floor landing of the backstairs.

After an endless evening of waiting and plotting in the underground dungeon, TC finally texted. She swore when she saw it was nearly ten PM.

'Come up the backstairs. Now. All's arranged.'

Earlier in the day, she tried to meet up with her fellow sleuth for strategic planning. No luck. The man was too busy. When she outlined her intention of trapping Herb into a confession, TC was underwhelmed. She sensed his lack of interest during the brief phone call she'd insisted on in her SMS. 'Leave it to me,' was his sole comment.

Minutes before her afternoon class, he texted, 'On campus tonight. Plays hooky from mom's dinner - ttyl'

She'd been so distracted the few students who showed up yawned and fidgeted. Well, no one liked Friday PM classes. Later, alone in her office after a quick bite at Tim Horton's across the park, she continued plotting her approach to the Herb interview. The grading pile and lecture planning could wait until the weekend.

Only when her steps echoed off the concrete walls in the

stairwell did reality sink in. This was not a fun philosophical thought experiment or intellectual game. She was on the way to confront a killer.

With infinite care, Agnes eased the fire door open. Heart racing not merely from the ascent, she stood rooted to the spot.

Mouth dry and knees wobbly, she peered around the steel door into the dimly lit upper hallway. Not a soul about.

She slinked around the door and shut it with hardly a sound. A movement across the corridor startled her.

Her breath escaped in an audible whistle. TC leaned against a doorframe.

Fingers raised to his lips, he beckoned her to join him. They didn't speak until he'd ushered her inside and closed the door.

"Pretty dark in here. Can we have some light?" she asked, unnerved by the unfamiliar space.

A floor lamp lit up, infusing the den-size room with mellow light.

Agnes gasped. Wooden bookshelves lined the walls, chock full of antiquarian hardcover volumes. Overawed, she approached to examine the titles. Classic literature rubbed shoulders with philosophy, poetry, natural science, and more. Works in English, German, French, Greek, and Latin jostled for pride of place. A scholar's dream refuge.

Her fingers caressed the spines of superbly bound editions. To be left here in blissful peace of an evening, enshrined at the ornamental desk—surely, it must be cherry wood—how marvelous. The office owner had invested in heavy curtains to shut out reality. Cocooned in one's own world.

"You like it?" asked her companion. Proprietorial gratification spoke in his tone and glance.

"Fantastic. How come you've got access to it?"

"Serves as my office," He waved at the walls in a dismissive gesture. "My former mentor, old Grace Cavendish, insists I use it. She's professor emerita. Comes by once in a blue moon. They can't allocate the space to other faculty because

Grace founded the humanities department in the days of yore."

"Some have all the luck," Agnes said as she tried the comfy desk chair. "I'd give— Um, whatever to use this place."

The proximity of his body as he settled on the edge of the desk, idly swinging one leg, disconcerted her.

His glance from above searched out hers. The smooth voice insinuated, "Well, maybe we can arrange something."

Uncomfortable where this might lead, Agnes sat up straight. "Okay, why don't we concentrate on our task? I've worked out how to approach Herb. Here's what I—"

"Leave it to me. I know the perp better than you."

To be thus sidelined raised Agnes's hackles. As she remonstrated, TC pulled out his phone and glanced at it. He slid off the desk, flicked off the light, and moved to the door, ignoring her feeble protests.

"Time to tackle him. Stay in the background and let me deal with things." Not waiting for her, he exited without a sound.

In frustration, she felt like shouting. Instead, she followed. This was not how she'd envisioned the showdown. She hurried to catch up with TC, who strode toward Herb's office.

After a perfunctory rap, TC entered without awaiting encouragement. Agnes stayed close on his heels.

Afraid to enter, she stood rooted at the doorpost. Vision blocked by her companion's back, the stench of booze nauseated her.

TC prompted her to pass. "Close the door," he hissed.

She obeyed without a word. As her eyes adjusted to the gloom, a sense of déjà vu caused her to mutter, "Not again."

Slumped over his desk, Herb remained oblivious to their presence. The empty liquor bottle spoke of excess. A rivulet trailed its way from an overturned tumbler to the fedora resting precariously on the edge of the barren desk.

"Bloody hell," said TC.

Agnes could have kicked herself—or TC—or Herb—for

leaving things too late. They'd given him plenty of time to get sloshed in solitude.

Maybe Herb realized their intentions and put himself out of commission to foil the attack. Not sure if shaking him would do any good, she stepped closer. The man seemed awfully still. No heaving chest with every breath. What if he'd done himself some harm? Like Cass...

No. Cass did nothing ... if their theory held.

Torn between concern—the man might need medical attention, and anger—her plans come to naught, Agnes swore silently.

"What do we do now?" she demanded. "He might need help."

"Nothing doing. I'm not playing the good Samaritan again."

"What if he attempted to—"

"Give me a break, Agnes," muttered TC. Still, he went up to Herb and placed his fingers on the side of the exposed neck.

A moment later, he said, "We go back to my office and talk. It stinks in here."

Chapter 29

Jacqueline smiled in agreement as AD Martha Muller balanced a sliver of moist Camembert on thinly sliced baguette, pronouncing it, "Delicious."

Their leisurely dinner at *Le Bistro* mellowed their mood. Shared reminiscences of Paris relegated Jac's worries to the background. Martha was just as fond of the Seine metropolis as Jacqueline. A gifted storyteller with a wry sense of humor, she'd delighted Jac with lighthearted anecdotes.

Now, Martha's expression grew somber. She sipped her Beaujolais. Thoughtful eyes searched Jac's face. "The evening is far too pleasant for serious subjects. But needs must."

A juicy black grape Jac just bit off from a small bunch threatened to choke her. Did Martha hear of Agnes's exploits? No. They'd not be here at dinner if she did.

The older woman regarded her with concern. "Not a topic one likes to raise at table. Leaving it until after the weekend feels awkward, too."

Her nerves stretched taut by the preamble, Jacqueline said as non-committal as possible, "I'm sure it must be important."

"Yes, indeed." Martha stopped a passing server. They both ordered espresso.

Another sleepless night awaited her, Jac figured. More bad news and caffeine guaranteed wakefulness.

"Gordon Gable called me this afternoon. I spoke to him and Emma. Incidentally, they thanked me warmly for connecting them with you and Agnes." A kind smile enveloped Jac. "They were most favorably impressed by your kindness and understanding."

Surprised at the praise, Jac searched the AD's face. Its sincerity was genuine.

"They stressed Agnes's astuteness." A tiny chuckle lightened the atmosphere. "To be expected in a philosopher, don't you think? Apparently, their son already paved the way for such an assessment of his favorite professor."

The positive remarks lulled Jac's fears. Why the caution about a topic perfectly fit for table talk? "Yes, Dorian and Agnes enjoyed their philosophical chats."

"The Gables reached out to let me know they planned to depart for Florida tonight." The AD consulted her old-fashioned gold-link wristwatch. "In fact, they'll be leaving as we speak."

This news further relaxed Jac.

"The climate down there agrees with Emma, they said. The past week taxed her health beyond endurance, one suspects. Did they make the funeral arrangements?" Jac asked.

"That's what I wanted to share. They opted for cremation and taking the urn to Florida. Did I mention the memorial service to you? The parents plan a celebration of Dorian's life either in Toronto or in Florida when the extended family can attend. Gordon will contact me with details."

Jacqueline murmured what was proper, yet her mind raced over the implications.

Ashes. No body, no postmortem to prove Agnes's wild surmises. It meant closure for the bereaved parents.

Unease mingled in. If Dorian died by the hand of another,

the murderer had nothing to fear. Herbert must breathe a sigh of relief. But surely, Agnes must be wrong—

"...was also Timothy's impression. Did Agnes mention anything of the kind?"

"Sorry, Martha." Startled out of her cogitation, Jac was clueless. "Thoughts about Dorian's family and their grief distracted me. I didn't quite catch your question about Agnes."

"Emma told me Dorian expressed horror at the idea of interments and believed in the dispersal of ashes as a return to nature. I wondered if Agnes mentioned discussing this rather philosophical topic with Dorian."

"Not to me. I can ask her about it."

An overwhelming urge to share with Agnes what she'd just heard caused Jac to fidget. Her fingers reached for the espresso cup, only to find it empty. She couldn't recall anyone serving it, never mind drinking it.

Across from her, Martha signaled to the hovering waiter for their bill. When Jac reached for her purse, Martha waved it aside. "My treat to celebrate your successful application," she smiled.

"So sweet of you to invite me tonight. Memories and stories of Paris are a delightful respite from...from the dreary weather."

"If things work out, I plan to visit you during your stay at the Sorbonne."

"I'd love it," said Jac, confident now the looming threat retreated mile by mile with the departing Gables.

She must catch Agnes first chance to prevent her from doing anything foolish. Earlier this evening, she'd caught Agnes grabbing a sandwich at Timmy's, fortifying for a long stint of grading. Though she couldn't smell the donut shop over the phone, Jac had shuddered at the thought of dinner there.

Now, she regarded the restaurant's stylish interior with renewed approval. For a few hours, one might fancy oneself at Montmartre.

"Ready to leave?"

"Ready for anything," Jac said, and meant it. A mental vision of the narrow winding streets on the famous hill in Paris lit up her face and her mood.

When they parted outside to walk home in opposite directions, they embraced and kissed each other's cheeks in French fashion.

Once alone, Jac whipped out her phone and dashed off an SMS to Agnes. 'Home in 10. Must talk.'

Every couple of minutes, she checked the display, not trusting the notification setting.

No response.

Chapter 30

Back in TC's loaned office, Agnes threw herself into the chair. It creaked in protest.

Frustration seethed inside her gut. She stared at the shelves. The peaceful vibe no longer charmed her. Nor did her fellow sleuth please her. His aimless meanderings from shelf to shelf, picking up books at random to flip their pages, irritated.

"So, what now?"

"*Eh?*"

"You heard me. With Herb dead to the world, we can't squeeze out a confession, can we?" Snarky but true. No reason to hide her annoyance. "Why did you leave it so late?"

"Did you want to tackle him while the cleaner was about? Slim chance our poet laureate owning up to his misdeeds when he's still sober. It's him screwing up my timing."

Angered by TC's sarcastic retort after he'd sidelined her earlier, she said, "I had it all worked out. The other day, you offered to assist me. Sounds now you have zero confidence in me."

"C'mon, Agnes. This is real life. Murderers don't break down and confess to some amateur. What evidence have you got, anyway?"

At least he turned to face her. Though the stance, leaned back against a shelf, legs crossed above the ankles, didn't show rapt attention.

"Of the eternal triangle, motive, means, and opportunity, I've figured out the first two. For the third, I need your input."

She'd recaptured his attention. In one swift motion, he loomed over her, palms grabbing the edge of the desk. "Oh? Let's hear the means. The motive we've ticked off in his filing drawer."

Pleased with her audience, Agnes rolled back in her chair—until she hit the bookcase behind her with a thump.

It took a moment to recover from the jolt and sit up dignified, ignoring his mocking grin. "To explain the means, we need to backtrack. The paramedics found a Warfarin vial when they came for Cass."

"Who told you that? You never mentioned it before."

The anger in his tone and stare surprised Agnes. "There's a lot you don't tell me, either. Let's stick to the point." She'd no intention of involving Andrea and Mel.

"Have it your way." He sounded peeved. "Cassandra probably filched it from her friend Dorian. Wasn't she the one who found him?"

"Yes, but we're assuming now Herb attempted to kill her after he'd killed Dorian." She paused for effect. "With an overdose of Warfarin."

Her fellow sleuth appeared stunned. He swung around and paced like the caged lynx she once saw in a zoo.

Not bothering to look at her, he asked, "How do you make that out? Didn't you say before Herb slipped him stuff that interacted fatally with Dorian's prescription med?"

"It dawned on me last night. Mrs. Nessbit suffers from high blood pressure, she told me. Plus, she's overweight. Hence, a candidate for Warfarin, depending on other conditions. Like heart issues."

When TC rolled his eyes, she admitted, "Okay, speculative, but probable."

"Tenuous at best."

"Hey, didn't you say your mom works at Rexall?"

"She's not a pharmacist. Where she works has nothing to do with anything."

To judge by his grumpiness, he'd guessed her sudden idea. Wouldn't be fair to drag in Mrs. Elliot to find out Mrs. Nessbit's prescription, Agnes realized and apologized. "Sorry, didn't mean to suggest…" Flustered and disheartened, she admitted, "Goes to show you, it's a case for police. I can't prove my surmises."

His icy look chilled her. "Let's leave the cops out of this, shall we? I don't want to lose my precarious teaching gig." Her nods earned a warmer gaze and kinder tone as he asked, "Any other conjectures? About how he did it, for instance?"

No longer sure of her deductions, Agnes hesitated.

"Exactly where I need your input. We assume—for argument's sake—Herb slipped Dorian Warfarin, thus overdosing him. The question is 'when?' We must figure out opportunities within the last three days of Dorian's life."

"Eh? Why three?"

"Because Warfarin takes effect in 48-72 hours, a doctor told me."

TC's eyebrows shot up. She'd beat him at smart sleuthing.

"I figure he might have shown signs of being unwell," she said. "In my class on Thursday, he was fine. My other class he took is on Tuesdays. He passed away on Monday night. Did you notice any change in him? When did you last see him?"

She watched TC ambulate again, eyes scanning the books like they held answers. "Why do you ask? The question is Herb's opportunity to mess with Dorian's meds. The million-dollar answer is: Friday afternoon, Dorian was in Herb's poetry class."

With a thump, Agnes brought her chair against the desk and sat bolt upright.

"Wow. We've nailed the opportunity. I can just see it." Her mind raced ahead as she visualized the scene. "Dorian always brought a reusable coffee mug to class. Slip a few pills in there. Must be doable."

Doubts snuck in as she spoke. Wouldn't one taste the stuff? Spit out the coffee or whatever was in the mug? Did Warfarin have a noticeable taste?

Aloud, she said, "We need to reconstruct what Dorian did all weekend. Who he was with. Friday afternoon may prove irrelevant."

"Why?"

"Too early. He died Monday evening before ten PM." Something stirred in the back of her mind. "Oh, hey, Friday night. You guys all were at the HCC, weren't you? Did you notice Herb and Dorian together? I mean, near enough for him to get at Dorian's drink. What did Dorian have, anyway?"

"Bloody Mary. Alcohol-free," said TC, his mind clearly on other ideas. "Dorian gets the bartender to make it after his own recipe."

"Did you see Herb with Cass there?"

"How do you know any of this? What are you holding back?"

No way she would drag in Jac and her eavesdropping episode. All this was far too complicated. Too many interests to protect.

She sighed, exasperated. "If only Cass could say what happened to her. The rest would follow. Oh, well, the police will figure it out once Cass regains consciousness. Amateurs lack investigative means and access to info. It's so frustrating."

TC's pacing ceased. He slotted a book into place and faced her. Impatience marked his handsome features. One hand reached to swipe back his hair, making strands stick out.

"You go from one extreme to the other," he said. "First, overconfident in your snooping ability, now total despondency. Reminds me of a manic depressant. Anyway, your sudden faith in the police astounds me. Have they talked to you or anyone you know?"

"No, but it's time we did." Aware of her mood swings, she resented the reference.

"You are nuts to suggest it. We'd be done for."

The dismissive tone hurt. She did her best to stay reasonable. "It may sound priggish, but doesn't justice trump self-interest? A killer will strike again—it gets easier—"

His laugh discomposed her enough to stop.

"Oh? Experience speaks?"

"Quit your misplaced humor, TC. This is serious. It's a truism. Murderers do anything to protect themselves."

"If you say so." The shrug didn't improve things.

Determined to action, she pushed her chair back and rose. "Never mind. If I can't convince you, I'll try convincing the police tomorrow. Now, I might as well go home and sleep."

She moved toward the door. TC stood in her path. For all she cared, he could stay in "his" office all night.

"I'll check on Herb on my way out," she said firmly. "No matter how I feel about the man, I can't leave him passed out in his office."

"You his nanny? The man drinks himself into a stupor most nights. Leave him be."

Though unsure how to get Herb home, she was too annoyed to admit defeat or beg for help. "Stay here if you like. I'll find a way to deal with this."

They stood facing each other. Neither of them smiled. Why had she let the atmosphere grow so tense?

"Sorry, TC," she muttered in the same breath, wondering about the Canadian need to apologize for no fault of their own. Well, maybe she was partly to blame. Yet, she compounded the *mea culpa*. "I'm just tired. This whole affair is getting me down."

His clenched jaw relaxed. "Tell you what. One last time, I'll play the good Samaritan. You can help."

Relieved by the offer, she exhaled. After all, he'd as much as promised to play Hastings to her Poirot. No reason to allow him to feel magnanimous, though. "Okay. Thanks. What's the plan?"

"Stay with my car at the loading dock while I maneuver him down the backstairs. We'll go out there now. No one will see us."

"Wait. I'll first make sure Herb's alright," said Agnes.

"No. Someone's bound to see us if we go twice. Two or three minutes won't matter. He's drunk as a skunk anyhow."

"But—"

"Don't stall. The bloody poet usually sleeps it off in there without needing a chauffeur.

Worried TC might back out of his offer, Agnes reluctantly agreed.

As they slunk into the dim corridor a moment later, Agnes again experienced an eerie sense of déjà vu. Made no sense because the fire door was right across. TC held it open for her to pass.

The smell of concrete hit her nostrils, dry and dusty. She thought she'd heard a metallic sound but couldn't tell if it came from above or below.

A few steps above her, TC eased the door shut. Must have scraped as it closed, she figured. In the emergency lighting, his tall body threw a gigantic, crooked shadow onto the bare wall. The tousled hair sticking out like horns.

Agnes laughed uneasily at her vivid imagination.

Chapter 31

All the way home through the lamplit streets, Jac clasped her mobile, begging it to vibrate. No response from Agnes.

When she reached her old brick pile of a house, she rushed up the stairs into the kitchen. It lay deserted. The wheezing of the fridge's compressor broke the silence.

Moshi or Paul had left the dishwasher gaping wide open. In annoyance, she banged the tripping hazard shut.

She dropped her handbag on a chair before striding across the hall to the living room. Except for an abandoned sweater and newspaper strewn on the floor, no sign of life. Agnes might be in her bedroom. Just to be sure, Jacqueline checked her study, though she trusted none of the others entered it when she wasn't home. It lay dark and soothing, tempting her to turn on a floor lamp to find comforting tidiness.

She resisted its allure and climbed the stairs to the upper landing. Her knock on Agnes's door yielded no results. The house brooded in gloomy stillness. No point in looking for her male tenants on the third floor. Friday night on the town, they called their weekly revels.

Despite Agnes's assurance to enter her sanctuary if she ever needed to borrow something, Jac felt reluctant. Unease won out.

She inched the door open, softly calling Agnes's name. Neither blackout blind nor curtains were drawn. The room was unoccupied.

If Agnes stayed this late on campus, why didn't she answer texts? Jac turned on the overhead light, a flush-mount globe with soft LED bulbs. One glance confirmed her suspicion. The phone charger lay on the nightstand. Mobile's battery dead, no doubt. So much for prearranged SOS signals, Jac thought, equally frustrated and anxious.

She went into her own bedroom to change into sweats. Back downstairs, she sought the refuge of her study to wait for her friend's return. Restless, she fingered a book, only to place it face down on her desk. The armchair felt just as confining.

Unable to stand the tension, she jumped up. In the hallway, she grabbed a light running jacket, slipped in her keys and access card. Her feet in trainers, she rushed back out into the night.

The cool air tempered her overheated imagination. Foolish to jog to campus at this hour in search of her friend, a mature adult. Yet, she told herself, nothing wrong with dropping by the part-timer office. Pick up Agnes and stroll home together.

It wasn't the first nighttime jog, she reassured herself. When unable to sleep without AC in the summer, she often went for a slow trot. This wasn't Toronto. Small towns were safe, she'd always assumed.

Her mind circled and looped back to the deeper cause of worry. Did Agnes seriously plan to confront a killer?

An image of Nessbit, somewhat pathetic yet belligerent, easy to offend and anger, rose to her mind's eye.

Jac sped up.

Chapter 32

"What's up?" asked TC. "Seen a ghost?"

Aware of staring at the tall figure elongated by the odd perspective—he on the edge of the landing, she a few steps below, putting her at eye level with his square-tipped ankle boots —Agnes suppressed another shiver.

The concrete walls chilled the space. Cold enough to numb her hand clutching the steel railing.

"Can't you turn the light on?" she asked, seeing a switch at the side of the door behind him. The stuffy dimness of the stair-well was claustrophobic.

"Let's not call attention to ourselves," TC said.

Made no sense as the space was windowless.

"C'mon. Down you go." His boot kicked playfully forward as if to prompt her to move.

Mesmerized, Agnes watched it swing. Her mind whirred. Fragments of speech and images rose from her subconscious and fused.

She got it all wrong. Through a mental fog, her words came muffled.

"It was you, wasn't it?"

There was a silence, like a tear in an old film reel.

Then, his laughter ricocheted through the narrow space.

"Agnes, come off it. Don't be ridiculous. You can't try on suspects like shoes. We've nailed the poet. Give it a rest."

"You were there at the club Friday night."

"Come again?"

"As Dorian's close friend, you had far better opportunity to tamper with his drink than Herb."

"So had x-number of other people. The one with the motive is the loser of a poet. You yourself found the evidence in his office."

"Planted there by you."

The sharp edge of his boot jerked forward. She ducked her head in reflex. A smile flickered over his face.

"That's wild." His laugh didn't sound amused. "Stuffed it in the drawer, did I? Really, Agnes. You were right there with me. Did you see me plant anything?"

"No, but J—" Agnes broke off. No way she'd drag in Joel the Spy. "Rumor has it someone saw you go into Herb's office at night. No one mentioned me with you. Since I was right behind you when we entered, they'd have seen me too. Which they didn't."

"Of all the flimsy reasoning, this takes the cake. As a sleuth, Agnes, you suck." He took a step forward. "To accuse me." He tsk-tsked and leaned toward her. "Either desperate or reckless. In here alone with me. What if I really were a killer?" His hands made a neck-wringing motion to faked delirious giggling.

Her wobbly knees conceded the point. Reckless, for sure. Yet, her gut told her she was right. Run for your life, part of her mind shrieked. Back off slowly, then bolt down to the loading dock. Must have cameras outside to guard the entrance…

Her mouth gaped. He never meant to ferry Herb out that way.

No—Nor did he mean for her to leave…alive.

She scanned his face for confirmation. He scrutinized her dispassionately.

Stubborn anger mounted at the blatant assumption of superiority, entitlement, his belief in his right to harm others for his own good. She wanted to lash out and hit—with wounding words. Fear aggression, her mom had called it, referring to one of their rescue dogs, Agnes realized in a flash.

Unable to stop herself, the words tumbled out.

"You betrayed yourself when you told me what *The Betrayal* was about. No one could know unless he'd read it."

"My young friend discussed it with me. I was his mentor, remember? He wanted a beta reader."

"An obvious lie. Dorian never shared with anyone prior to submitting his work. Not even with his mom." A shaky claim to test the ground.

"Lucky guess. A 'what if' conjecture was all I intended. With such a title and the fact his girlfriend dumped him for another lover, it stands to reason a sensitive writer like him would churn out a tragic romance. The shoe fits Nessbit, not me." Maybe merely to illustrate, he jerked his foot at her.

Her body swung backwards by instinct. Only the hand clutching the rail saved her from falling.

"Watch it." He chuckled at her clumsiness.

"You framed Herb. Cass would never pick a lover like him. It all fits you."

"Ah, you recognize my irresistible charm. Fell for it yourself," he said smugly. "A bit long in the tooth for my taste. Younger chicks to fry."

Ouch. A low blow. Still a few years before she'd reach forty. If she ever did… Maybe if she stalled him long enough, flattering his humongous ego, security would come to throw them out. And save her.

The image of her mom, Sera, arose. A lifelong example of bravery. They'd faced a murderer before. This time, she was

alone and couldn't hide behind anyone's back. Her mom's childhood advice floated through her consciousness. 'Never turn your
back on a bully.'

Agnes stood tall—not letting go of her safety grip on the
handrail—she gritted her teeth. Lure him into an irrevocable
admission, her ego prompted, if it's the last thing you do. Her
sane self urged her to keep him talking.

She struggled to calm her voice. "Right you are. Cass is far
more attractive. A liability, though. Didn't you say she's unstable? Over-dramatizes? Quite a worry for you."

"Changing tack, are we? Amateur psychology?"

"Just musing. Trying to understand and empathize." Don't
lay it on too thick, her mind warned. He's too smart for obvious
cajoling. Susceptible to flattery... "You've got to admit,
though—"

"I admit nothing."

"No, no. I didn't mean—" Mimicking embarrassment, she
averted her glance, focusing on the central stair column while
watching for his every move in her peripheral vision. The steely
solidity of the poles anchoring the entire staircase infused
strength.

"Only," she said, "Herb is far too weak to carry out a bolt
scheme like this. It takes a higher intellect to plot this stratagem
to eliminate Dorian in an ingenious way. Herbert never received
the manuscript. You found it in the admin office, didn't you? On
the floor. Or Giuseppe put it on the table for Fraser."

A covert glance caught rage flickering up. So, she'd guessed
correctly.

When he spoke, he betrayed no emotion other than
contempt.

"Flattery won't get you anywhere. Just spin your yarn.
Tested your loony ideas on your pal yet?"

Agnes hesitated. Claiming she'd told her friend meant a
modicum of safety. No, it would put Jac in danger. If Elliot

planned to eliminate her—shivers contracted her skin—Jac would be next.

She bit her lip and aimed for a distracted drawl. "Oh? Discuss my theories with Jacqueline Xavier? How could I? Only worked it out now."

The man's stance slackened. Not yet ready to pounce, she thought. This predatory-prey game suited him too well. Sadly, no game for her.

"Carry on, pocket-Poirot," he said. Arms crossed, he leaned against the wall, feet apart, and asked, "How was the ingenious plan carried out?"

She sensed self-congratulation beneath the surface sarcasm.

"Nothing to it. A few Warfarin tabs popped into Dorian's Bloody Mary at the club Friday night. The Clamato juice and Worcester sauce they use masks other stuff added, I'd say."

While she spoke, Agnes picked up a faint noise from below. In the vain hope someone down there might listen in, she'd clanged her silver bracelet against the railing and spoke louder.

Nothing in TC's face betrayed he'd heard the sound. "You forget your own argument about Nessbit's means and opportunity, dear Agnes. His motive is indisputable. Everyone on campus will agree. Yes, Cassandra is unstable, liable to do just anything. Plus, they found Warfarin in her room, you said. Ex-girlfriends never lack motives. None of it applies to yours truly."

His lips twisted to one side. Never noticed the cruelty in his smile, she thought, what a devilish smirk. To think how he beguiled me.

Her shudder triggered an idea. "Your mom works at Rexall. A job at a drugstore provides opportunity—"

"Leave my mother out of this." The hiss held darker menace than all his posturing.

"Fine with me," she said. "As a friend of Dorian, you probably visited him and gained access to his medication."

A shot in twilight. His face said she'd missed the mark. To judge by his earlier reaction, Mrs. Elliot's pharmacy connection was the source. The problem was she couldn't prove her hunches. If she ever got out of here.

"Just to entertain me, finish this off. Anyone with brains will agree I lack motive. Why would I steal a student's literary outpourings? Drivel, not worth the paper they're written on."

He yawned and pushed back his hair to expose the eminent forehead. A studied gesture, she recognized now. It triggered her combative academic spirit. Neither narcissists nor academics can ever resist showcasing their intellect and ingenuity, she thought, realizing the irony of the moment.

"Hah, now you're tripping yourself, my dear Timothy." The enraged gleam in his eyes cautioned her not to mock a killer.

She reigned in her temper and continued in sober tones, "Substitute Elliot for Nessbit in your rendition of *The Betrayal*, and there's your motive. You alienated Cass from Dorian and seduced her. If Herb reads the story, or if Dorian had publicized it, your chances of a permanent job here would be nil. Probably won't even get sessional work afterward. You'll be done for once the story comes out. Cass is a danger to you, so you tried to eliminate her."

Elliot's raucous laughter drowned her last words. In the narrow confines of the stairwell, its echo multiplied. A chill crawled along Agnes's arms into her neck and face.

Still sputtering, he taunted her. "Get real. No one would kill for bloody teaching contracts."

"People have killed for less. A trite cliché but true. The police will gather enough evidence once Cass comes out of the coma."

A spasm contorted his body. Not pain or fear. Uncontrollable guffawing. She watched in consternation.

When the sound subsided, he wiped his mouth with his upper sleeve. The calmness of his voice shocked her after the insane merriment. "A nice theory, dear Agnes. What you don't appreciate, it's doomed to remain pure speculation. We'll never know what killed my friend Dorian. Nor by whose hand he died."

"Oh, yes, we will. After police talk to Cassandra, they'll apply for an autopsy."

"I hate to break it to you. They cremated Dorian Gable today."

Chapter 33

Jac's heart pounded when she reached the main entrance to the humanities building. The jog wasn't the reason. To calm down, she paced back and forth in the darkness of the landscaped forecourt.

Upon entering the foyer a few minutes later, an elderly guard greeted her. He stood, hands behind his back, in front of the security office's service window.

"Good evening, miss. We close at eleven." He pointed to the dial-faced clock high on the wall behind him. "In about twenty minutes."

"Yes, I know. Just. A quick trip up to my office. Forgot something."

He nodded in fatherly understanding of the younger generations' frail memory capacity.

"Everyone else gone?" she asked.

The senior guard chuckled. "Our officers are rounding up the stragglers. A job for the youngsters." One hand reached forward to pat his sizable stomach. "A few professors and students are still on the loose."

Not exactly a criminal act to work late, she wanted to point out. Instead, she said, "I promise to hurry."

The gent waggled a playful finger as his ruddy cheeks wrinkled benignly.

She sprinted to the main staircase and, ensuring his back was turned, escaped through the rubber-padded swinging door down to the basement.

No one was about. The corridor down here smelled musty despite the overtones of institutional cleaning agents. Her trainers issued sticky squeaks as she hastened on to the part-timers' office.

The narrow, rectangular glass inset on its door revealed no overhead lights. The opening was a mere four by twelve inches, enough for taller people than Jac to see inside or out.

Bouncing up several times, she didn't glimpse anyone. Agnes's desk was not within her range of vision. Her friend might be working away there, divided from the door by several partitions, without a desk lamp casting a noticeable gleam.

Jacqueline's card gave no access to this office. She dug out her keyring and stretched to rap-tap a staccato on the window. The sharp noise startled her as it resounded in the empty hallway.

No reaction from inside.

Now what? Get security to check? They'd believe her officious for keeping tabs on a colleague. Agnes would hate it if she made a fuss for no good reason.

Unsure how to proceed, she decided to run up to her office as she'd claimed to intend. Armed with a file folder, her late-night campus visit would pass muster.

The backstairs were closer than returning to the main staircase at the center between classroom and office wings. Her feet opted to retrace their steps. The noir mystery vibe of the stark concrete and steel of the fire escape deterred her by day. Far too creepy at this hour. Veritably spine-tingling.

A marginal difference, she scoffed at her fanciful imagination. Windowless, the stairwell was immune to the passage of time.

Chapter 34

Agnes gaped at Timothy's grinning visage.

"Who told you that? I don't believe it!"

He laughed at her. "Puts a damper on things, doesn't it? Emma called me. Another of my conquests. Didn't want to leave for Florida without thanking me."

Nausea rose from her stomach. The horror of Dorian's mom thanking his murderer!

"You monster. How could you—"

"Easy. I encouraged them to opt for cremation. The mother hen agonized over leaving her baby behind. So, I said, why not take him along to Florida? Phrased piously, of course. Told her the genius confided his terror of waking up in a coffin buried alive. He believed in indigenous burial traditions. The parents were impressed." He smirked, self-satisfied.

"You lied to them." As if that mattered after his horrific crime.

"Oh, you mean about indigenous practices? Some traditions opt for funeral pyres."

"About Dorian." Her shout ricocheted. Maybe someone heard her, she hoped.

Hatred of this man threatened to choke her. Evil. Pure evil.

Cassandra's tortured face flashed into consciousness. Cass recognized the evil in this ogre.

How could she, trained in philosophy and critical thinking, have missed the signs?

"Agnes, Agnes," Elliot tut-tutted. With studied deliberation, he came a step closer. "What shall I do with you? Such an inflated sense of self-importance. Philosopher you call yourself? The immortal Nietzsche would be ashamed of you."

His scorn no longer touched her. Despair engulfed her in waves. If Dorian's remains were indeed cremated, this killer would evade justice. Her mind revolted at the thought.

A gleam of hope flickered. "Cass will tell police—"

Derisive laughter cut in. Not aware she'd spoken aloud, Agnes sucked her lower lip between her teeth. Too late.

"Oh no, she won't. I'll make sure of that."

Sweat dripped into Agnes's eyes, stinging, blurring her vision. Now, she'd endangered Cassandra's life.—No. He stood no chance to get in.

Not relinquishing the railing she still clutched with her benumbed right hand, her left reached to swipe droplets off her brow.

Her tormenter noticed her relief. "Reckon Cass will survive long enough to blabber? Think again," he taunted her.

"No one's allowed to see Cass. Only next of kin."

"Watch me," he mocked. "Ah, sorry. Afraid I've got to take care of you first."

He's enjoying himself, Agnes's mind shrieked as he made a playful lunge at her.

When she flinched, he crowed. "Scared witless, aren't you? For all your fancy degrees and high morals, you lack the virtue of bravery. No backbone."

He leaned against the banister. The eyes dissecting her face craved his victim's reaction. "They'll let me in alright. I'll play uncle come home from abroad, bushy beard and all. Nurses are gullible and starved for attention like all you women."

"You won't get away with it. I'll make sure—"

An insane cackle shook his tall frame. "Stupid cow. Still don't get it? This is the end of you. They'll find you tomorrow. A sad accident." His voice rose an octave in mimicry. "Too bad she tripped over her own feet. No worries. We'll mourn you."

Tears of merriment coursed over his cheeks. "The workplace safety crowd will insist on brand new signs. 'Watch your step.'"

By now frantic, Agnes tried to figure a way to escape even while he spoke.

Bolt down the stairs? An easy target for a swift shove or kick from his square-toed boots.

Attack him? No chance in hell.

Her eyes latched onto the inner stair column's vertical poles the railing attached to. Reach between the balusters below the handrail to hug a pole tightly with arms hooked around it, she figured in desperation. Would take force to pry her loose. No faking an accident—Her mind stalled.

Her body swung to the right, left hand grabbing the pole while the right hand released its grip to slither her arm around the cold steel. Her narrow feet followed in swift motion through the gaps below the railing.

As she clung tight, a flashback to her high school gym days flickered behind her tightly closed lids. She'd hated pole climbing with a passion.

Above her, Elliot swore obscenities. She craned her neck to await his jeering approach. "Playing monkey now, are we?"

Agnes clenched jaw and fingers as he loomed close.

"The ape act won't help you. Down you go."

Chapter 35

On her way up the well-lit central stairs, Jac didn't meet a soul. Along the office corridor, illuminated only by emergency lights, all doors were shut. In the silence, she distinguished the faint hum of the overhead ventilation system. Despite the dimness, here she felt at home.

Maybe Agnes went to the admin office before going home. The chance of happening upon her friend there was infinitesimal, Jac assumed. Still, she might as well pick up her own mail. After a day away from campus, memos and interdepartmental stuff mounted. A pile of mail under her arm ought to validate her late visit.

The glass door to the admin area showed no bright lights. She swiped her access card when faint voices reached her ears. A glance back over her shoulder detected no movement along the deserted hallway.

Probably her imagination.

She pushed the office door. Nothing happened. Relocked after her hesitation.

Just as she swiped again and waited for the release click, muffled laughter made her stop dead.

She glanced towards the fire escape door a few steps away. The ventilation system might carry noise from there.

Security rounding up night owls? Nothing wrong with asking them quite casually whether they'd seen Agnes. The admin office could wait.

Jac pocketed her card and made for the steel door to the backstairs.

Chapter 36

Agnes yelped. Excruciating pain seared her insides. Her attacker's fingers dug mercilessly into the soft tissue below her ribs. A knee kicked against her spine. Breathless, she went limp.

Like a ragdoll, he hauled her up from her monkey crouch, her arms smarting as they scraped against the balusters.

"Told you—down you go." His breath grew ragged as he heaved her upright.

"No, she won't!" A squeaky shout reverberated.

For a split second, Agnes sensed her aggressor's grip loosening. Her shoes scrabbled to gain a foothold.

Pounding feet from below.

"Stop!"

"Let her go!"

Blood roared in Agnes's ears, making her doubt the reality of the high-pitched shout followed by a deep bass. Her arms pinned to her body, pressing the air out of her lungs, Agnes lost any strength to fight. Conscious of the sour sweat smell and blackness of the killer's shirt, she jerked her head back.

A violent shove launched her. Her mind froze.

A dull thud. The pain on impact never came.

Instead, she felt herself cradled by brawny arms.

A low boom in her ears. "You okay, Agnes?"

The puff of released breath might have been her own.

"Man, we almost blew it. Sorry. Waited too long."

Gentle arms lowered her to her feet without letting go.

"You tried to kill her!" The familiar tenor voice—Joel's unmistakably.

Awareness returned like a brutal awakening. Wedged between Kalen, who had her back, and Joel two steps above guarding her front with—Lester!

Higher, in retreat on the narrow landing, her attacker, now babbling and laughing insanely, "Just a joke, guys. No harm meant. I swear—"

"Your game is up. I recorded every word." The tenor voice vibrated.

Not sure if she wanted to laugh hysterically or cry, Agnes felt like planting a smacking kiss on brave Joel's head.

"Yeah, Chuck. We heard it all," hollered Kalen over her head. "Can't weasel out of this one. Man, you're some disappointment. We trusted you."

"I never did," Agnes heard Lester say. "Bloody fake."

Suppressed anger underscored the contempt in Lester's voice.

Like a rugby player ready to charge, his bony frame curved.

"No!" Agnes yelled. "Lester–Don't!"

She tried to wrench herself free, arms stretched out to grab the kid as he propelled upward.

"Nah, Kafka's okay. Jiu-jitsu black belter."

Kalen's off-hand tone didn't calm Agnes.

Frozen in terror, she watched Elliot, his hand clutching the door handle, swing around to face his assailant.

With an oath, he pivoted again to yank at the steel door. It flew open violently, throwing him off balance.

Elliot pitched backward and lost his grip.

Agnes gasped as the momentum forced him over the edge of the top step.

Kalen whipped her against the railing away from the path of the body crashing down the stairs.

A scream pierced her ears.

The metal steps shuddered on impact.

Then silence.

"Oh, my God!" An agonized scream from above. "I've killed him!"

Agnes tore her eyes from the still form below to seek the speaker.

Up on the landing stood Jac, hands clasped over her mouth. Stunned.

Chapter 37

Jac's stomach heaved. Her fingers painfully digging into her lips, she couldn't retract the outcry. Nor did the pain caused by her nails distract from the afterimage of a face distorted by hatred. She quaked and forced her lids to open wide, dislodging the vision.

The scene in front of her made no sense. Everyone stared at her. There was Joel at the railing, his arm hanging onto Lester, just rising from a crouch. Their expressions frozen, unreadable, as if caught in a still life.

Below stood Kalen holding Agnes, who made no move to free herself.

Nothing made sense.

Her eyes strained to what she tried to avoid. An immobile figure. Like funeral clothes stretched to dry, spread across the landing where the stairs turned at a sharp left angle out of sight.

"Is he dead?" She coughed to mask the shakiness. "I didn't mean to—"

"It wasn't you, Jac," said Kalen. His voice carried conviction. "Tripped. Didn't watch where he stepped. We saw him tumble, didn't we?"

No one responded.

As if awakening from paralysis, Agnes removed Kalen's arms with gentle care, it seemed to Jac. Her friend's voice sounded foreign, like drained by spent emotions. "Thanks, Kalen. I owe you. And Lester and Joel, too." The timbre belied the simplicity of the words. Agnes turned to point at the still figure below. "Now, we'd better look after *him*."

Torn by numbing fear of finding him dead, a need to understand what happened here, and the hope of helping the man who lay prone on the metal grid, Jacqueline rushed after the others. A human life took precedence.

"You guys got CPR training," Kalen said. "See what you can do."

Amazed but relieved, Jac realized he meant Lester and Joel, not faculty. First aid was not among her skills.

The two students approached Timothy without flinching and hunkered down to check cautiously for vital signs.

"Is he…" The sentence formed in Jac's mind but trembled on her lips. In her heart, she felt certain. She had pushed the safety bar of the heavy steel door with both hands in a rush to speak to the guards. Her mistake. The door flew open. Timothy recognized her before he went over the edge. She felt sure. Why else the hateful grimace?

Agnes's voice summoned her to reality. "We must call an ambulance. Security, first."

Crouched on his haunches a step above the landing, Kalen watched his peers. "What do you say, man? Is he gonna make it?"

The words struck Jac as callous. She glanced at her friend, expecting her to protest. To rush to Timothy's side. Agnes appeared preoccupied, hands rubbing her sides as if cold or in stitches as from an unaccustomed sprint. But Agnes never jogged.

Bewildered, Jacqueline turned to Lester, who spoke now, not lifting his glance, "Breathing's shallow. Weak heartbeat. We can't move him. See the angle of the neck? A goner, I'd say."

Jac gasped at the cruelty of the verdict and appealed to Agnes who didn't even flinch.

Joel pushed up his granny glasses. They slid to the tip of his nose when he nodded along with his peer's assessment.

"Right," said Agnes. "We'll phone for help." She pulled her mobile from her pants pocket. "Dead."

"I'll call," offered Jac. Time to pull herself together, she, who aimed at leadership, a useless bystander to their lackadaisical emergency response. Besides, she must talk to Agnes away from prying ears.

"Come upstairs with me, Agnes. The signal is stronger in the hallway."

"Won't be a minute," her friend told the students.

By unspoken consent, they kept silent until the heavy steel door shut behind them with a metallic clunk. A glance down the corridor confirmed no one was about.

"Agnes, speak to me! What happened here? Timothy. The poor man. I should have thought— Why were you two with the students? What did you say to them?"

"Stop this barrage of questions. Better you don't know. You saw nothing." Agnes's hand shot up. "No. Don't interrupt. Trust me—for now, you play dumb. I'll fill you in at home."

"Agnes, I refuse—"

"If you love me as a loyal friend as I love you, Jac, you must trust me with this. I swear I'll come clean later. There's no time —call them. Please."

The pleading yet stubborn expression meant no room for negotiations, Jac knew only too well.

"Tell security there's been an accident. Someone tripped on the stairs and is badly hurt. Oh, say to come in this way so as not to hamper the paramedics. Closest for them to enter from the loading dock."

Amazed how Agnes's logical mind worked out strategics while the man she'd seemed to care for lay unconscious below,

Jac shook her head and touched the key on her mobile programmed for campus security.

A few minutes later, they joined the waiting students.

Kalen, squat in a Bowman College sweatshirt, reclined against the outer wall, legs stretched out. Baseball cap visor sideways covering his ear, he contemplated the railing at his leisure. A step above crouched Joel, skinny arms hugging lean legs, chin resting on the knees of his grubby jeans.

Below, hunched black-garbed Lester, his back to them.

Was he gloating over the body? Irritated, Jac pushed away the uncharitable thought. No matter how sinister he struck her, he probably monitored the injured man.

"Security will arrive shortly," Agnes said.

"What's our story, then?" asked Kalen, his guttural voice so quiet Jac strained to hear him. "Like, I saw Chuck step back without looking when he heard the door release. Lost balance and plunged backward. You guys saw it too, didn't you?"

Lester nodded but remained focused on Timothy's immobile body.

Joel straightened, pushed back his glasses to seek Agnes's attention. "My own observations confirm this, Dr. Taylor."

Perplexed yet unable to pinpoint the undercurrent, nor willing to reveal her ignorance and ask the students for answers, Jacqueline strove to read her friend's face marked by exhaustion.

Agnes slumped on the step beside Joel as though her legs refused service. "A purely theoretical question for you guys. Do you think Dorian's parents would be better off knowing or not knowing?"

Jacqueline shuddered in confusion. Why talk about the Gables now? Indignation displaced empathy with Agnes's anxiety for the life of a new friend. Were the students in Agnes's confidence? They shouldn't discuss— She cleared her throat to draw attention.

In a low voice more captivating than his usual boom, Kalen intercepted her remonstration.

"If I were Dorie," he said, "last thing I'd want is my mom hurting all over again. You saw them. They suffered so much. No way I'd want the media dragged in—and the courts." He pointed at Timothy's prone figure. "It'll kill Dorie's mom."

Joel's head kept nodding assent to every word.

This time, Lester turned, his intense gaze directed at Agnes. He uttered one word, "Ditto."

"I think you're right," Agnes said with perplexing emphasis.

What was going on here?

The sound of the fire door above compounded Jacqueline's bafflement. How could she assume leadership in dealing with security when at a loss to comprehend the situation?

Her friend rose and pulled her into a quick hug, murmuring, "You know nothing."

With unexpected agility, Kalen jumped up and muttered under his breath, "Let me do this." He squeezed past them.

Two security guards paused on the landing to survey the scene.

The female, about a foot shorter than the towering male guard, issued a brief command, prompting her colleague to flick a switch next to the door frame. Glaring white light made everyone blink. The guards' uniforms and the male's turban appeared almost black from where Jac stood.

She moved to join them. The woman barked, "Stay," as if they were a pack of dogs.

Wordlessly, the female guard approached. Her determined gait brooked no resistance. They hastened to get out of her way as she descended to the injured man.

The male remained a few steps above, addressing them curtly, "What occurred here? Who reported the incident?"

Jacqueline pushed her shoulders back, curving her spine inward. "I did."

In a swift movement, Kalen loomed next to her, his broad six-foot frame making her feel diminutive.

"I saw the accident happen, officer." The bass filled the tight space. "Me and my friends were just coming up around the bend here when Dr. Taylor," he indicated Agnes respectfully, "passed Chuck on her way down. Chuck headed upstairs." Kalen pointed to the inert figure. "That's him there."

"The injured man is Timothy Charles Elliot, one of our sessional instructors in the Humanities department," Jacqueline felt duty-bound to clarify. The student's account struck her as wordy. Why the tedious details?

The guard, however, scrutinized Agnes when Kalen rushed on, "I stopped Prof. Taylor to ask about my presentation for next week. Chuck went on up, didn't he?" His massive head arced to seek his peers' confirmation.

Joel's squeaky voice did as bidden. "Yes. Mr. Elliot was in a great hurry, I noticed."

Behind the curtain of Agnes's dark hair flickered a tiny smile, it seemed to Jac.

Lester, hunched by the wall, nodded assent as Joel spoke.

Her attention reverted to Kalen, now facing the officer again. "Next thing, the door opened just when Chuck reached the landing. Without looking, he took a step back and tripped. We couldn't do a thing. He came tumbling down. I pulled Dr. Taylor back, or she would've crashed, too." Again, he sought affirmation.

"Exactly. My own observations confirm Kalen's statement, officer." The student's index finger pushing the slippery glasses into place. An optician should adjust them, Jacqueline thought irrelevantly. Close up, she perceived the twitching eyelid. "Lester and I were unable to intervene. Before we heard the click of the door, we'd been listening to Dr. Taylor behind us. She is our professor too."

"Can you confirm the students' statements?" the guard asked Jac.

Lester swung around. His fringe lifted by the momentum long enough for his stare to pierce Jac. Fear gripped her. Was a trick of light causing the glint in the charcoal pupils?

"Professor Xavier came in *after* Mr. Elliot went over the edge. She saw nothing of the accident."

A wave of relief and gratitude flooded Jacqueline. The exoneration from guilt despite his dislike for her counted immeasurably. The young man's enunciation struck her as cultured and mature, restoring her own confidence to contribute meaningfully.

"It was a profound shock to find Mr. Elliot badly injured and unconscious. These young men—Lester and Joel—are skilled in first aid and CPR. They proceeded to check carefully for vital signs, as far as possible under the circumstances. We alarmed security, as you know."

The male guard's attention swayed to his colleague. Their glances followed his. The second officer stood up and shook her head but remained in place.

The questioner turned to Agnes, saying, "And you, ma'am?"

Chapter 38

The security guy's question knifed Agnes's overstrained nerves. She swallowed. Or tried to, her palate dry like cracked leather. "The shock ... Give me a minute." Her mind raced. To gain time, she leaned against the wall and closed her eyes.

Doubts tormented relentlessly. Lies will out. No, theirs were not lies of commission but of omission. Not active lies but withholding information. A lot. Ends did not justify means—her default belief. Now she'd incited her students to...

Seek oblivion in a hot bath at home, soak the aching back. Bruised flanks and scraped palms—

"Ma'am, can we hear your account?" Security was losing patience.

Loyal Kalen shifted his body to insinuate a barrier. Lester and Joel sidled right and left of her. A questioning glance from Jac. Say something, her own mind prompted too. Don't contradict.

"The students were in a better position to give an accurate account. I can vouch for them."

Loud clanging echoed through the stairwell.

"The paramedics are here," she said as if others couldn't infer what the hurried foot treads meant.

The collective attention shifted to what lay below. TC, a mere body awaiting removal. They'd now styled the killer a victim. An accident victim was innocent. To be pitied, not blamed.

Lester pronounced him a goner. What if he survived?

"Everyone out of the way." The bellow from below set them in motion, herded by the guy who'd questioned them.

They didn't get far. More uniforms entered above.

The police.

Another female-male pair. This one matched in size. Their uniforms toned with the midnight blue of security. The constables—or whatever their rank—wore hats with shiny bills crowned by emblems.

Smooth roleplay too. The woman cop strode, blond ponytail bobbing below the hat, to meet the ambulance crew. Unlike her security counterpart, she said, 'excuse me' and 'thanks,' as they scurried to let her pass. Polite or assured of her authority, Agnes figured.

Their group's attention followed her to watch the paramedics ready TC for transport.

The sight of the fallen would-be friend tugged at her heart. Regret for might-have-beens if TC hadn't lost his moral footing —long ago.

Cruel and callous words returned to shatter the illusion. Timothy Elliot never regretted the horrific things he'd done and intended to do. A merciless killer.

For a moment, she sensed Jac's closeness. Poor Jac must feel sick with worry and no clue how they slid into this.

They bumped arms in a tiny gesture of reassurance.

"I need to take your statements."

Each pivoted to face the other cop. Like naughty kids caught ogling the forbidden, thought Agnes.

"Where can I take them?" he asked the security guy.

"Our admin office is closest," said Agnes automatically. "Dr. Xavier and I have access to it." Of course, so had security. "Lots of room for all of us," she added in haste. On their home turf, Jac would feel securer. And she herself gained a few moments respite.

The cop took his campus colleague's shrug as agreement and instructed him, "Stay right here and let no one in. Send anyone coming from the upper floor straight back. Tell your partner to do the same down the next level."

To Agnes, he said, "Please show the way."

"Kant's tossing in his grave," murmured Lester as he helped her wheel desk chairs to join the two-seater sofa in the reception area. Agnes spun to regard him. Had he read her mind about the lying conundrum? The grin was genuine.

"He'd condemn us without a hearing, he would," she muttered. The German philosopher of moral absolutes drew no distinctions. Lying was wrong, no if ands or buts.

"I'm Constable Pozo. Let's get your names and addresses," said the cop when all were seated. Without his hat, he looked younger, mid-twenties at the most. Tight black curls framed an almond-toned face naturally more inclined to joyous laughter, Agnes suspected, its somber expression ready to dissolve any minute.

His presence reassured rather than alarmed. If she stayed focused on the now, the haunting images might recede. The scream never would.

"Would it suit you if we would use a notepad to provide addresses and phone numbers, officer?" asked Jac, poised and sophisticated in sweats and trainers, her professional persona taking over. "We strive to uphold confidentiality at the college."

"Fine with me, ma'am," he acquiesced. "May I put you in charge of it?"

Jac wordlessly obliged and filched a sticky pad, plus exam pencil stubs from Fraser's desk.

"Let's hear what happened back there. Lady faculty first, *eh*?" The officer's musical diction contrasted pleasantly with the security lot's sharpness. With an appreciative smile, Agnes shook her head to the cocked eyebrow he aimed at her.

When Kalen leaned forward, the chair creaked in protest. "Officer, if it's okay with you, I'll start. My calling as a writer trains me to be hyper-observant."

"Sure. Mind if I record you? It's fast and accurate." Constable Pozo waved his iPhone at them.

"Be my guest," said Kalen.

Pozo recorded time, location, and persons present. "Ready? Tell it in your own words. Minus the poetic license. In short, just the facts, man." The contagious smile transformed his features and eased their tension.

Kalen's reiterated account stayed true to the earlier version without repeating verbatim. It sounded unrehearsed.

Burly Kalen never ceased to amaze her. The chameleon ability to adapt tone and diction to his audience and purpose, convincingly portraying 'the life or the party dude' just as convincing as the 'respectful junior' boded well for his novelist career. Yet, coming to her aid tonight showed the authentic Kalen, she'd wager.

Asked by Pozo, he described his view of their various positions on the stairs. He and his friends faced the upper landing. While in conversation with Kalen, Agnes had her back turned toward TC, he asserted. In echo to Lester, he insisted Dr. Xavier entered after the fall.

Unsure how she felt about this rendition of events, she let her mane curtain treacherous cheeks and pondered her knees. An untimely blush might alert the constable.

As Kalen's recital ceased, she glanced up. Pozo appeared bemused, overwhelmed perhaps by the profundity of detail.

"Officer, can I have my turn now?" Joel bounced in his seat. "I'm a trained observer. I mean," a shy look at Agnes, light sparkling off the round lenses, "I'm studying to be a private investigator." The mentioning of his career goal buoyed him. As if the raised chin pulled his strings, the posture straightened.

A corner of the constable's lips twitched. "Future colleague. Glad to hear it." No trace of amusement colored the words. "Please proceed."

Under the weight of responsibility, Joel buckled. Glasses precariously teetering on the tip of his nose, a pulse ticked on the side of his slender neck. Everyone held their breath in empathy.

"Private investigators are lucky." The soft purr soothed not only Joel. "You'll be your own boss. First time I reported to my sergeant, I tell you, I was shaking in my regulation boots. Was alright after I got lots of practice."

The kind words triggered recollection. Joel the Spy proffering evidence of cheating. A video. 'Your game's up... recorded every word.'

Agnes's ears roared. Interior and exterior images fused. He's going to blurt it out—chased by a fatalistic, he's got the right to tell the truth.

Shoulders slumped; she bowed her head to let the world crash over it.

The tenor timbre launched into a repetition of the earlier statement. With each sentence, it grew in confidence and Agnes in calm. Not a word betrayed their omissions.

"Is it okay if I add my deductions, officer?" he inquired after the report wound to its end.

The constable's pencil, used to scribble occasional notes on a pad, tapped against even, white teeth. Agnes suspected the note-taking was a courteous sign of gravitas rather than a necessity.

"Strictly speaking, a statement must stick to facts," he said.

Joel's features pinched. The mouth puckered.

"Now, it's different when I ask you—between colleagues, you know—what's your opinion, Joel?"

The eyes behind the thick lenses sparkled. "Based on the

observed facts, I deduce—I mean, I opine Mr. Elliot's square-toed boots, plus his large feet, caused the fall."

Puzzled frowns all around met this revelation.

"*Eh?*" said Pozo. "Come again?"

"It's quite simple." The treble voice rose a notch in triumph. "Kalen and I stated Mr. Elliot stepped backward. The left foot tried to shift his weight to the lower stair tread. His feet being large—I estimate size 13, the length increased by the narrow, square toe cap—his heel was suspended over the edge. The momentum threw him off balance. Down he went."

Agnes gaped. He'd convinced her, at any rate. An accurate description, she imagined, of such a fall. Joel's last phrase sent a chill over her aching back. Might've been you, her mind said.

Pozo, who'd listened closely, remarked, "Off the record, you do your professors proud. Smart observation."

The witness beamed.

Kalen leaned over to slap his friend's knee. "He's a smart cookie," he told Pozo.

Asked to contribute his account, Lester confirmed the facts already stated, minus Joel's inferences. Instead, he praised the shorter guy for saving him. "He lunged to push me off to the side. Not as puny as he looks. No offense, Joel."

The mischievous grin from under the wayward, dark hair was catching.

A smile curving his generous mouth, the cop turned to Agnes. "You're next. Let me ask, first, do you know the victim well?"

Agnes dropped the dead phone she'd been holding on to.

While she bent to retrieve it, she heard Jac say, "Dr. Taylor just recently joined our department. Timothy Elliot taught here on a term-by-term basis for several years."

"Thanks, ma'am," Pozo said. "I was thinking of next of kin to be notified."

Oh, no. Poor Mrs. Elliot, Agnes thought. Someone must tell her.

"We don't have information about his private life," said Jac with finality.

Agnes took her cue. "We've talked occasionally as one does among faculty," she said. "Not to the extent of sharing about family, Constable Pozo." Quite true as far as it goes. "About the accident, the students were in a much better position to observe. I only remember clutching the stair pole when Kalen pulled me off to the side."

She glanced at the ceiling to avoid the constable's gaze. "From a logical point of view, Joel's inference strikes me as sound."

Since Jacqueline's sparse statement shed no new light on events, Pozo seemed anxious to leave. "We might be in touch if questions arise."

As Jac walked the cop to the door, Agnes nudged Kalen beside her. "Stay behind. There's something I need you guys for," she whispered and got up.

When the constable's broad back disappeared out of sight, she said aloud, "What we need is coffee. The shock got us frazzled. Jac, give me a hand, will you?"

"Security wants us out of here," said Jac. "The campus closed a while ago."

"No worries, they're still busy."

Not waiting for a reply, Agnes left Jac to follow her to the makeshift kitchenette. She rummaged through the cabinet above the Keurig, unearthed two mugs and a couple of paper cups, and plunked pods into the machine.

"Agnes, really. Is this necessary now? I don't want coffee."

"You won't get any," said Agnes while she filled the canister at the water cooler. "Coffee's for me and the guys. I need to have a word with them after you leave. We don't want more rumors, do we? Besides, there's something I must take care of."

"It's late. Do it tomorrow. Walk home with me now."

"No. You've got to hurry back and call Martha. You don't want her to find out on Monday—from the police or someone."

"Oh my God, I didn't think," cried Jac. "What's wrong with me? I—"

Agnes shushed her.

"Help me carry the mugs and then run."

Shortly after, she and her helpers were alone.

"I don't like coffee," said Joel in a small voice.

"Consider it a prop for camouflage," said Agnes. "I've got another mission for you guys."

Chapter 39

Out of breath after the fast jog home, Jacqueline gulped water from the kitchen tap. She refilled a glass twice. The fright on campus, more than the short run, left her dehydrated.

Silent and deserted like the Marie Celeste, the house seemed. Paul and Moshi seldom returned before the wee hours on Friday nights.

No one to disturb her difficult conversation with the AD. Phone already in hand, she opted for a trip to the bathroom before the ordeal.

Minutes later, she balanced on the edge of the desk chair in her study, psyching herself up to punch the numbers. A chronic bedtime procrastinator, Martha wouldn't be asleep for quite a while.

At least, after the questioning by security and the police, she could share how the accident occurred, Jac thought. Just the straight facts, not her mistaken impressions.

How small-minded to assume the worst upon seeing Agnes in Kalen's arms. She blushed at the memory.

A minor consideration compared to Timothy's tragic accident. Guilt for disliking him pricked her conscience.

His poor family. Someone must contact them. Admin required emergency contacts. The AD had access.

Here, she dawdled, postponing the inevitable when she might have called from her office. No, the residue of her Catholic upbringing still tethered her to rule compliance. The campus shut down at eleven; her sense of duty had urged obedience. She sighed, exasperated.

"*Allez-y*," she exhorted herself, "get on with it and stop stalling." Another gulp of water.

Her fingers tapped in the numbers from memory. Five buzz tones later, when she readied to disconnect and text instead, a sleepy voice answered, "Yes?"

"So sorry. Did I wake you, Martha? It's Jacqueline."

"No, no, I just nodded over my nightcap."

"I hate to disturb you at this hour, but I'm afraid it can't wait. There's been an accident."

She heard the AD's sharp intake of breath.

"Jacqueline, are you playing messenger to my Job? Am I to dread your calls?"

For a second, Jac's mind groped for the meaning. Then it clicked. The benefit of a religious past. Job received one devastating message after another.

"Don't shoot the messenger," she murmured and rushed to recapitulate the students' account of Timothy Elliot's accident.

Silence greeted the end of her recital.

A resigned exhale from Martha. "Bad things come in threes. Heaven forbid more misfortunes."

Chapter 40

Halfway along the corridor, Kalen by her side, Agnes glanced over her shoulder.

At the far end, past the admin office, stood Lester and Joel, paper cups in hand, blocking the fire exit.

When she'd explained their task of ghoulish loitering at the door, one of them waylaying security or police with questions while the other was to alert Kalen via SMS, Joel's face crumbled.

Theirs was a brain job requiring quick wit, she'd assured him. Hers and Kalen's amounted to mere grunt work. No time for details now; she'd debrief them after mission accomplished.

At this rate, she'd told herself, she'd soon be applying to become the spy's sidekick.

Lester's mouth had barely twitched over the solemn assurance, "You can count on us." What a guy.

Now, she signaled thumbs up with her free hand. The other cradled a full coffee mug. Her buddy carried the second.

They'd reached their destination.

Agnes took a steadying breath.

"Let's get it over with," she whispered. Only half briefed, Kalen followed unquestioningly.

One last glance in both directions.

With trepidation, she twisted the doorknob. It didn't resist.

Caught in a time loop akin to *Groundhog Day*, she once more inched open the door marked 'Nessbit' to be hit with the familiar reek.

"Herb, are you there?"

Stupid question.

Slumped forward over the surface of the desk, he showed no sign of life.

Sweat broke out on her forehead and trickled onto the lids. She thrust a slopping mug into Kalen's hand, adding coffee smell to the stifling air. Heating's cranked up, her mind diagnosed. Swiping her wet fingers on her pants, she neared the desk to check for a pulse as TC had done.

An explosive snort shook the head just as her fingertips touched the clammy neck. Her hand flew up. She jumped back like a startled thief.

Behind her, Kalen snuffled in ill-suppressed laughter. She turned to shush him and almost knocked the mug out of his left.

"Don't spill—"

A phlegmy rasp interrupted her.

"N' offis'our t'day," slurred Herb.

The blotched skin of his right cheek bore the wrinkled impression of tweed punctuated by three buttons.

Agnes motioned her ally to deposit the mugs.

"Glad you're back among the living, Herb," she said. "You'll down a lot of coffee now, and then home you'll go. No more midnight labor for you."

An unsteady hand fumbled for the liquor bottle. The drunken voice needed three attempts to enunciate, "Cur … curt … courtesy of Tim …Timothy."

Ah, I see, thought Agnes. "Oh no, you don't," she said and removed the bottle gently from his grasp.

To her immense relief, he didn't fight her.

"Here, let me play nursemaid. You've taken a chill working

late," she said, observing his shaking hand sloshing coffee when she handed him the first mug.

Tactfully, Kalen browsed among the books on the shelf while she steadied Herb's hand. The boozer appeared to enjoy her ministrations and sipped obediently like a toddler from a beaker.

The second mug he managed to cradle with both hands.

One eye on him, she told Kalen, "We'll call a cab once we get him outside."

"No need. My motor's in the student lot."

"Perfect. Time's up, Herb."

"Gotta pee," said the patient.

"Let's get out of here. Kalen, check the coast is clear."

When her helper beckoned from the door, she lent Herbert her arm, guiding his lurching step safely out of his cubbyhole.

The rearguard still stood sentinel. Joel gave a discreet thumbs-up, echoed by Kalen.

Once they reached the men's loo, she said, "Kalen's going to wait here with you. Forgot my phone and didn't lock your door, Herb. Back in a tick."

A few minutes later, they entered the elevator, Herb in the middle, supported on both sides by his escorts.

Agnes held herself very straight, hoping the elastic waistband of her undies sufficiently secured the wad of loose paper stuffed inside her clothes. Dangerous staple removed to avoid stabbing her tummy. She'd have to drag her feet or something to mask the faint crinkling sound when walking.

Over the squishing of the closing elevator panels, she said, "Once we're outside, you get your car. We'll wait in the passenger pickup zone off to the side. Got that?"

Her fellow passengers nodded in eager agreement.

"You'll get to bed in no time," she told her charge.

Bleary eyes met hers. "Home, James," Herb said and winked.

Chapter 41

Jacqueline wielded a fork, beating eggs in a glass bowl, just like her mother had taught her when she was a little girl. French toast drenched in maple syrup was the family's Saturday morning ritual for as long as she could remember. It took little persuasion to convert Agnes to the comforting tradition.

Last night, Jac woke in her armchair at two AM. A note from Agnes, taped to the door, said, 'Back safe and sound–talk tomorrow.'

Delicious espresso aroma wafted from the cafetiere on the stove. She placed bowls of vanilla-flavored low-fat ricotta, fresh berries, and a mixture of chopped nuts and seeds on the table, her health fad addition to her mother's cholesterol-rich recipe.

Jac reduced the heat under the milk pot and wiped her hands on the blue-white checkered dishcloth tied around her slim waist to protect the black leggings. Time to wake the sleeping beauty.

Back at the stove minutes later, she used a spatula to flip the golden toast.

A heavy tread on the stairs announced Agnes's arrival. Mobile held at waist level, she thumbed the screen furiously without looking up.

"And a good morning to you too," said Jacqueline when the typing ceased.

"Sorry. Hi." Agnes's nose twitched like a rabbit's, inhaling the scents. "Smells wonderful." Still eyeing her phone, she slid onto a chair. Its Barbie-pink padding released somewhat rude-sounding air.

"Thanks," she said when Jac placed café au lait in front of her.

The hope of a restorative meal receded as Jac went back for the platter heaped with sizzling French toast. "Any news about Timothy?" She watched Agnes's face closely for a reaction. None came.

"No. Here. Read. From Andrea." Agnes held out her phone. Jac sank onto a chair to peruse the SMS thread.

ANDREA
'Cass woke last night'

AGNES
'OMG! So happy to hear! Did you see her?'

ANDREA
'Not yet. Her aunt did. Arrived from EU.'

AGNES
'How's Cass? Did they say?'

ANDREA
'Not sure. More later.'

AGNES
'Yes, please. Keep me posted. Thanks!'

"Thank goodness. What a relief for the parents," said Jacqueline as she returned the device.

"Makes my day." Agnes wiped syrup from her upper lip and grinned. Then, she grew sober. "Let's hope there's no permanent damage."

Her fork spearing a small piece of toast, Jac sighed. "I just hope Timothy pulls through, too. We might get back to some sense of normality."

"I don't."

Unsure she heard correctly, Jac asked, "Pardon? What do you mean?"

"Just that." Agnes, uncharacteristically, stopped eating and laid down her fork. "Last night, I promised to come clean, remember?"

"Oh, but the students explained. I relayed it all to Martha. A severe shock for her, of course."

"Only the finale, not the brunt of it. Prepare yourself for a major shock." Agnes leaned over to cover Jacqueline's hand. "I'm sorry, Jac. There's no gentle way of telling you. TC is the killer."

A sudden lightheadedness made Jac clench the metal tubing of the chair. Her vision blurred. Mind benumbed, she vaguely sensed Agnes rushing to the fridge.

"Here, drink some cold water. You look deathly pale. Shouldn't spring things. Worse on an empty stomach. You hardly touched your food."

Nauseated, Jac pushed away her plate. The proffered glass, wet from condensation, almost slipped from her fingers. Agnes reached out to steady it until Jac was ready to manage on her own. The icy water hurt the sinuses at the root of her nose.

In slow sips, she drained the glass to Agnes's, "Much better. A bit of color's back in your cheeks."

As if fossilized, Jac's mind refused to absorb the earlier message. It took minutes for her to say through stiff lips, "Tell me. All of it."

"You sure now?" Agnes's hand stroked Jac's lying next to the empty glass. "Okay, here goes. TC was to help me coax a confession from Herb. When we found him passed out in his office, we retreated to TC's office. It's like a library. Some professor emerita loans it to him."

Mechanically, Jac said, "Grace Cavendish."

"Oh? You knew he uses it?"

"Everyone does. She was Elliot's mentor and reference to get him hired as a sessional."

"Well, I didn't. Anyway, I was furious we'd missed our chance with Herb. Come to think of it, TC scoffed a killer wouldn't confess to an amateur sleuth. The irony of fate." Tsk-tsking finished the sentence.

"Agnes, please. You make my head spin."

"Bear with me. My recall is not the greatest in the morning. TC and I hashed over what facts we got. In retrospect, I figure he plumbed me for what I might suspect. Things I mentioned raised his alarm bells, I guess."

"Oh, my God. If he's a killer, you could have been next."

"Well, yeah. He tried—"

"What? He attacked you?"

"Calm down, Jac. I'm sitting here at breakfast with you, am I not?" Agnes scooped up a handful of blueberries and used them to punctuate every word before popping them into her mouth one by one. "I believe my subconscious—or survival instinct—put me on alert."

"You never SOSed me." A senseless reproach, Jacqueline allowed. "The battery ran dry, didn't it? I found your charger next to your bed."

Agnes looked sheepish.

"When you didn't show up, I grew worried and jogged to campus."

"Ah, I wondered why you showed up. In the nick of time."

Jac's stomach cramped. Too much black coffee. Fear returned with a vengeance. She needed to have certainty.

Quietly, she asked, "Was it my fault he fell? The door flew out of my grasp when I pushed the crossbar. I leaned my full weight on it, I think."

"You heard the students. Quit your guilt trip, Jac. Anyhow, back to my story. Have some berries to sustain you."

"Agnes, you are trying my patience," said Jac, pushing the unwanted dish aside.

"Won't be any left if you wait too long."

The misplaced levity annoyed Jac into a stern, "Pray continue," which merely prompted her friend's laughter.

"Oh, Jac. Did you binge eighteenth-century novels again? Okay, okay. Call it a delayed reaction to a traumatic experience. It's exhilarating to be alive. I promise appropriate solemnity. When I insisted on getting Herb home, TC suggested I should wait by his car down at the loading dock while he went for Herb."

"Ah. I wondered why you were on the backstairs."

Agnes nodded. "The cunning rationale TC concocted. Not sure how it suddenly dawned on me. An epiphany as we entered the barren concrete confines. Like being trapped in an elevator shaft."

The imagery chilled Jac.

"Without meaning to, I said something like, 'It was you who killed Dorian.'"

"*Mon Dieu*," murmured Jac, appalled.

"Yeah, well. Your God must have looked out for me. Stupid to blurt it out, but effective in prompting a kind of confession. Your old priest in Quebec would give me kudos for confessional skills."

"Don't joke about it," said Jac, unsure if she meant the danger Agnes exposed herself to or the religious allusion.

"Sorry about the Catholic toe-stepping. Anyway, TC bragged how cunningly he eliminated Dorian. He meant to finish off Cass for good after taking care of me."

"Agnes, this is horrific." Jac felt her blood drain. Her cheeks felt icy when her hands flew up to clasp them.

"Should have seen me. Like a chimp, I hung on to one of those poles at the center of the staircase. The man had the gall to call me a monkey when he tore me away from my perch to chuck me down the stairs. Hey, a pun. Chuck chucked me."

"Agnes!"

"Jeez—Don't screech, Jac. You'll wake the guys. They need their beauty sleep."

"I think you're enjoying this. How can you be so flippant? Didn't you care for that man before? To find he is a killer, I'd be devastated."

"Believe me, Jac, if I'd let myself dwell on emotions and my trusting stupidity now, I'd be crushed. Unless I make light of it, I'll have nightmares."

Jacqueline reached across to stroke her friend's arm. "How did you manage to stop him?"

"Our incredible students did." A grateful smile lit up Agnes's features. "I'll never forget. There's TC yelling, 'Down you go,' when the repartee follows in the best opera style from the tenor, 'No, she won't.'"

"Joel?" Why she sounded so incredulous when she'd seen him right there, Jac couldn't say.

"Exactly," grinned Agnes. "Still, TC launched me like a rocket. Okay, more like a deflated beach ball. Kalen's rugby or football practice paid off. Caught me mid-air, it seemed. I landed unharmed in his muscular arms."

"I wondered why." Embarrassed about her suspicious mind, Jac didn't finish.

"You would, wouldn't you? Never mind. Elliot, the villain, fled up the stairs. Lester lunged for him but missed grabbing his leg. Then, enter Jac, the avenging angel. No, don't look like that. TC stepped backward on his own accord. The rest is history."

They regarded each other across the congealing mess on Jac's plate. She draped a napkin over it. The smell of stale

French toast turned her stomach. She'd have to resort to a different Saturday morning treat for a long time.

Pieces of last night's interchange resurfaced and clicked.

"Your question if Dorian's parents need to know. The students eavesdropped on you and Timothy, didn't they? You left them to decide whether to cover up for him."

"My concern is not the killer but those victimized. You heard Kalen. I agree with the three of them. Emma and Gordon suffered unbearably. Let them come to peace. The cremation brought them closure. It also ended the hope of bringing the murderer to justice."

"I realized the implication when Martha mentioned they opted for this form of burial." Her thought at the time had been entirely selfish, she admitted silently. She hadn't even told Agnes about Paris. Maybe later today. Or tomorrow. To mention her success now was in poor taste.

Instead, she said, "I understand what you meant earlier about Elliot surviving. A killer free to kill again."

The vibrations of Agnes's mobile knocked a tattoo on the Formica tabletop.

While Agnes checked messages, Jac stacked dishes yet covertly watched the fleeting expression of relief followed by worry pass over the other's face.

"Andrea?"

"Yes. They allowed her to visit Cass, accompanied by the aunt. Andrea brought in toiletries and nighties and whatnot. The thing is, Cass only remembers having a splitting migraine and twice taking a couple of capsules prescribed by her MD. She has no recollection of a note."

"Then you were mistaken about Timothy trying to kill her."

"No way. He admitted as much. The scrawled message on a mere slip of paper he might have found among Cass's study notes. Or, most likely, cut from something she wrote to him." Agnes stared into her cup as if to read non-existing tea leaves.

"Could have been the last line of a letter breaking off their affair. Who knows?" With a sigh, Agnes looked up again to add, "The question is, will Cass recollect more as time goes by? And will she talk?"

Defeated, Jac sank back onto the kitchen chair. Her fingers clutched the spongy padding.

"Will this nightmare never end?"

Epilogue

With deepest regret and sadness, we share the passing of our valued colleague, Timothy Charles Elliot. Our hearts reach out to his family and friends.

Timothy, affectionately known to colleagues and students as TC, passed away peacefully on Sunday …

So, he died yesterday.

R.I.P.?

Was it peaceful, Agnes thought, to slide from a coma into eternal oblivion? Maybe.

Made one wonder about divine retribution. Or another irony of fate. You reap what you sow? His second victim woke up. He didn't. Nor had his first victim survived.

His death meant safety for Cass. At least from his evil machinations.

A sobering reminder to Agnes of what had been in store for her on Friday night—if Elliot had succeeded. If her amazing students hadn't rushed to the rescue.

Speaking—or thinking—of which, she needed to rush to meet them for the promised debriefing session.

Agnes closed the email app, grabbed a jacket, and stuffed the phone into a pocket. Her backpack with the laptop for class waited on the kitchen table among breakfast debris. No time to clean up. She'd need to beat Jac going home tonight and remove all traces of sloth. First things first.

In true private eye fashion, Joel insisted on a private spot, yet open enough to observe potential eavesdroppers.

From afar, she saw the three hunkering on the bleachers, Lester two rows up, slightly off to the side. Off-season, the baseball diamond looked tired and unloved, balding turf and grit. The overcast sky didn't help. Perfect for an assassination with the curious trio.

The PI held forth, animated and earnest. Kalen played along. Like watching an imaginary game, ready to be sent into the fray, he sat shoulders hunched up to his ears, feet planted apart, fists gripping the bench's edge.

Behind them, Lester's bony fingers scrabbled at his knee, chin to his chest, the forward-falling hair shrouding his gaunt features. Yet, Agnes sensed him listening intently.

Joel spied her first. Of course he would. She smiled to herself and waved.

She settled with Lester, two or three feet apart, to give him space. The others turned to face them. When she praised and thanked them for saving her, they demurred, not quite hiding their pleasure.

"You received the obituary email?"

They nodded.

"Might sound callous," Kalen said. "Best outcome, I'd say. Leaves us off the hook. What a bummer if he'd pulled through."

Beside him, Joel's legs bounced as if the untied, bulky sneakers were electrified. The shoulders under the faded, oversized sweatshirt jiggled. Now, his hand shot up like in class.

"A murderer strikes again if no one stops him," he said. "We would have told the police, wouldn't we? Dr. Taylor?" Anxious for reassurance, he looked up to her.

"And they'd have done what?" muttered Lester. "No body— no proof."

They'd heard TC's taunt about cremation.

Which reminded her, "How come you three were on the backstairs so late at night? Doesn't security shoo students—Hey, no complaints from me," Agnes hastened to explain, "I'm forever grateful you thundered to the rescue like avenging angels."

"Ask Joel," said Kalen. "He talked me into trailing Chuck." Lightly elbowing his buddy, his imitation goon growl prompted, "Spill the beans, chum."

No encouragement needed. Granny glasses nudged into place, their arm held between thumb and index finger just in case, Joel's chin pointed at Agnes as he reported from below.

"I had Mr. Elliot under observation for quite a while."

"You suspected him?" Agnes interrupted, astounded at his acuity.

"Not as perpetrator." Joel's free hand pulled at his lips as if ashamed. "I thought Mr. Elliot intended to prove Professor Nessbit stole Dorian's novel. When I told my friends about my deductions, I mean, opinions, no one believed me." His glance at Kalen spoke of hurt loud and clear.

"Nothing mysterious about Chuck dropping by Nessbit's lair. They're friends, or so we thought back then," Kalen said.

"Renata and Cleo laughed at me." The smaller guy's lips pinched tight.

Beside Agnes, Lester muttered, "They would," condemning the scoffing girls to irrelevance.

"You'd seen Elliot enter Herb's office at night, didn't you?" Agnes asked to get them on track.

"Yes. When he went in, a brown envelope—you know, the kind the department uses—was under his left arm but not when he came out. I thought dropping off mail was part of his cover for sleuthing."

A shy smile at Agnes. "You figured out he was planting evidence, Dr. Taylor. I never suspected him."

"Yeah. Chuck fooled us alright," grumbled Kalen. "Ticks me right off. It was him creating the shitstorm about Herb. Private Eye, here, decoded the username. 'Toksy.'"

Kalen spelled it for her. The Snapchat alias she'd heard mentioned but misunderstood the night Dorian died.

"A kind of anagram of Chuck's names," Kalen said.

"Wow, you realized Elliot was spreading the faked accusations? Joel, you are terrific."

"No, I'm not. Like a goofy, I believed it was the truth." He gazed at her, desolate. "You teach us critical thinking, and I never used it."

Welcome to the club, sighed Agnes. "Nor did I."

"If you had pooled your observations and knowledge," remarked Lester, matter of fact, "you would have figured it out."

"Thank you for your vote of confidence, Lester." Agnes smiled at him. "But, guys, you haven't explained what brought you out Friday night."

"Neither cunning plot nor conspiracy" said Kalen, grinning in self-mockery. "We stayed late on campus to finish assignments at the library and in the computer commons. Saves lugging laptops on club night. I'd just logged out when Joel spotted Chuck go up the main stairs. Couldn't let our PI Joel roam the dark halls of academia alone, could I? So, I tagged along."

"Mr. Elliot never spied us," the PI took up the tale. "Our observation post was the men's washroom. With the lights turned off and the door open a hand-width, we kept surveillance. Our target entered Professor Nessbit's office but came out approximately 90 seconds later."

Agnes couldn't help grinning, so sure was she Joel had noted it down to the second should the evidence be required.

"But I did not video him, Dr. Taylor," he assured her. "After what you said the other day, I felt it would be wrong."

"Right you are," she said. "Carry on, don't mind me."

"The target then proceeded to the far end of the hallway. To keep him in view, we had to risk being seen."

"Felt like the old Maxwell Smart minus the shoe phone," said Kalen. "Ever heard of him, Agnes?"

"You won't believe this, yes, I have."

Kalen grinned appreciatively.

"Clouseau's better comedy," said Lester.

"Different genre," countered Kalen.

"Guys, let Joel continue," said Agnes.

"Mr. Elliot met you at the backstairs, and you both went back to Prof. Nessbit's office."

"Sure clinched it for me," said Kalen. "Convinced me Joel was right. Why else would the two of you go there at night unless you were snooping?"

"You left again in less than three minutes and proceeded to Mr. Elliot's office."

"We wondered what that was all about and decided to get closer," Kalen explained when Joel hesitated. "PI Joel ordered this sweet bug online. It picks up talking within a certain range. We figured the backstairs made it easy to get close and scamper if needed."

"You listened to us talk in his office?" Why this should offend her surprised Agnes the moment it slipped out.

"I'm sorry, Dr. Taylor," murmured Joel. "We never did. Honest."

"The hand of fate interfered with Kafka as its instrument." Kalen pointed at Lester, who smirked affably. "Man, we tried to shake him off when he stopped us in the foyer. Kafka shadowed us." Kalen leaned over toward Lester. "You had a hunch, didn't you, man?"

"You realized all along it was—"

But Lester cut off Agnes's question. "No. I'd seen him

upstairs with you and once or twice sniffing around the back of your place at night. Seemed off."

"So, you decided to play bodyguard," said Agnes. "Might have told me."

Lester resumed fraying his tattered jeans.

"When we entered the staircase," piped up Joel as if to break the tension, "we heard you arguing. I recorded it because I thought there was a threat, which justifies recording. Doesn't it?"

"Yes, threats of harm do. And you acted on it, too. That was very brave. If you guys hadn't intervened, the obituary this morning could bear my name instead."

Three pairs of eyes widened at the bald reminder.

Agnes's phone vibrated.

"Excuse me. I'd better check." She inched toward the end of the bleacher and pulled out her mobile. An SMS snippet showed.

ANDREA

'Cass wants to go home and not come back. Her parents finally reached New Zealand and contacted the doctors here. Requested a transferal to a BC clinic ASAP. The aunt is at my place packing up. She'll arrange transport. I'll miss Cass!'

AGNES

'Thanks, Andrea. Best for Cass to be with family. We'll all miss her. Tough on you and Mel. Keep me posted, please."

ANDREA

'Will do.'

Agnes slid back to the guys who were chatting softly.

"I've got to run now," she said. "But we'll talk again soon. It's been quite a stressful ordeal for you guys—"

"No worries about us," said their spokesperson, and his buddies nodded. "But before you go, Agnes, can we get clear going forward? We think it's best to keep quiet about the affair. Unless you give us the word. Herb's innocent. Easy to spread the word on Snapchat and TikTok. Like a troll stalked him and won't post again. Or something. It'll die down, eventually."

"Sounds fair to me. Herbert did nothing wrong. The malicious gossip is stressful and hurts his reputation." In silent supplication, she asked the dead writer's absolution for committing his creative labor, not to the flames, but to Jac's shredder.

She got up to thank each of them. "Let's hope things at the college come right again."

As she hastened to campus to pop by Jac's before her afternoon class, the sun peeked out behind darkly brewing clouds.

A good omen, she thought.

Armored with coffee and ham and cheese from Jac's favorite French bistro's takeout, Agnes cut the corner into the office wing and promptly bumped into the poet of all people.

"Watch it," he snarled, sounding like he breakfasted on gravel.

"Sorry," she yelped, concerned about the coffees rather than his tweeds.

His head kinked onto his neck to squint at her from below the rim of the fedora.

"Agnes. My apologies. I did not recognize the whirlwind swooshing in." A benevolent, close-lipped smile let his red-veined cheeks protrude like a squirrel's stuffed with nuts.

Unsure if he recollected their Friday night encounter—he'd dozed all the way home in Kalen's car—she opted for the Canadian default small talk.

"Did you have a good weekend? The weather was rather iffy, wasn't it?"

"Ah, I felt kissed by the muses. Saturday morning, let's be honest, it was afternoon," he winked at her, "I woke inspired, transported, elated. On the wings of Pegasus, I flew to my old Remington and hammered out the marvelous opening chapter of a beautiful romance."

"Glad to hear it, Herb. You feel thrilled, I bet." Another of TC's lies. The poet worked at home, after all.

"Oh, yes. I'm under a spell. Words tumble onto the page faster than my fingers can transcribe the lyric flow." He raised stubby digits for her to admire.

"Wonderful," said Agnes, and sort of meant it. The man deserved a break after the wrongful accusation and being framed as a scapegoat, a victim of TC's malice. She shuddered at her own contributions to that plot.

"I'm glad we ran into each other, almost literally," he chuckled. "With your consent, the mater would like your email address. May I share it?"

Surprised Mrs. Nessbit meant to follow up on their brief acquaintance, Agnes assented.

"Expect an invitation to afternoon tea." He wriggled his fingers at her. "She was delighted with your company on Thursday."

"Your mother is a remarkable woman, Herb. I found her charming."

"You don't have to live with her," he muttered, his mood morphing from sunny to sullen.

"Nor do you," said Agnes without thinking.

"She's getting on in years and would be lost without me in that grand mausoleum."

"Don't kid yourself, Herb. I hate to disillusion you, but I'm convinced the mater would be just fine."

"You think so?" He sounded genuinely astonished.

"Ask her," Agnes said with a broad smile. "Must dash. Coffee's getting cold."

The fedora lifted with a bow. "A pleasure chatting with you, Agnes. Have a nice day."

"Same here," she called after his retreating back, noting a jaunty spring in his step.

Minutes later, she deposited the pulp fiber tray holding their lunch onto Jac's desk. Her friend wriggled a few fingers in greeting without interrupting an ongoing phone call.

Agnes carried the visitor chair to join its mate by the window and added a small folding stool to hold the goodies. Tuning out of the conversation behind her, she contemplated the view over the campus grounds. Errant sunrays spotlighted a massive pine tree in the distance, reminding her of the Canadian Group of Seven paintings her mom, Sera, showed her at a gallery on the outskirts of Toronto when she was just a kid. It would be fun to chat with the forthright Mrs. Nessbit, who loved Sera's artwork.

"That was AD Muller," Jac interrupted Agnes's mental meanderings and arranged herself in the other chair. Skirt straightened and legs elegantly crossed, she reached for the paper cup Agnes pointed at.

"Thanks, I need a pick-me-up badly. Too much happening today. First, this morning's announcement about Timothy. You saw it?"

Agnes gave a careful nod, cup at her lips.

"Now, we heard Cassandra decided to withdraw from the program. The aunt contacted Martha this morning."

"Andrea texted me. The parents want Cass home. Understandably, she's anxious to be with family."

"Oh? You knew?"

"Found out not even an hour ago. It's for the best, don't you think?"

"Will you visit her in hospital before she leaves?"

"No. I don't think so. She won't want a reminder of our last

encounter. I'll always remember her as Medusa in the rain."
The vision materialized for Agnes as she spoke. Her fingers
tugged at the skin below her temple. "Like her namesake in
myth, Cassandra's portent of evil went unheeded, at least
by me."

"Agnes, don't beat yourself up. Elliot fooled everyone. The
man is dead."

"You were wary of him from the start, Jac."

"But for all the wrong and selfish reasons. I saw him as an
ambitious schemer out to harm colleagues when it comes to
hiring. Not for a moment did I suspect him of anything worse."

"Joel decoded a Snapchat alias and discovered TC was the
source of the rumors against Herb," said Agnes between bites
of her sandwich.

Jac appeared to digest the news. She drank coffee and
picked at her croissant.

"It makes some terrible sort of sense," she said and rested
her cup on the table. "One feels for Elliot's mother. Mercifully,
she will remain ignorant of her son's true character."

"I kind of doubt it," Agnes said. "Did you notice the desig-
nated charity for donations instead of flowers? The funeral is
private, too."

"Pardon? What do you mean? I'm afraid the details didn't
register."

"A local shelter for battered women."

Pupils dilating in distress, Jac's hands fell to her lap. "You
mean he beat her?"

"No idea. Just stuck out for me. There're all kinds of
reasons for the choice of the recipient charity. Still, wouldn't
mothers intuit their child's true nature by adulthood?" She
thought of her own mom. Sera probably had few illusions
about her.

Jac shrugged. "Speaking of character, one thing I've realized
over the past week I'm not cut out for admin executive
leadership."

Agnes spluttered flaky pastry. "Come now, Jac. You're over-reacting."

"No, Agnes, I'm serious. It's humbling to recognize one's inadequacy. I just crumbled under the stress."

"Anyone might with so much at stake," said Agnes.

"No, let's be honest. My primary concern was my own future. I was on the cusp of sacrificing truth and justice. You pursued them faithfully."

"Argh, don't make me cringe, Jac," groaned Agnes. "I screwed up royally. Okay, truth time. Might as well admit it. I'm ruled by the appetitive part of my soul instead of the rational, as Plato would say. To use our students' lingo, drop-dead charmers are the curse of my life."

As she had predicted, this drew a giggle from Jac, who'd missed the ill-chosen adjective that made Agnes really cringe now. Were callous words her own way of coping with the horrendous experience of the past week? Better than bawling her eyes out. Agnes sighed.

Her friend gazed at her in concern. "There's one more piece of news, Agnes."

"Oh, no. Paris didn't withdraw their offer, did they? You're so looking forward to getting away."

"No. It affects you, I'm afraid. Martha mentioned management froze hiring for the Humanities. My sense is they don't wish to draw attention to recent events. They might post the full-time position next year." Jac reached over to stroke Agnes's arm. "You still have your one-year contract."

Agnes chewed this over, not just mentally. Only when she'd washed down the remnants of her croissant with the dregs of cold coffee was she ready to reply.

"Not to worry." Wiping crumbs from her chin and dusting her sweater and pants, she grinned at Jac, who'd watched in apparent solicitude.

"Hey, I might go into the sleuthing business with Joel the Spy."

Their sputtering laughter released the penned-up emotions.

Life would go on, Agnes felt confident as her glance considered Jac's almost untouched croissant.

For more Mysteries by Eva Bernhard

Agnes Taylor Mystery Series
amazon.com/dp/B099436TY2?

Louise Penfold Mysteries
amazon.com/dp/B0FR6M4CTL?

For new release alerts follow me at
amazon.com/author/evabernhard

Dear Reader

Dear Reader,

Thank you so much for reading *Writer's Death*.

I love writing mysteries for you. Happy readers make my day!

May I ask you a big favor? If you've enjoyed reading this mystery, please recommend the Agnes Taylor Mysteries to your friends and to your local library.

Just cite the ISBN found on the copy right page of each book.

Mystery lovers with vision challenges will appreciate the **large print editions of *Agnes Taylor Mysteries*.**

I'd love to hear from you. Please share your thoughts and insights in a review of Writer's Death on the Amazon Review Page.

Thanks for your continued support and kindness!

Warmest wishes,

Eva

The Perfect Gift...

Treat yourself and Loved Ones and tell your Friends about the Agnes Taylor Mystery series

Standard Font and eBook Editions
amazon.com/dp/B099436TY2?
amazon.co.uk/dp/B099436TY2?
amazon.ca/dp/B099436TY2?

LARGE PRINT – AGNES TAYLOR MYSTERIES

amazon.com/dp/B0D8K71ZMM
amazon.ca/dp/B0D8K71ZMM
amazon.co.uk/dp/B0D8K71ZMM

My sincere thanks for your support!

Acknowledgments

It's often said that writing is a lonely business. Yet, we are embedded in a terrific community of writers, readers, and all kinds of helpers. I am most sincerely grateful to all of you!

I'm enjoying the company of the writers in the Sisters in Crime (SinC) community and that of my other writer friends.

So many have provided astute constructive critiques at various stages of this novel. Sisters in Crime, Heather McLeod and Paris Grey, set me on the right track with their comments on parts of the first draft. Dr. JP, well-known for her *Pick Your Poison Podcast*, advised me on a critical point. I was fortunate to receive lots of feedback on the opening chapters from several Critique Circle members. The encouraging comments of Mark Roman and Writely spurred me on.

Most of all, I'd like to thank my critique partners from Critique Match, Rebecca Markus and Ione Huhtala, who read drafts of the entire manuscript. The thoroughness and insightfulness of their critiques was just outstanding. Nothing escapes your eagle eye, Ione. Thanks!

Before my wonderful editor, Pam Clinton, scrutinized the manuscript, Kelly Sweeney from Critique Match, gave important feedback from a reader's point of view.

Of course, with so much helpful feedback, one is bound to get conflicting advice. In the end, the decision rests with the author based on the intention for the novel and the series. Pam Clinton ironed out the remaining kinks—thanks so much, Pam!

The editing is always subject to intentional idiosyncrasies of my characters and my writing style. Hence, any remaining perceived errors are mine.

This labor of love is solely for you, my Reader. May you enjoy it!